BLOODSHED

A JOHN JORDAN MYSTERY

MICHAEL LISTER

PULPWOOD PRESS

Also available in audiobook, paperback, and hardcover.

Book Edited by Aaron Bearden

Book Design by Tim Flanagan of Novel Design Studio

Paperback ISBN: 978-1-947606-16-6

Books by Michael Lister

(John Jordan Novels)
Power in the Blood
Blood of the Lamb
Flesh and Blood
(Special Introduction by Margaret Coel)
The Body and the Blood
Double Exposure
Blood Sacrifice
Rivers to Blood
Burnt Offerings
Innocent Blood
(Special Introduction by Michael Connelly)
Separation Anxiety
Blood Money Blood Moon
Thunder Beach
Blood Cries
A Certain Retribution
Blood Oath
Blood Work
Cold Blood
Blood Betrayal

Blood Shot
Blood Ties
Blood Stone
Blood Trail
Bloodshed
Blue Blood
And the Sea Became Blood

(Jimmy Riley Novels)
The Girl Who Said Goodbye
The Girl in the Grave
The Girl at the End of the Long Dark Night
The Girl Who Cried Blood Tears
The Girl Who Blew Up the World

(Merrick McKnight / Reggie Summers Novels)
Thunder Beach
A Certain Retribution
Blood Oath
Blood Shot

(Remington James Novels)
Double Exposure
(includes intro by Michael Connelly)
Separation Anxiety
Blood Shot

(Sam Michaels / Daniel Davis Novels)
Burnt Offerings
Blood Oath
Cold Blood
Blood Shot

(Love Stories)
Carrie's Gift

(Short Story Collections)
North Florida Noir
Florida Heat Wave

Delta Blues
Another Quiet Night in Desperation

(The Meaning Series)
Meaning Every Moment
The Meaning of Life in Movies

DEDICATION

For all the victims of school rampage shootings and their family and friends, teachers and coaches, principals and custodians.

HOW TO READ THE JOHN JORDAN BLOOD SERIES

The Blood Series

This *New York Times* bestselling and award-winning series features a conflicted detective—a cop with ties to Atlanta who also works as a prison chaplain in Florida. He's a man of mercy and justice, compassion, open-mindedness. He's also a smart, relentless detective.

The John Jordan mystery series is character-driven and realistic—thoughtful mystery thrillers involving the hero's journey of a good man trying to be even better, as he helps others along the way.

Like John Jordan, the author, Michael Lister, was a prison chaplain with the state of Florida before leaving to write full-time.

If you're new to the John Jordan series, you can begin with any book, but we recommend one of these 3: *Power in the Blood, Innocent Blood,* or *Blood Oath.*

Power in the Blood, the first fiction the author ever wrote, was published over 20 years ago, and though it's recommended, the books in the John Jordan series don't have to be read in order.

All the books in the series are novels—mystery, thrillers,

whodunits—except for the 3rd book in the series, *Flesh and Blood*, which is a collection of short stories featuring temporal and metaphysical mysteries. If you don't care for short stories, feel free to skip *Flesh and Blood* and continue with the fourth novel *The Body and the Blood*.

If you decided to skip the short stories and continue on with the novels, we recommend that you read the short story "A Taint in the Blood" in the book *Flesh and Blood* to find out what happened to Laura Matthers from *Power in the Blood*.

The 7th book in the series, *Innocent Blood*, is a prequel going back to John's very first investigation. Though the 7th in the series, it can be read 1st or 7th since it's a prequel.

The 10th book in the series, *Blood Cries,* is the second in the "Atlanta Years" series within a series following the 7th book *Innocent Blood*. It can be read 2nd or 10th.

The 17th book in the seres, *Blood Stone*, is the 3rd book in the "Atlanta Years" series within the series following the 10th book *Blood Cries*. It can be read 3rd or 17th.

John Jordan is an ex-cop in books 1-10, but once again carries a gun and a badge beginning with book 11, *Blood Oath*.

All of the John Jordan novels are available in high quality hardback, paperback, ebook, and audio editions.

Interspersed throughout the "Blood" books there are other related books that are part of the John Jordan universe. These books are extremely important to the series and provide essential backstory for characters, connections, and locations of series regulars. Most of all they answer the questions most readers want to know. They include *Double Exposure, Burnt Offerings, Separation Anxiety, Thunder Beach,* and *A Certain Retribution*. These are "Blood Series" books without being John Jordan Mysteries.

We hope you will enjoy all the books in the John Jordan series and eagerly await each new entry.

Be sure to join Michael Lister's Readers' Group for news, updates, and special deals on the John Jordan series.

THANK YOU

Thank you for your invaluable help and support with this book:

Dawn Lister, Aaron Bearden, Tim Flanagan, Mike Harrison, Terry Lewis, Debra Ake, and Micah Lister.

AUDIOBOOK

BLOODSHED is also available as a high quality audiobook.

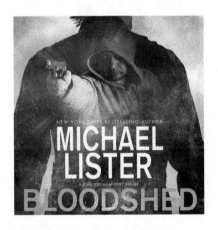

Get a FREE audiobook when you purchase BLOODSHED in audio. Just email your proof of purchase to MichaelLister@MichaelLister.com and we'll send you another John Jordan audiobook absolutely free!

INTRODUCTION

Some crimes are so incomprehensible as to not seem possible. School rampage shootings are just such crimes—acts so inhumane they may as well have been perpetrated by a different species.

I am haunted by school shootings, their cold, arbitrary evil, their pitiless brutality, their indiscriminate injury, and fatality.

As a student of human nature, a seeker of truth, an asker of questions, I find the massacres taking place at our schools as perplexing as it is disturbing.

In *Bloodshed*, I attempt to explore the phenomena of school rampage shootings with care and respect, while also writing what I hope is a fast-paced and entertaining mystery thriller. In doing so, I honestly have no agenda, no message, no ax to grind—only the need to examine and express. That is, after all, what art is for.

For me, there's no better way to delve into a subject than through a detective novel, no better way to investigate an area of interest than through the moral maze of a mystery novel.

While writing *Bloodshed*, I've kept school shooting victims and survivors and their families and friends in my heart and mind. This work seeks to honor and memorialize them. I have often thought of Kelly Fleming, the sixteen-year-old Columbine student who wanted to grow up to be a published author, and felt like I was undertaking this with and for her.

As always, I attempted to write a truly engaging, suspenseful, exciting story with the goal of entertaining and inspiring while also handling the delicate subject matter and the fragility of humanity with care and compassion. That's the goal. Whether it succeeds or not can only be answered by each individual reader. My sincerest hope is that it succeeds for you.

This is a particularly devastating case for John. It had to be given the weight of what he's dealing with. He will forever be changed, adding new wounds to the fine, fibrous scar tissue already present. No one survives a school shooting unscathed.

In preparation for writing this novel, I invested a lot of time in study and research. In that process, I found these three books particularly helpful: *Give a Boy a Gun* by Todd Strasser, *Ceremonial Violence* by Jonathan Fast, and *Columbine* by Dave Cullen. I highly recommend them all.

At the beginning of each chapter are fictionalized quotes based on actual, similar sayings surrounding school shootings—by students, teachers, parents, cops, gunmen, media reports, pundits, and engaged citizens. I have rewritten and fictionalized them but they were taken directly from those far more involved in this epidemic than they ever thought they'd be.

Thank you for taking this journey with me and John. I hope you are the better for it, and that the experience is both entertaining and enlightening.

—Michael Lister
July 2018

You, in the schoolyard I am ready to kill
and no one here knows of my loneliness.

—*White Flesh* by Rammstein

BLOODSHED

1

Dear Mom and Dad, by the time you read this it'll be too late to do anything. I'll already be gone. I just wanted you to know that it was too late long before now and there was nothing you could have ever done to stop this. I know you would if you could. You guys always tried your best for me. If anyone doesn't believe that or tries to blame you, show them this. It wasn't you. It was me. I'm not right. Never have been. I don't think I could ever really explain any of this, but I've never been happy and I genuinely and truly believe I will never be. How can I keep living when I know that every day of my life will be miserable? What's the point?

"What if you could've prevented Columbine or Sandy Hook or Parkland?" Chip Jeffers asks.

It's late.

We're sitting at a booth in the back of Rudy's Diner. As if in an Edward Hopper painting, we're the only customers in the dim, lonely all-night establishment.

The night is dark and quiet, the rural highway out front

empty, the lone streetlamp reflecting off the asphalt, damp from a brief early evening rain.

"You would have, right?" he adds. "Don't know a cop in the entire world who wouldn't. Well, we have something none of them ever had—an actual chance to stop one of these things."

Chip Jeffers, the Potter County deputy sitting across from me, is a middle-aged white man with a thick, wiry mustache, large, black plastic-framed glasses, and a pale, dome-shaped balding head haloed by brown-going-gray hair.

"Somebody could've stopped all those school shootings from happening," he says. "So, I guess they had a chance. A parent, a teacher, a coach, a cop, another student. Somebody heard something, saw something, knew something that they chose not to act on. We can't afford to do that. Guarantee if any of them could go back, they'd do it differently, they'd've stopped them. We don't want to be in that same position, standing over the dead bodies of kids knowing we're responsible for their deaths."

Jeffers has been a deputy for a long time—going back to when Dad was sheriff here. In fact, it was Dad he had asked to speak with. But because the clandestine meeting had to be late at night, because Chip Jeffers has always been a bit of an alarmist, and because of the politics involved, Dad asked me to meet with him.

Since I take every opportunity I can to see little John Paul Pearson and check on his mother, I said *yes*.

I glance over toward mother and child.

Carla is sleeping on one of the barstools at the front counter, her head lying on her outstretched arm on the faded Formica countertop, her baby boy asleep in a car seat next to her. Like his mother, he is sleeping sitting up—something his mother has spent most of her life doing. Perhaps she is training him to do the same or perhaps she is preparing him to do something she never could—ride out of this town and never return.

Looking at them sleeping rough like that causes a certain slippage inside me as if something at my core is sinking a little, shifting around a bit—and not in any kind of good way.

"You okay?" Jeffers asks. "What is it?"

I nod. "Go ahead with your story," I say. "You sayin' we have a chance to stop a school shooting?"

"Think about it," he says. "We always come in after a crime has been committed, after it's too late for anything but picking up a bunch of broken pieces and arresting some poor, sad, shot-out bastard who would take it back if he could but he can't, so . . . But what if we could stop it from ever happening? I think it would not only prevent loss of life in this particular situation but inspire other agencies to do the same—make them more proactive and all. Like us. What if we started a movement that transitioned from law enforcement to crime prevention? Serious crime prevention—like school shootings and . . . things like that."

Ignoring his grandiose plans to transform police work, I say, "You think there's going to be a school shooting? Here? In Pottersville?"

He nods. "I know it."

His certainty is as hollow and annoying as his visions of grandeur.

He frowns. "I can tell by your expression that you don't believe me. Your dad used to give me that same look."

"I don't *not* believe you," I say. "Tell me why you think there's going to be a school shooting here and why you're telling me and not the new sheriff."

"You don't have to take my word for it," he says. "Kim and LeAnn will be here in a minute with evidence."

Kim Miller and LeAnn Dunne are the school resource officer and the guidance counselor of Potter High.

"And as far as Glenn . . . I *did* take it to him. He didn't take it seriously. Like everything else I've ever taken to him. But he told me I could look into it, just keep Kim in the loop. Dismissive like. Giving me busy work the way you would a kid."

Hugh Glenn, the current sheriff, is the former deputy and detective who beat Dad in a closely contested general election, handing Dad his first defeat. Ever. Glenn had been a lazy deputy and investigator and is now a lazy sheriff—far more politician and administrator than law enforcement officer.

Headlight beams sweep across the dim diner, and I turn to see Kim and LeAnn pulling into the parking lot in Kim's cruiser.

I jump up and quietly step out to greet them so I can keep the cowbell above the door from clanging when they come in.

I reach their car just as they're getting out.

"John Jordan," Kim says. "Been too long since we've seen your handsome face around here."

"Hey Kimmy," I say, and hug her.

Kim Miller is a petite woman with a pretty, pale face and big, brown eyes, and longish, silky black hair she almost always wears in a ponytail. There is the slightest hint of something Asian in her features that, if it's there at all, must come from her mother's side.

Though it's late and she's off duty, she's in uniform.

"Wow," she says. "Haven't been called that in a while."

LeAnn walks up with a big smile and says, "Class of eighty-six. Where you at?"

"Hey LeAnn," I say as I hug her. "How are you?"

LeAnn Dunne is a large, solid woman with smallish blue eyes and curly, blond babydoll hair. Nearly my height, muscular with no hips and very few curves, she has the build of a slightly above average man.

"I'm good. Real good. Don't know if you heard but I figured out I was a lesbian since that last time I saw you. Life got a lot better after that."

I hug her again and tell her how happy I am that her life is better.

Both LeAnn and Kim were in my graduating class, and though we weren't extremely close, it was a small class in a small school in a small town. We knew each other well and liked and respected each other, and we shared the bond of having survived high school together.

"I'm still straight," Kim says, "but that's no picnic, lemme tell you. Think I could get another hug?"

We pull her in, and the three of us hug in what resembles a small football huddle.

When we release each other, I tell them about Carla and the baby being asleep.

"And here I am thinking you rushed out here 'cause you couldn't wait to see us," LeAnn says.

"Poor things," Kim says.

"We had heard you and Anna were going to adopt the little fella," LeAnn says.

I frown and nod. "We were."

"What happened?" Kim asks.

"What so often does," I say. "Carla changed her mind after she held him."

"I get it," LeAnn says. "I changed my mind after holding a man too—but to quit them, not keep them. But I know you've got to be disappointed, John. I'm sorry."

She pats me on the shoulder without having to reach up to do so.

"Me too," Kim says. "So sorry to hear that. How is Anna?"

"We're both sad and disappointed, but . . . we're okay. Getting used to the idea."

"So," LeAnn says, "instead of being safe at home in bed with you and Anna watching over him, he spends his nights inside Rudy's disgusting diner."

"We're working on that," I say.

Their eyes widen and they perk up. "On getting him?" Kim asks.

"No no, nothing like that. On making it so Carla doesn't have to be here with him. It's just taking a little time. Trying to get her low-income housing and some assistance."

"Oh."

"We've offered for them to stay with us, but . . . she won't take us up on it. I think she feels . . . I don't know . . . guilty or something for changing her mind. We've tried and tried to reassure her, but . . ."

They nod and give me sympathetic looks.

We are all quiet for an awkward beat.

"Well," I say finally, "shall we go in and hear what Chip has to say about starting the crime prevention revolution?"

They laugh and the awkwardness is instantly gone.

I ease open the door and hold the old cowbell that dangles above it while Kim and LeAnn come in, and, after a brief pause for us to look at little John Paul, we make our way over to where Chip is waiting.

I've always tried to make an extra special effort for those students who are most vulnerable or stressed. I've done that my entire career. And I'm not the only teacher to do it. Several of us do our best to stop bullying and to make sure every student feels safe and cared for and even loved. That's as much a part of teaching as reading, writing, and arithmetic. I've taken so many students aside and reassured them, bragged on them, let them know that it will get better. And I don't just mean school, but life. I tell them their lives will get better. I promise them that. It catches most of them completely by surprise. And I've seen many of them actually blink back tears.

"What took so long out there?" Jeffers says. "I just got a call. I've got to go in a minute."

"Sorry," Kim says, "we were just catching up. Haven't seen John in a while."

We slide into the booth—LeAnn on my side, Kim on Jeffers'.

"Well, let's go over everything real quick so I can go," he says. "Show him the letter."

LeAnn reaches into her enormous purse, leaning into me as she does, and withdraws a manila file folder. Opening it, she hands me a sheet of copy paper. On it are copied fragments of handwritten notes that appear to have been ripped from a lined journal.

I read them as quickly as I can, which isn't very quickly since cyphering the handwriting is challenging.

Swear to God I will kill every fucking one of them. Every asshole that ever tortured a poor soul just trying to make it through the goddamn day. We've had enough and we're not going to take it another motherfucking second.

Mom, I'm so sorry about all this. I wish I could have told you what I was dealing with. I tried a few times. But you couldn't understand and even if you could there was nothing you could do about it. None of this is your fault. I know you will get blamed and that's the only regret I have, but this is not your fault. Show the bastards this and tell them I said there was nothing you could do and that you didn't do anything wrong. It's them and the horrible human beings they're raising. It's them and their kids. Not you. NOT YOU!

K and H had it right. Time to continue the revolution. Blow the fucking lid off the whole thing, then go down in a blaze of glory. Unless. What if there was a way to keep doing it? Strike fear, keep it burning, be there to watch it? I'm a goddamn genius. Revolution 2.0.

I look up from the paper. "K and H?" I ask.

Kim shrugs.

"Harris and Klebold," Jeffers says, the pitch of his voice rising. "Columbine."

I look from Kim to LeAnn. "Could be, I guess," she says. "But we can't be sure."

"Yes we can," Jeffers says. "In the context of the notes it can't be anything else."

"Where'd you get these?" I ask.

"Janitor saw them in the boys' bathroom trash," LeAnn says. "Brought them to me. Chip was filling in for Kim that day. I shared them with him. Here we are."

"The original notes are on journal paper," Kim says. "Like they had been ripped out of someone's diary. It was a few different pages—some wadded up, others just laying in there."

"Any ideas on who may have written it?" I ask, looking from Kim to LeAnn and back.

LeAnn says, "Got some good candidates."

Kim nods. "I can think of a few that fit the Harris-Klebold profile."

"We need to identify them and stop this from happening," Jeffers says.

His radio sounds again, louder this time, and I glance over toward Carla and John.

"I gotta go," he says.

Kim stands and lets him out of the booth, then sits back down.

"You guys talk some more and see what you come up with," he says. "Report back to me and let's get together again tomorrow. Or I'll swing by later to see if you're still here."

"We won't be," LeAnn says. "Mama needs her beauty sleep."

"Your level of commitment to saving lives is inspiring," he says, and turns and leaves.

"That bald fat fuck just zinged me as his exit line," she says. "We can't stand for that. Shoot him, Kim. I know it will wake the baby, but it'll be worth it."

Though I reminded him before he left, Jeffers doesn't hold the cowbell as he exits the diner and its brassy clanging wakes Carla and the baby.

"What do you think we should do, John?" Kim asks. "I know Chip is a classic overreactor, but . . . do you think this could be something?"

"Could it be what he thinks it is?" LeAnn asks.

I shrug. "I don't know. The fact that he threw the pages away might be a good sign. But I think we have to look into it—even if there's the slightest chance it could be true."

They both nod.

"I agree," Kim says.

"All we have to lose is a little time," LeAnn says. "Maybe a little beauty sleep. And the downside is too deep for doing nothing."

"The question is—*what*?" Kim says.

"It's not a lot to go on," LeAnn says, "and we don't want to run this risk of targeting the wrong kid and ruining his life."

I nod. "We certainly don't. Why don't we do this . . . First, have you notified the principal?"

They nod.

"I'm assuming he notified teachers and staff to be on alert," I say.

"He did," Kim says. "He handled it very well."

"He does such a good job," LeAnn says, "and everyone responded well. You can tell a difference in how things are being done."

"Okay," I say. "Good. So . . . we've got at least two things to go on—the content of the notes and the handwriting itself. Very quietly . . . without telling anyone . . . why don't you two make a list of the most likely students, but do it independently so we can compare your lists—see if anyone is on both. And keep your eyes open for suspicious behavior or absences of anyone you suspect. Once we have the list, we can ask their English teacher for a sample of their writing to compare to the notes."

"I've already made my list," Kim says.

"Me too," LeAnn says, nodding. "And we've already compared them."

"Excellent," I say. "You're way ahead of me."

"You have no idea," LeAnn says, leaning into me and pulling another folder out of her purse. "Here's our lists and a little info on each kid."

"Wow," I say.

"Don't be too impressed," Kim says. "We didn't even think about getting samples of their handwriting."

"You would have," I say.

"Yes we would," LeAnn says.

"This is great work," I say, opening the folder and glancing at its contents.

"You didn't think we were just another pair of pretty faces, did you?" LeAnn asks with a wide smile.

I nod at the folder. "I'll look over this tonight."

"First thing tomorrow we'll get samples of their handwriting," Kim says.

"See if you can do it without singling out the individual kids," I say.

"How?"

"Get an assignment from the entire class, not just a few students."

"As guidance counselor," LeAnn says, "I'm in and out of classes having the kids fill out forms all the time. It wouldn't raise any suspicions if I went in and had them fill out a survey about vocational interests."

"Even better," I say. "That's perfect. Great thinking."

She points to her large, heavily and brightly made-up face. "Told you. I'm far more than just this."

"You certainly are."

"So," Kim says. "You study our lists and the information about the students from an outside perspective. LeAnn will collect the samples. What do I do?"

LeAnn smiles. "Somebody has to report back to Super Cop Chip. That can be your job."

3

To all you pathetic people of Pottersville, I hope each and every one of you read this! I hope they print it on the front page of the paper and post it everywhere on the internet. I know you don't give a good goddamn about me being dead, but you want to know why I took so many of your kids with me? I'll tell you why. You each and every one of you have made my fuckin' life a living hell. How could you raise your kids to be such horrible people? How can you all hate anyone who isn't just like you?

I look down at the good-natured little baby boy with the enormous brown eyes who just a few short months ago was going to be my son, and feel, as I always do, a complex mix of sadness and joy, regret, longing, and love.

Sliding my hands behind him and easing him out of his car seat, I say, "Let's let your mama sleep a little more. Whatta you say?"

I lift him to me, kissing his forehead and gently placing his head on my shoulder, rocking him in my arms and patting his back.

I couldn't love him anymore if he were my own son.

"You're so good with him," Carla says. "I feel so guilty for not . . . for keeping him."

I look away so she can't see me, pretending to be adjusting John Paul in my arms, and blink my stinging eyes.

"There's no world," I say when I can, "in which you should feel guilty for keeping your own child. Please let that go. You have absolutely nothing to feel guilty about. You did nothing wrong. You did everything right."

I mean what I'm saying. She did nothing wrong. And of course, she should keep her baby. But that doesn't change the fact that the entire experience has been complicated and painful for me and for Anna. For months before he was born, we thought he was going to be ours. We rushed Carla to the hospital, worried the baby was coming too early, concerned for his and her safety, believing he was ours. We stayed with him in the hospital for weeks, taking care of him in his vulnerable, premature condition and helping his mom physically and emotionally, believing he was ours.

For months we believed we had another child. It didn't matter to us whether he was a boy or a girl, we were just happy to welcome another child into our home. It didn't matter that he was a boy, but it was significant. Years and years ago I had a dream of being at the beach with my little boy. A dream I truly believed had finally come true.

Anna and I had something we were no longer able to have on our own—a baby, a child together. And then Carla changed her mind. It would have been difficult under any circumstances, but for us to have him, care for him, receive him into our family only to have him snatched away, taken from us, had been only slightly less emotionally devastating than if he had been kidnapped or succumbed to SIDS.

"I'm sorry for getting your hopes up and . . ."

"You didn't," I lie. "You didn't do anything wrong. Our family is complete. It's not like Anna or I feel like we have to have a son or that we're incomplete without a boy somehow. It's not the case. Not at all. We love our girls and they are more than enough. We feel like the luckiest parents in the world. We were going to take him because you asked us to, because you needed us to, and we would have loved him like our own—we still do—but we weren't actively looking for another child. You didn't do anything wrong."

She gives me a sleepy smile. "You're almost convincing."

"Even if you thought you got our hopes up and that we were disappointed when we didn't get him, you have nothing to feel guilty for. He's *your* baby. You made the right decision."

"I feel guilty . . . I feel guilty because y'all could give him a better life than I can," she says.

I shake my head. "Absolutely not. No one can give him a better life than you can. And we're going to help you—as much as you'll let us—give him the best life you possibly can."

So far she has been unwilling to let us do much of anything for him or for her, and I think I know why.

"You really think he's better off with me?"

"His own mother?" I say. "Of course. Absolutely."

"And you're not mad at me?"

"Of course not," I say. "We love you. We want you in our lives. Want you to let us do more for you and your baby."

She nods and gives me something between a smile and a frown.

"Are you not letting us help because of the guilt you mentioned?" I ask. "Or because you think we might try to take him from you?"

Tears appear in her eyes. "I'd never think you guys would try to take my baby from me," she says, "but . . . y'all are so good with him, with your girls, and I fuckin' suck as a mother, and . . . it just points out how good y'all are and how bad I am and how selfish I'm being not to let y'all raise him."

"Oh, Carla," I say. "You're a great mother and you're not being selfish. He's *your* child. You can't be selfish with *your* child. Something would·be wrong if you didn't want him."

"I knew you wouldn't try to take him, but I did think that others would see how much better y'all are than me and report it to Children and Family Services and they'd take him away from me and give him to you."

"Would never happen," I say. "Not in a million years. You have nothing to worry about. And nobody thinks you're a bad mom or that we would be better. No one. And there wouldn't be anything to compare. It wouldn't be like we'd have him and then you'd have him and someone could compare the two. We're just wanting to help you with him. We'd be doing it together."

She starts crying. "I . . . that sounds so good. I . . . could really use some help. I feel like I'm going crazy. I'm so tired all the time and I'm having some crazy ass thoughts."

"Like DCF taking your baby and giving him to us?" I say.

She laughs. "Yeah, like that."

"Come home with me tonight," I say. "Stay with us until we can get you your own place. Let us help you get some sleep, some rest. Let us help you with your baby. You're his parent. And I promise you Anna and I will never try to be. But you could let us be your parents and his grandparents. How about that? That could work, couldn't it?"

4

---

*I will kill every fucking one of you motherfuckers. That's a promise.
I'm the real pirate of Pottersville. It's going to be Columbine all over
again. Only better. Harris and Klebold had it right. Blow the whole
fucking school up then blow yourself the fuck away. God, how I wish
I would have had the chance to meet them. Maybe I will someday.
Maybe there's a special place in hell for people like us. But then again,
maybe I'm not ready to go out just yet. Maybe I'll go underground
afterwards, travel the earth like fucking Kung-fu and help other
outcast kids kill their fucking foes. Keep this revolution going or start
a new one. Keep fighting until they bring you down in a volley of
bullets. Mark my words, Columbine was just the beginning and soon
they'll say Pottersville the way they do Columbine or Parkland or
Sandy Hook.*

Driving back to Wewa, Carla sound asleep in the seat beside
me, John Paul just as soundly asleep in his carseat in the
back, I call Sam Michaels.

"Hey," I say softly. "Sorry to call so late. Did I wake you?"

"No. It's good to hear from you. Why are you whispering?"

I tell her.

Sam Michaels is an agent with the Florida Department of Law Enforcement who I have worked with over the years and who had actually lived with Anna and me for a time while she was recovering from a gunshot wound. She and her husband, Daniel Davis, had moved back to Tallahassee recently, and we missed them terribly. Because of her brain injury, Sam is no longer physically able to be a field agent, so instead she's becoming one of the keenest investigative minds I know. I often call her for advice.

"What can you tell me about school shootings?" I ask.

"Some," she says. "Kids who do it have so little to love that everything seems meaningless to them, and yet they're out for revenge—it's the one thing that seems reasonable and valuable to them. Makes them both suicidal and homicidal. I can tell you that school rampage shootings are acts of random terrorism without an ideology. Those who perpetrate them often cobble together some sort of ideological justification, but it's usually just some bullshit mashup of Ayn Rand, Nietzsche, shock rock, and pop culture glamorizing of violence. Why?"

"Trying to prevent one from happening."

"*Really?*" she says. "That's interesting. In every case I know of there were plenty of warning signs—clues if someone were looking for them. Most adult mass murderers operate in isolation, but adolescent ones inevitably share their plan with one or more friends. How incredible would it be to stop one before it happened? But what makes you think there's potentially going to be one somewhere?"

I tell her.

As I do, I realize that I owe Chip Jeffers more respect and credit than I give him, and that if it weren't for him, none of the rest of us would be doing this.

"Fascinating," she says. "How long you got?"

"Just the drive from Pottersville to Wewa, I'm afraid."

"Then I'll talk fast and give you a little to start with and you can call me when you have more time."

"Perfect."

"School shootings are a pretty recent and nearly exclusively American phenomenon," she says. "What we think of as school shootings, what we mean when we reference them, began in 1996 with a fourteen-year-old kid somewhere in Washington—Moses Lake, I think—named Barry Loukaitis, who walked into Frontier Middle School dressed in a black duster carrying two handguns, seventy-eight rounds of ammunition, and a hunting rifle. He killed two students and wounded a third before shooting his algebra teacher. But the one everyone references, the one that inspires nearly all of them now, is Columbine. Harris and Klebold created a script that now nearly everyone follows."

I think about the K and H from the note the janitor found at Potter High.

"Three years after Loukaitis, in April of 1999, Eric Harris and Dylan Klebold created a blueprint for mass rampage shootings schoolhouse style with what they did in Littleton. They made it a media event—first by creating media themselves, the videos and short films and basement tapes recordings, but then by the way the media covered it and the ones that've followed. Harris said he wanted to start a revolution and in a way he did. The attention and sensationalism and rock star-like coverage feeds the phenomenon—inspires, triggers, instructs the troubled and bullied and mentally and emotionally ill kids who've come after them. I'd be willing to bet when you find who you're looking for you're going to find references to Eric and Dylan and probably even similar videos or journal entries."

I tell her about the K and H referenced in one of the note fragments.

"See?" she says. "Guarantee it's Klebold and Harris. And it probably means you really are looking for a school shooter and might be able to actually prevent a school shooting from happening."

"What should I look for?"

"In almost all cases, the kids tell other kids about it," she says. "It may seem like they're joking at the time. They'll say, *Oh that's just Joe. He's crazy. He says shit like that all the time.* They'll be obsessed with guns and gun culture. Be huge fans of the movie *Natural Born Killers* and other films like it. Very dark music. Disturbing internet activity. Obsessive-compulsive behavior in general. Big into first-person shooter games. Probably been bullied by other kids at school. Rejected and embarrassed by a girl. He or they will have journals and audio or video recordings of rants. He's probably shown his guns to other students—or at least bragged about them. Maybe even taken them shooting. He'll be into explosives—building bombs. This is all evolving, so some of it is changing. But more than likely there will be clues, warning signs, something or several things to let you know you're on the right scent."

"Thanks, Sam," I say. "I really appreciate your help and all the great info."

"Most of these kids make a goodbye video," she says. "Justify and explain themselves. Say their parents aren't responsible, didn't know anything about it. They then pose with the gun, pointing it at the screen, then their own temple—because this is almost always murder-suicide—then at the end they wave goodbye."

"Interesting."

"Got to do what Eric and Dylan did," she says.

I think about that as I pull into our driveway.

"And John, the kid you're looking for may not be very fringe at all—not a complete loner, no black trench coat, no outlandish behavior, could be just a quiet, sort of shy boy that nobody really even notices. But there'll be real rage right behind his eyes."

I let her know we're here, thank her again, and tell her to tell Daniel I said hello.

"Be careful with this one, John," she says. "Case like this is far more dangerous than most—and with more potential pitfalls. And don't for one second be fooled by their juvenile appearance. He may look like a kid, but he's a vicious, merciless, calculating coldblooded killer intent on shedding as much blood as quickly as possible."

5

You know what? I went to three different high schools growing up and in none of them did I for one moment feel safe. Not one. High school was horrifying. And you want to know why? I'll tell you. It was the casual cruelty of the popular kids and the indifference to the rest of us by the coaches and teachers who adored them that made it a ticking time bomb ready to explode.

Anna stirs when I ease into our bed.

"Hey," she whispers sleepily.

"Hey."

"Missed you. How'd it go?"

"Missed you more," I say. "I'll talk to you about it tomorrow. Go back to sleep. But before you do, guess who's sleeping in our guest room?"

"Somebody from the class of eighty-six?"

"Carla and John."

She pushes herself up on her side, leaning on her elbow, instantly awake.

"They're going to stay with us until her apartment comes through."

"Really? Wow. Why the change?"

"She wasn't letting us do much because she felt guilty and threatened. I assured her there was need for neither. We're happy for her and only want to help and we'd never try to take her child from her. We're not trying to be his parents, just trying to help her parent him."

"What do they need?" she asks. "I should go and check on them and get them some—"

"They're all settled in," I say. "They're getting what they need most—sleep."

"I have the strongest urge to go and wake him up and hug and hold him for the rest of the night."

"Resist that urge, sister," I say. "Be strong. Hug and hold me instead. You'll get a crack at him first thing in the morning."

"Thank you so much for bringing them home," she says.

"I knew it would make you happy," I say, "and I took a chance it wouldn't make you too sad."

"Not too, no."

"Good. So why don't you slide over here and hug and hold me and let's get some sleep? I have a feeling we're about to be getting less for a while."

After Anna is sound asleep again, I roll back to my side of the bed and begin to look up information about school shootings and the kids who commit them on my phone.

Most school injuries are sports-related. Most school crimes involve petty theft. Most teenage deaths are accidents, followed by homicides, then suicides. The number of teens who die in school rampage shootings is less than one-hundredth of one percent.

Most murders are unplanned, spur-of-the-moment, spontaneous acts—a fear and anger-induced response to a perceived imminent threat. But mass murders, the murdering of multiple victims by a single murder within a relatively short period of time, accounts for less than one percent of all violent crimes. These tend to be predatory, planned, and purposeful, but without emotion.

Kids who kill other kids in mass rampage attacks at school feel persecuted and bullied—whether they actually are or not. Some live a long while under the constant threat of attack and injury and some experience extreme forms of bullying and harassment for long periods of time.

In one study, Catherine Newman, a sociologist at Princeton University, identified five common conditions present in most school-related shooters.

First, the shooter perceives himself to be socially marginalized—whether he actually is or not. Second, he suffers from some form of psychosocial problems—such as learning disorders, psychiatric disorders, dysfunctional families—all of which magnify his marginality. Third, he follows pop culture notions of violent problem-solving—if you're being mistreated respond with force to retaliate your way to respect. Fourth, he flies beneath the radar. His serious, severe, and problematic behavior goes unnoticed or unidentified by parents, teachers, friends, guidance counselors, school psychologists, and social workers. Fifth, he has access to firearms. Without the availability of weapons, there are no school-related shootings.

L ater, when sleep comes, I have the same dream I had so long ago.

It's interesting. I didn't have it before John Paul was born, nor even after he arrived into the world. It was only after Carla decided to keep him, only after he was lost to me, that I started having the dream again. But since then I had been having it nearly every time I slept.

A cruelty and simultaneously a kind of salve, it is bittersweet but not unwelcome.

The last of the setting sun streaks the blue horizon with neon pink and splatters the emerald green waters of the Gulf with giant orange splotches like scoops of sherbet in an Art Deco bowl.

A fitting finale for a perfect Florida day.

My son, who looks to be around four, though it's hard to tell since in dreams we all seem ageless—runs up from the water's edge, his face red with sun and heat, his hands sticky with wet sand, and asks me to join him for one last swim.

He looks up at me with his mother's brown eyes, open and honest as possible, and smiles his sweetest smile as he begins to beg.

"Please, Daddy," he says. "Please."

"We need to go," I say. "It'll be dark soon. And I'm supposed to take your mom out on a date tonight."

"Please, Daddy," he repeats as if I have not spoken, and now he takes the edge of my swimming trunks in his tiny, sandy hand and tugs.

I look down at him, moved by his openness, purity, and beauty.

He knows he's got me then.

"Yes," he says, releasing my shorts to clench his fist and pull it toward him in a gesture of victory. Then he begins to jump up and down.

I drop the keys and the towels and the bottles of sunscreen wrapped in them, kick off my flip-flops, and pause just a moment to take it all in—him, the sand, the sea, the sun.

"I love you, Dad," he says with the ease and unashamed openness only a safe and secure child can.

"I love you."

I take his hand in mine, and we walk down to the end of his world as the sun sets and the breeze cools off the day. And we walk right into the ocean from which we came. A wave knocks us down and we stay that way, allowing the foamy water to wash over us.

He shrieks his joy and excitement, sounding like the gulls in the air and on the shore. He plays with intensity and abandon, and for a moment I want to be a child again, but only for a moment, for more than anything in this world, I want to be his dad.

We forget about the world around us, and we lose track of time, and the thick, salty waters of the Gulf roll in on us and then back out to sea.

6

I could have just gone off and killed myself quietly. Everybody always asks why guys like me don't. I'll tell you why. That would have been an even bigger waste. If I go out this way, taking as many of the fuckers who made my life miserable with me as I can, then maybe just maybe it will send a message. Maybe something will change and some other poor miserable kid in some other shitty school will get treated better and maybe find a reason not to do what I'm doing.

I wake up later than I intended to the next morning and reach for my phone.

To my surprise, it's not on the bedside table next to my gun, badge, books, and bottle of water where it usually is.

I search for it a few minutes before realizing Anna must have taken it—something she does on the rare occasions when I have a day off.

She keeps the phone with her and monitors my calls and texts, waking me if there's ever anything that can't wait. This simple, kind act makes me feel cared for and loved and provides genuine, measurable benefits for my mental health and wellbeing. I'm an owl being taken care of by my robin.

I stumble down the hallway to the living room to find Anna lying on the couch, both Taylor and John Paul lying on her asleep.

She looks up at me and smiles.

She has no makeup on, she's still in her pajamas, and her thick, brown hair is still morning mad—and she couldn't be more beautiful.

"Morning," she whispers. "How'd you sleep?"

"Great, thanks to you," I whisper back.

"Your phone's on the counter," she says, glancing back toward the kitchen. "Nothing that couldn't wait so far."

I smile. We have differing ideas on what can and can't wait.

"Carla took my car to get a few things," she says. "You hungry?"

I shake my head. I'm not a morning eater—no matter how early or late in the morning it is, and though she knows this, she always asks me anyway, a practice nearly as endearing as her taking my phone so I can sleep.

I can't help but notice that her question was phrased a little differently than it normally is. Clearly, even with the children asleep, she didn't want to take the chance that I would give her my typical response when she asks some variation of is there anything I'd like to eat.

Before I can point this out, my phone starts vibrating on the counter and I step over to get it.

"You had a chance to look over our lists of names yet?" Kim asks.

"Not yet, but—"

"Why are you whispering?" she asks in a whisper of her own.

I tell her.

"And you really haven't read the lists and info yet?" she says.

"Plan to as soon as we hang up."

"What in the world you been doin'?" she asks in mock outrage. "Wait'll I tell Chip. He'll probably fire you from his task force."

I stifle a laugh to keep from waking Taylor and John and walk into the mudroom but continue to whisper.

"LeAnn and I are both meeting with everyone on our lists today," she says. "Using a variety of excuses so we don't raise any suspicions. And she's doing a short safety presentation in their classrooms because it can't hurt and so she can get handwriting samples."

"Great," I say. "That's—"

"Think you can bring yourself to look at the lists and read the info about the kids on it in time to meet with us about them after school this afternoon?" she says.

"I think I just might."

"Don't want to overburden you or anything."

"What time?" I ask.

"Let's do four," she says. "Give faculty and staff time to leave too."

"See you then."

"Only if it's not too much trouble," she says.

As I'm finishing up my conversation with Kim, I see Dad pull into our driveway in his new pearl Platinum F-150. Slipping on a pair of shoes, I ease open the door as quietly as I can and step outside to meet him so we can talk without disturbing the little sleepers.

He comes to a stop beneath the shade of the three oak trees near the far end of our driveway. I reach his truck before he gets out and he rolls down the window.

"Tried to call," he says. "Decided to drop by, make sure Chris didn't get reanimated somehow or Randa didn't break out of jail."

"Anna took my phone when she got up to let me sleep," I say. "Haven't even checked it yet. Sorry."

"Don't be. Glad you got some sleep. You don't get enough. Just checking about last night, see what Jeffers had to say."

"I think he might be on to something," I say.

"Really?" he asks, his voice rising in surprise. "Guess it was bound to happen eventually. What's the saying about a stopped clock?"

I tell him what Chip, Kim, and LeAnn had to say and about the fragments of the journal notes.

He shakes his head. "Still can't believe the deputy who cried wolf got one right this time," he says.

"Well, we don't know that yet, but I certainly think it's worth looking in to."

"Got to do something," he says, "stop all these kids from getting killed."

I nod. "Yes, we do."

"Let me know how I can help," he says. "I'm in a bit of a bind since I'm not the sheriff anymore. Try not to do anything that looks like I'm trying to do Hugh Glenn's job or work against him in some way, but . . . none of that matters if it comes to savin' kids."

"I'll let you know, but hopefully we can just locate the kid and intervene, get him some help, keep anything from happening."

"Certainly hope so," he says. "Just let me know."

He cranks his new truck and puts it in reverse.

"And John, thank you. Would've been easy to write this off since it was Jeffers who brought it to us. A lazy investigator would have."

7

High school sucks. It's one of the truly universal truths. Whoever said high school is supposed to be the best days of your life is a sad, pathetic, delusional fuck. The truly pathetic thing about high school is everyone tries so damn hard to be something they aren't. Even the staff. Maybe it's that way everywhere but it's worse in fucking high school. My problem wasn't that I didn't fit in with the popular kids. It was that I didn't fit in anywhere. I didn't even fit in with the misfits. I hated high school and I've never trusted anybody who didn't. Show me someone who liked being a teenager and I'll show you the most fucked up person of all.

E ntering my old high school—even when it's dim and after-hours empty, elicits complex and conflicting thoughts and emotions. Now, unexpectedly, a measure of nostalgia and bitter-sweet homesickness is mixed in with old feelings of adolescent banality, cliquish confinement, and quiet desperation.

I feel a certain amount of hesitation and trepidation about assisting with an investigation here. Pottersville will always be home to me, Potter High will always be my school, but I'm an investigator in another county, and even though we have a Mutual Aid Agreement in place, I feel awkward and out of place.

The Mutual Aid Agreement has been signed by all sixty-seven sheriff's departments in the state of Florida and means that any sheriff or deputy can enforce the law and even make arrests in any county. But it doesn't cover coming into another county and conducting an investigation. There's a world of difference in being in another county and intervening when you witness a crime taking place versus assisting in an investigation to stop one—especially when the county in question is where your father used to be sheriff until he lost his last bid for reelection.

Kim and LeAnn's offices are next to each other on the back-side of the front offices which include reception, accounting, and administration. And though they have back doors that open into the main offices, their front doors are in the back corner of the commons, between the stage and a bank of microwaves built on surprisingly high shelves along the beige block wall.

I pass the huge built-in trophy case and walk over an enormous seal on the floor that reads *PHS Home of the Fighting Pirates* encircling a logo of the school's mascot—a cartoonish pirate with a black eye patch, tricorne hat, and swashbuckling sword—to the brightly backlit glass doors of Kim and LeAnn's offices.

I find them waiting for me in LeAnn's office with two students —a pale, pie-faced, blond-haired, heavyset white girl named Sierra Baker and a tall, skinny, light-skinned black boy named DeShawn Holt.

I'm surprised to find students here and shocked when I'm told they've been recruited to help.

"Sierra and DeShawn have helped us a lot in the past with valuable information," LeAnn says of the two kids who are obviously some sort of schoolhouse snitches. "They know the other kids far better than we could ever hope to."

I shoot a glance at Kim and I can tell she understands and shares my concern.

"Could you two wait out in the commons for a minute?" Kim says. "Let us talk to Mr. Jordan for a moment before we begin."

The two overly helpful teens are more than happy to comply, and quickly vacate LeAnn's office.

"What's up?" LeAnn asks.

"I'm not comfortable discussing possible student suspects with other students," I say.

"Oh," she says. "Okay. I just . . . They've been very helpful in the past and I thought we needed all the help we could get on this thing."

Kim says, "What if it got out or they said something to one of the suspects or a parent?"

"They've never said anything to anyone but me," LeAnn says, "but I see what you're saying. I'll just tell them to keep an ear out for anything suspicious and bring it to me if they hear anything."

"I think that would be better," Kim says.

LeAnn jumps up, comes around her desk, shoves her door open hard by the flat metal crossbar, and steps out into the commons, and I am unable to tell if she is angry or if it's just her normal way of doing things.

"I'm glad you said something," Kim says. "I was trying to think of how to. Couldn't believe it when I walked in and they were sitting here."

"Sorry about that," LeAnn says when she returns. "I was just trying to give us our best chance at stopping this thing—and I've worked with them a lot over the years to get information. Didn't think about . . . the other."

Kim says, "It's no problem. And you're right. We need all hands on deck. I think the difference is between them bringing something to us versus us talking to them about other students."

"No, you're right," LeAnn says. "My bad."

"It's all good," Kim says.

LeAnn moves back behind her desk and Kim and I take a seat in the two chairs across from her, previously occupied by Sierra and DeShawn.

"Where do y'all want to start?" LeAnn asks.

"Why don't we start with what we're looking for more broadly," Kim says. "Then talk about the people on our lists."

"Sounds good to me," she says. "From what I've read and learned from the training I've done, we're not looking for a girl—think there's only been one of them—and we're not looking for a black guy. That's part of the reason I felt safe involving Sierra and DeShawn."

Though there may have been other girl rampage school shooters, the only one I had ever heard about is Brenda Spencer —the troubled teenager who in 1979 killed two adults and wounded eight children in a school shooting in San Diego, California. And though there may have been African-American school shooters before, I am not familiar with any.

"So," Kim says, "we're looking for a white male—rampage shooters and serial killers have something in common."

"Based on the statistics I've read," LeAnn says, "most of them struggle with suicidal tendencies and depression. They feel persecuted or victimized, but more in a general way than specifically being bullied. They don't act on impulse or snap in some way, but painstakingly plan their attack. And most if not all talk about their plans with someone they know before they carry them out. And if not that, then at least their violent fantasies in some way."

"I read that something like ninety-three percent did something that deeply concerned someone close to them before the shooting," Kim says.

"Exactly," LeAnn says. "That's from the secret service report from a few years after Columbine. That's why I'm convinced there are signs. We just have to see them. It's why I thought students could help."

"They absolutely can," I say. "Just in general, not a specific way. We need them noticing any alarming behavior from anyone, not focusing on just a few."

"I get that now," she says.

"Where is Chip?" I ask. "I figured he'd be here by now."

They both smile.

"We may have told him the meeting started a little later," LeAnn says.

"Give us a chance to go over everything together first," Kim says.

"It's an old trick we used to pull in high school too," LeAnn says.

I think about how in many ways they're still in high school, how it's like they never left.

"Speaking of . . ." LeAnn continues. "We better keep moving or we won't finish before he gets here."

Kim nods and says, "It's counterintuitive or at least contrary to conventional wisdom, but most school shooters are from two-parent homes, are in the mainstream crowd in school, make pretty good grades, don't usually get in trouble, aren't extreme loners, and aren't addicted to violent video games and movies—though a lot of them are into first-person shooter games and the Oliver Stone film *Natural Born Killers*."

"A big factor seems to be difficulty coping with loss or failure," Le Ann says. "Especially if it's significant and they are young. Things like failed romances, family illnesses and deaths."

"So we need to be thinking about these factors when we look at the kids on our lists," Kim says.

"Let's talk about them," I say.

Kim says, "You know how we each have four guys on our lists and only two of them show up on both lists. We were talking and neither of us thinks the two that show up on both lists are significantly more likely to be the shooter than the other four that weren't on both our lists."

"Interesting," I say, glancing down at the lists.

Kim's list includes Mason Nickols, Dakota Emanuel, Evan Fowler, and Zach Griffith.

LeAnn's list includes Mason Nickols, Dakota Emanuel, Tristan Ward, and Chase Dailey.

"Either of you had any other thoughts or questions since making your lists and talking about them?" I ask. "Anyone else to add? Anyone you've reconsidered and want to take off?"

They look at each other and then me, shaking their heads.

"Okay," I say. "Now I want you to make a new list independent of each other—no conferring. Exclude white guys and include girls. See who comes to mind."

Kim's eyes widen as she nods appreciatively. "Because less likely isn't the same as impossible."

"Do we have handwriting samples for all of them?" I ask.

LeAnn nods and hands me a file folder from her desk.

"I'll look at these while y'all see if anyone makes the new list," I say. "Cool?"

It must be because both of them are so busy thinking and writing that neither responds.

A few minutes later I look up from the folder to find them looking at me. "I'm assuming Potter High doesn't have a penmanship class," I say.

"Did it back when we were here?" LeAnn asks.

"I'm not sure I could exclude anyone from the list based on these handwriting samples," I say.

"That's what I said," Kim says.

"I thought Zach's was different enough," LeAnn says, "but..."

"What're the ages of the boys on the list?" I ask.

"Mason, Dakota, and Tristan are juniors," LeAnn says. "Chase, Evan, and Zach are sophomores."

"Anyone make the new list?" I ask.

Kim looks at LeAnn, nodding for her to go first.

"Denise Royal," LeAnn says.

"I put her too," Kim says.

"She's our only truly goth girl," LeAnn says. "Always writing dark poetry and drawing dark pictures. I'm not sure I could see her doing it as much as helping someone do it."

"Does she hang out with any of the guys on the list?" I ask.

"Tristan Ward a little," LeAnn says. "She doesn't hang out with anyone much—and he's got a girlfriend, but they do hang out some."

"Anyone else?" I ask.

"Not really," LeAnn says. "Besides a little with Tristan she's a loner."

"No," I say, "anyone else make your lists?"

They both shake their heads.

"She's the only possible girl," Kim says, "and I just can't see any of our black kids doing it."

"I agree," LeAnn adds.

"Okay, let's talk about our suspects," I say. "What came out of your meetings with them today?"

"I was thinking . . ." LeAnn says. "Right now there's drama and band practice happening out in the arts building and a home baseball game at the baseball stadium. Between all three, most if not all of these kids are on campus. We could take you around to them so you can either put a face with the name or actually talk to them if you want to."

"Absolutely," I say.

"Great," she says, "but we should warn you about the approach we take. Our focus is on at-risk kids and our best hope is to maintain a rapport with them. These are often the most fringe kids and we let them be themselves. They can not only be odd but disrespectful and foulmouthed. We don't strain out the gnats."

8

You want to hear something interesting? Dylan Klebold grew up in a home with no guns. Not even toy ones. Dylan's dad was adamant. Said they didn't need guns in their house because they weren't going to play with them. I've got no father, but my mom said the same thing about our house. Boy, will she be shocked if she looks at the arsenal under my bed.

The main building of Potter High is a circle—a huge round hallway with classrooms on the right and a large library on the left.

What was known as the band and agriculture building in our day and is now the arts building is a smaller detached circular building in the back. Beyond it is yet an even smaller circular building that used to house the auto-mechanics program but now sits empty.

We walk up the dim hallway of the main building and around toward the arts building in the back.

I can remember walking these very same halls a lifetime or

two ago—Merrill beside me, my mind often somewhere else, except when I hoped to catch a glimpse of or have an actual encounter with Anna.

I'm a step behind them and get to observe the enormous size difference. Kimmy looks like a kid next to LeAnn—even in her green deputy's uniform. She walks with energy, kind of bouncing down the hallway, her ponytail swinging back and forth as she does. Next to her, LeAnn, who looks like her clothes come from a mens' big and tall shop, lumbers along, one of her strides equaling three of Kimmy's.

"Is it strange for you to be back?" Kim asks me.

I nod and smile. "Some, yeah."

The school smells and feels the same, though much has changed. Unlike when we were students here, the hallway is carpeted and the lockers line the walls between the doors instead of being located all together in an alcove.

There are far more pirate mascots around than when we were here—painted on the glass of windows and doors, on the cinderblock walls, splashed across lockers and on welcome mats and rugs. The building seems cleaner and better maintained, but it's the same.

The single biggest difference—both in the hallways and the entire school—is the seemingly excessive amount of security cameras. If there ever is a school shooting we should have plenty of angles on it.

"Do y'all ever miss being in school?" LeAnn says. "I miss it. We had a good class and a lot of fun back then, didn't we? And no adult shit to deal with—like paying bills or watching the world fall apart around us."

Kim shrugs. "Sometimes, I guess. I guess I miss certain things about it, but I wouldn't want to go back."

"What about you, John?" LeAnn asks.

I shake my head. "Don't miss a thing about high school," I say.

"Except getting to hang with us," Kim says.

"I'm doing that now."

"You were always so . . ." LeAnn begins.

"I was always so what?" I ask.

"I don't know exactly," she says. "You didn't really act like the rest of us. I can't think of the right word, but you were—"

"Self-contained," Kim says. "More mature."

"Yeah, I guess that's it," LeAnn says. "You were so focused—but not on anything school or normal teenager-shit related. Sort of set you apart."

I think about that. "That's interesting and I think you're right, though at the time I just felt like I didn't fit in."

"I can tell you what he was into," Kim says. "He was focused on God, the Atlanta Child Murders, and Anna Rodden."

I laugh. She's right, but I would've never guessed she or anyone else would know any of that.

"None of us stood a chance because of Anna," Kim adds. "And you wound up with her."

"Sometimes the guy gets the girl," LeAnn says. "You got Ace Bowman."

Ace Bowman, who is now the head football and baseball coach and athletic director of Potter High, was two grades ahead of us and a star athlete when we were in school here.

"That's true," she says.

"I didn't know you two were—" I begin.

"It's a world class workplace romance," LeAnn says. "Both of them had a yin for each other back in school. Neither of them knew it. Years later, after relationships and kids and whatnot, they're back in high school and available. Hell, the kids set them up. It was so— I'll tell you what it was like. It was like one of those damn Lifetime Christmas movies—'cept without the snow or Christmas or cheesy lines and ridiculous plot lines. But it had every bit of the romance."

"Our first dance was at the prom," Kim says. "We chaperoned last year."

"It was," LeAnn says. "I'll tell you what it was. It was romantic as a son of a bitch. That's what it was. The kind of shit that gives the rest of us single girls hope."

"Which is what you should have," Kim says. "You're going to find someone soon. I just know it."

"Sure," LeAnn says, "some massive cornfed female who likes big-mouthed Amazon women with frizzy blond hair and saggin' tits is gonna come walking through the front door to apply for the vacant driver's ed job and'll take one look at me and . . . 'Course when she tries to sweep me off my feet she'll break her back, but I won't leave her bedside until she can pee on her own again."

"I'm serious," Kim says. "She may not waltz through the door of PHS, but she's out there." She turns to me. "I keep trying to get her to try online sites or apps."

"What do you think, John?" LeAnn asks. "Should I get myself a Farmer's Only account?"

"Well, Cornfed Only, maybe, but yeah. You live in a very small town. Why not use the tools that give you access to the larger outside world?"

"That's a good point," she says. "And it's certainly not like I'm against using tools. I wear the hell out of some vibrators."

9

School shooters are able to easily acquire high-powered guns. Hell, in many cases their parents helped them get them, either directly or through negligence. Always seems to be a lot of negligence. Rampage killers prefer guns with rapid fire capability, weapons of personal mass destruction that spray bursts of bullets in a matter of seconds. More bullets in less time equals more victims. And that's what it's all about. It's a numbers game.

The art building is a microcosm of the main building—a smaller circle with classrooms around the theater in the center.

And bad student art on the walls.

When we were students here this was the band, ag, and shop building. Now there is no ag or shop program, so instead of soil and fertilizer and freshly sawed lumber or wood burning, it smells of spray paint, epoxy, latex, cooking clay, and creative teen spirit.

We find Tristan and Denise in the theater working on an original play written by Tristan and directed by Denise.

The theater is small and dim except for the stage. Tristan and Denise are sitting on the fifth row up from the front, watching as student actors in drag and blackface move overly dramatically across the stage—each overacting even for a high school musical.

Based on the words and lyrics, the costumes and casting, what we're witnessing is a heavy-handed exploration of teenage angst as it relates to identity, race, and sexual orientation. The production lacks both subtlety and subtext. Everything is self-consciously obvious and on the nose. They have an important message and want to make sure no one, not even the densest, unwokest adult misses it.

The setting is a school cafeteria, where students move around like cattle, herded into small cliques by loud and obnoxious jocks and cheerleaders and milquetoast goody-goodies.

Suddenly a half-male/half-female, half-white/half-black school shooter slowly walks in and begins shooting, each student singing about his or her crime before falling to the floor dead.

Kim glances at me, eyes wide.

LeAnn whispers, "Are we witnessing a confession?"

The crimes the students confess to are typical teenage trespasses.

I was too self-involved to even notice you.

I only thought of myself.

I was too insecure to let you be you.

I called you faggot because I was questioning my own sexuality.

I picked on you to make myself feel better.

As soon as Denise notices us, she points us out to Tristan and he stops the rehearsal.

"Good work everyone," he says. "We're getting there. Let's take five. Get a breath, grab some hydration, and we'll take it from the top."

He then stands and walks up the aisle to meet us, Denise trailing behind him.

"Miss Dunne," he says, nodding toward LeAnn.

He's a soft, pale boy with a bird's nest of blond hair, big, bright red lips, and odd blue eyes with large dark circles beneath them.

"There a problem?" Denise asks.

Neither kid makes direct eye contact with any of us.

Denise Royal is even more ghostly than Tristan—a fact emphasized by her jet black Flock of Seagulls hair and her black lipstick and eyeliner. Her myriad piercings make it look as if she fell face first into a tackle box.

"Why'd you stop the rehearsal?" Kim asks.

Tristan doesn't respond.

Denise, without looking at or acknowledging Kim, says, "This is a closed rehearsal. We've been given assurances from administration that we won't be hindered or censored." Nodding toward me, she says, "Who's this?"

"Just a guy who used to go here too," LeAnn says.

"Smells like bacon," she says, still talking to LeAnn. "They both do."

I smile.

"So we can't stay and watch your play?" LeAnn says.

"*You're* welcome to attend the premiere," she says, making it clear she just means LeAnn.

"Is your play about a school shooting?" Kim asks.

Tristan looks at her directly for the first time, disgust and disdain filling his pale, puffy face. "Art isn't *about* anything. It just is. It requires no justification or explanation."

He says all this like he's the first pretentious person to ever be on this planet.

"I won't explain my work to you. I'm sure you wouldn't *get it* even if I was willing to."

"There's nothing *to get*," I say. "Nothing to intuit. You *gave* it all. Forcefully. There's nothing left to explain. It's all there on the stage."

He nods and smiles as if I've just given him a compliment.

Denise nods. "It's like theatrical rape. We're sayin' *Take it hard, bitches. Whether you want it or not.*"

Kim nods. "Yeah, that's what it felt like to me."

Tristan lets out a sinister little laugh. "That's funny," he says, as if he's just received a new insight from his muse. "It's like *fuck the police*. Literally."

"Actually, it's not," Kim says. "If you're gonna be a playwright you should probably know what *literally* means."

"We'll be sure to get a *dick* . . . tionary and do that," Denise says.

"Anything else?" Tristan asks.

"When is your premiere?" I ask.

"Friday," he says. "Which is why we need to get back to work."

"We're performing it in front of the entire student body," Denise says. "During school. And mark my words . . . It'll be a day none of these losers will ever forget."

Kim looks over at me. "You marking it or should I?"

Tristan says, "This little piggy went to market. This little piggy made a joke."

"Soon no little piggies will be laughing though," Denise says.

"They'll be squealing all the way home," Tristan says.

10

You know what? Not everybody has to do what you say they have to or what you want them to. Does that come as a shock to you? You really do think you rule the world, don't you? Well, you don't. And high school isn't the whole world anyway. I know it's your whole world, but it's not the whole world. You should maybe know that. You should also know that you are only doing what every other stupid and ignorant person in history has done. You attack and torment people who aren't like you. You aren't even original. You ruined my life. All I've done is pay you back in kind.

"Please tell me at our adolescent worst we were never that bad," Kim says.

"Not even close," LeAnn says.

"I remember being far too earnest and taking myself too seriously at times," I say, "but I don't think I was ever that pretentious."

The three of us are back out in the hallway of the arts building, walking toward the music room and recording studio.

"You weren't at all," Kim says. "You were the sweetest boy. Always so nice to everyone."

"You *did* treat everyone the same," LeAnn says. "I always admired that. You could certainly be . . . serious . . . even humorless at times . . . like you were carrying around the weight of the world, but for an adolescent Atlas you were all right, and you certainly were so nice to everyone—no matter their race or socioeconomic level."

"And unlike John, you were *never* serious back then," Kim says to LeAnn.

"Still not if I can help it," LeAnn says. "Best defense mechanism I've found against the slings and arrows. How is that for some self-perception, and what about throwing in a little Shakespeare since we're at the theater lab? Are y'all as impressed with me as I am?"

"More," I say. "Of course, it would have been even more impressive if you hadn't felt the need, like Tristan, to tell us what you just told us."

She smiles. "What he and I have to say is too important to take a chance that you might miss it. It's our duty to break it down for you dullards."

"And I was always pining after some guy," Kim adds, looking away wistfully. "I'm sure we were self-absorbed and maybe even a little dramatic, but we weren't anything like that."

"See why we thought of them?" LeAnn says.

I nod.

"They could be our own little Mickey and Mallory, right?" she says.

I think about the mass-murdering couple from Oliver Stone's *Natural Born Killers* and try to picture the goth girl I just saw in the role of Mallory and the pale, puffy boy as Mickey.

The original Mickey and Mallory were victims of traumatic childhoods who became a rampage killing couple, a bloody Bonnie and Clyde sensationalized and spurred on by the media.

"I'm sure y'all had this thought," Kim says, "but . . . what if they . . . Do you think they could be planning on doing the shooting during or at the end of the play?"

I nod. "Very well could be," I say. "Send the actors out with real guns loaded with live rounds, or . . . more likely . . . make everyone sit through that dreadful drivel and then—"

"We'll all be begging to be shot," LeAnn says.

As we near the music room, we hear the fine fingerings of a skilled musician playing an acoustic guitar in an arpeggiated manner, and LeAnn tells us about Chase Dailey's alcoholic mom and the severe abuse he had suffered at her hands—hers and the parade of user-abuse boyfriends that had worn a path through their home and lives.

Kim taps on the door and we step inside.

As we do, Chase stops playing.

Looking up from his vintage-looking Guild guitar, his eyes widen when he sees the three of us.

Chase Dailey is a slight and slightly effeminate young man with long, dark hair and deep-set dark eyes. He has long, narrow fingers with nails in need of cleaning.

He's alone, seated at a music stand in a large carpeted music room, his bare feet on the round, silver circle near the bottom of the stool he's on.

"Everything okay, Miss Kim?" he asks.

She nods. "Everything's fine, Chase."

Foam egg crate acoustic panels mounted on the walls absorb much of the sound and all of the echo in the dead room.

"We were just walking by and heard your beautiful playing, thought we'd stop in and listen for a moment."

"Chase isn't just a great musician," LeAnn says. "He's an accomplished songwriter. Only problem is they're so sad you can only listen to a couple at a time."

Kim says, "Chase, this is John. He was in our class back when we went here."

He puts his hands together and gives me a small, heartfelt namaste nod.

"How's it going?" I say.

He shrugs. "Ah, you know . . . could always be better."

"Sorry to hear that," I say. "You play beautifully."

Music is his escape, this music room his only sanctuary—one he remains in to avoid going home until the evening custodians finish cleaning and kick him out of the building so they can lock up for the night.

"Be a shame not to do the one thing you do . . . well," he says.

"You mind playing a song for us?" Kim asks.

"I don't want to sing, but I'll play for you if you want."

"Please."

He does.

I'm not sure if what he plays is original or not—it's a testament to his skill that I can't be sure—but it's extraordinary, complex, moving, intricate, impressive.

When he finishes the three of us clap for him.

"That was incredible," I say. "Thanks so much for playing for us."

He gives me his little namaste nod again.

"Well, we'll go now and sorry to disturb you," LeAnn says. She turns to leave, but then turns back toward him. "Oh . . . before we do. Remember what I spoke to your class about today? Can you think of any students who seem particularly stressed right now—bullied or just broken up with someone? Anything like that?"

"Everybody I know is like that," he says. "And not just kids. The whole world is fucked. Whatcha gonna do?"

"Anything we can do to help you?" Kim asks.

He gives her a resolved look and shakes his head, his long, dark hair moving back and forth.

"Okay."

"Well," LeAnn says, "if you think of anyone who—"

"You thinkin' someone's gonna do something?" he asks. "Something violent or something?"

"What makes you say that?" she asks.

"Just from what you said today and how y'all're acting."

"Do you know of anyone who might do something drastic or violent?"

"If it were me . . . I'd look for someone who doesn't have a thing—you know, a girl or a sport or a hobby or a passion or a . . . something. It weren't for this guitar, I'd've offed myself a long time ago."

"We're glad you have the guitar," Kim says. "And you're so good at it. But we want you to have more. Come see me and Miss LeAnn tomorrow, okay? Let us help you get more, have a better life. Okay?"

He nods.

"I mean it. Promise me you'll come see us tomorrow."

"Okay," he says, but doesn't sound like he means it.

11

My thoughts and prayers are with you. May almighty God, the eternal father, hold you in the palm of his hand.

Baseball doesn't get the crowd that football does in Pottersville, but it's a good season, so the park is packed.

In the warm glow of a quiet, peaceful evening, the boys of spring stand in a greening field backlit by the sinking sun participating in the leisurely pursuit of their country's official favorite pastime.

The outfield fence holds the homemade signs of hometown businesses whose advertising dollars spent here won't net a single additional sale.

As LeAnn, Kim, and I walk up, the park lights buzz and wink and flicker on, the beams of those near the backstop catching the curling smoke from the concession stand grill.

LeAnn turns to us and says, "Who would want to shoot up this living Norman Rockwell painting?"

"*There are those . . .*" Kim says, shaking her head.

"I guess there are, but *damn* . . . Seems like some Taliban shit to me."

Kim nods. "That's exactly what it is. Same destructive impulse."

We stop along the back edge of the ballpark and take in the scene.

The announcer is a soft-spoken, twenty-something, African-American guy who was once a star here and went on to play in the minor leagues and even a few unremarkable games in the majors before returning home to become a roofer for his dad's company. His dad, who was a star some twenty years before his son, is doing color commentary.

"At the plate now is the right-handed-hitting catcher, Bradley Conroy, hitting two-seventy-three with eight RBIs so far this year. Short lead . . . and this one on one hop by the third baseman into left field. Well, Sanders was playing in, and that one was just over the glove by about a foot and a half."

"Back-to-back singles . . . Another nice piece of hitting by Conroy for the Sharks."

The home bleachers are mostly filled with parents and grand-parents and the siblings of players too young and small to be on their own. Most of the Potter High students are swarming around the park in small packs, socializing, seeing and being seen.

Because there aren't many visitors, the guest bleachers are filled with spillover from the home side, mostly teachers and faculty and the suck-up students who don't mind sitting near them.

Beyond the dugout, the right field fence is lined with clusters of students sitting in the grass or on blankets, paying far more attention to each other than the game.

"Watch them," LeAnn says, pointing to the two students she had in her office earlier, DeShawn and Sierra. "See how they move about the various groups of kids. They aren't part of any discernibly defined group, but they are friendly with all of them. It's like they haven't chosen a side—or been relegated to one—and so by not being part of any, they are welcomed by all. That's why they're helpful. That's why I thought we could use them."

"I'm sure we will be," I say, watching the two move about, greeting and being greeted by all the various factions just as she has described.

"Absolutely," Kim says, "we just couldn't give them information about other students. That's all."

"I get that now," LeAnn says. "I should've thought about that part. I just got excited about playing detective and being able to bring actual informants to the table like I'm on *The Wire* or some shit like that."

Kim and I both laugh.

"Just want to be a top cop like y'all," LeAnn says.

"Speaking of . . ." Kim says, staring off in the direction of the concession stand. "Look who's here and who he's with."

We follow her gaze to see Chip Jeffers standing in between the sheriff, Hugh Glenn, and the principal, Tyrese Monroe— Merrill's cousin and the first black principal Potter High has ever had.

"Shall we?" LeAnn says.

"Sure," Kim says as I nod.

And we begin to walk in their direction.

On our way, as we pass the Pirates' mostly empty dugout, we pause to talk to Evan Fowler, one of the sophomore suspects from Kim's list.

Evan is small even for his age, the high school baseball uniform too big for him. He wears his hat pushed way down on his head, just over his eyes, as if he's trying to hide, his bushy, too-long hair spilling out around it as if ready for a bowl cut.

"Hey, Evan," Kim says. "How's it going?"

He turns his red face toward us and uses his tongue to unstick his lip from his buckteeth before speaking. "Same old same old.

Ridin' the hell out of this bench. Doin' my job and keepin' it good and warm."

"Hang in there," she says. "You'll get your chance to play when you're older."

He shrugs. "Not likely."

I wonder if he's talking about getting older or getting to play.

"Hey," the coach and Kim's boyfriend, Ace Bowman, yells from the other end of the dugout. "Arrest that woman if she continues to harass my players."

His tone along with his big, easy smile is flirtatious.

He's a tall, broad, once athletic man who has gone soft. His fleshy face is both puffy and loose, and his wide hips appear even wider in the piped knicker baseball pants.

"Hey," Kim says, pointing at him, "you take care of baseball and leave policing to me before I arrest your cute ass for harassing a law enforcement officer."

"Honey, you got the cuffs, I got the time," he says, holding his hands out, wrists together.

As he talks, he has to shift the sunflower seeds around in his mouth. When he's not talking, he's chewing on them and spitting out the shells in a rapid, practiced manner.

In the stands closest to the home dugout, a set of male twins dressed identically in PHS T-shirts and jeans, the sleeves and legs of which are rolled up, and who look to be around sixteen or seventeen, are shaking pompoms and cheering loudly but insincerely.

Someone in the stands behind them tells them to hold it down, asks them why they're even here, it's obvious they don't know anything about baseball.

"If you can't be an athlete," one of them says.

"Be an athletic supporter," the other says, looking over at the dugout and adding, "Right coach?"

LeAnn notices me noticing them. "The Dupree twins," she

says. "Hayden and Hunter. Very troubled boys. Suffered horrendous abuse before being taken from their biological parents."

"Why aren't they on the list?" I ask.

"Never occurred to me," she says. "They're just so . . . soft and . . . I don't know . . . effeminate."

Kim steps over to us, "They'll fuck anything that moves—or be fucked by them I guess, but . . . can't see them hurting anyone."

I wince at students being described in such a way, and LeAnn says, "Damn, Kimmy, don't hold back."

When we continue on and are far enough away so Evan can't hear us, LeAnn says, "I just can't see that sweet little bucktooth boy sawin' down his classmates with a rifle either."

"You're probably right," Kim says. "Hope you are. But there's a lot of frustration and rage in that little body. I've seen it firsthand. Remember that fight he got in last year with that boy who had been bullying him? I thought he was going to kill him."

"Oh, shit," LeAnn says. "I forgot about that. You're right. Keep him on the list."

Up at bat is an enormous kid everyone calls Slow Stevie.

"Watch this," LeAnn says. "If he hits a home run, which is what he usually does, he'll walk the bases. Not run. Not jog. Walk every step."

"Not a fast walk either," Kim adds.

On the third pitch and his second swing, Slow Stevie drives a fastball so far past the right field fence it rolls into the swamp and nobody goes after it.

And as they described, he drops the bat and starts walking the bases.

When we approach the three men standing near the concession stand, Hugh Glenn steps toward me and extends his hand. "Hey, John," he says. "Good to see you. How are you? How's your dad?"

"He's good, thanks," I say. "Staying busier now than before he retired. Enjoying being a newlywed again."

"That's good. That's real good. I'm glad to hear that."

Like every extroverted politician, Hugh Glenn is warm and friendly and acts as if he not only cares deeply about you, but you're one of his closest friends. And mostly pulls it off.

While Glenn is talking to me, Chip is getting onto Kim for not being in her office when he came by earlier and not being at the game when it started.

"I made sure I stayed here until you got here," Chip is saying loud enough for Glenn to hear him.

"Leave her alone," Glenn says, turning away from me and toward them. "She's an outstanding SRO, and there's only one of her. She can't be everywhere all the time."

"No, sir, she can't. I was just letting her know I had it until she got here."

"What you *had*," LeAnn says, "is your head so far up the sheriff's ass you wouldn't've noticed if anything happened anyway."

We all laugh as Chip pushes back, trying to defend himself, and Slow Stevie just reaches third.

"John," Tyrese says to me, extending his hand. "Good to see you. How you been? Seen Merrill lately? Said he was gonna call me the next time you two headed to the gym for a little b-ball, remind y'all how springy young legs can be."

"I'll make sure he does," I say.

"Good, 'cause he says y'all still got game and . . . I'll have to see that to believe it."

Above us, on the second story of the concession stand, its piece-of-plywood window propped open, the press box towers over everything else. At this angle, nearly directly beneath it, I am unable to see the father-and-son team calling the game, but I can hear them.

"Tommy Hudson, the right fielder, the hitter. Two outs. One runner on base. He showed bunt. Laid down. Picked up. Nobody covering first . . . and he's on base."

"Hudson snuck one by the Pirates on that one."

"Can I speak to you for a minute?" Glenn is saying to Kim.

She nods. "Sure."

The two of them step a few feet away from the rest of us.

LeAnn says, "We're gonna step over here and see Zach while you do that."

LeAnn starts walking away and, after saying goodbye to Tyrese, I follow her.

She leads me over to a platform next to the visitors' dugout, and we climb up it.

"Hope they built this with big girls in mind," she says.

When we reach the top, we find Zach Griffith, the only other sophomore on Kim's list, videoing the game with one of the school's cameras.

LeAnn waves to him.

"You can talk," he says. "I'm not recording sound. Just video."

"Oh, cool," she says. "How's it going?"

"Seventh circle of hell," he says.

"Damn," she says. "That's pretty bad. John, Zach. Zach, John. Zach runs our school video production unit. He's very good."

I think of the many videos Harris and Klebold made and make a mental note for us to check Zach's work.

"This silliness is just point-and-shoot shit," he says. "You could train any monkey to do this."

The media tower is high above the field and provides a unique perspective on the game and the ant-like individuals swarming around it below. It makes me think of Charles Whitman, the Texas Tower Sniper, who climbed to the twenty-eighth-floor observation deck of the tower at the University of Texas in Austin and started picking off strangers with his hunting rifle—this, after killing his wife and his mother and three people inside the tower below. Before being shot and killed by Houston McCoy of the Austin police department, Whitman wounded thirty-one people and killed seventeen—sixteen on that day and a seventeenth who died thirty-five years later from injuries sustained back then.

"Why do it if you hate it so much?" LeAnn asks.

"Got in trouble. It was this or get suspended. Coach Ace Bighips thinks it's funny 'cause I hate sports."

"What'd he have to do with it?" she asks.

"He's the one who decided my punishment. Fucker."

She turns to me. "Coach Bowman is not only a coach and teacher and athletic director, he's also the principal designee. Takes care of most of the discipline around here. Makes more money than anyone in the county—including the superintendent."

There's nothing surprising in that. Coaches are kings in small southern town schools. And many, many are also serving in other positions like athletic director or principal designee.

"I'm just glad the motherfucker hates me," Zach says. "I'd hate to be one of the pretty people that gets the Sandusky treatment."

That one stops me. He says it in a playful manner, but is it a real accusation?

As Zach checks his camera, I glance at LeAnn, eyebrows raised.

She shrugs and shakes her head.

"Are you saying Coach Bowman has had inappropriate relationships with students?" she asks.

"Huh? Yeah, no, I was just kidding."

"That's not something to kid about," she says. "If there's any truth in it, it needs to be investigated. If there's not, you could ruin an innocent man's reputation."

"You can't ruin a coach's rep. They're untouchable. Fuckin' a student would only increase their schoolyard cred, but I was just talkin' shit. I don't know anything. We done? I need to get back to shooting the game. I'm missing plays."

"Can't have that, can we?" she says. "Know how important this job is to you."

As we reach the bottom of the media platform, Kim is walking up.

"See why these fine specimens made our lists?" LeAnn says to me.

I nod.

"I just hope we haven't left anyone off who could be the . . ." Kim says.

"What did Glenn want?" LeAnn asks.

"Asking what I thought about the probability of us having an actual school shooting," she says. "Mostly he wanted to know what John thinks. We're gonna have a meeting in the morning with him and Tyrese and Chip. Said he'd like if you two were there too."

"Me?" I ask.

She nods. "He has a lot of respect for you. Think he's takin' it more seriously because you are."

"Can you be there?" LeAnn asks.

I nod. "I will be."

"Good," Kim says. "I'm with Hugh on this one. I feel far better about having you involved. Too much at stake . . ."

"So," I say, "we've seen everyone on your lists except—"

"The two who made both of our lists," LeAnn says. "The two most likely to do it. Mason Nickols and Dakota Emanuel."

"They're not here," Kim says. "I've looked all over for them."

"Yeah, me too," LeAnn says. "Even from up on the media tower."

"That's a real shame," Kim says. "I really wanted John to meet them. They're definitely our Eric Harris and Dylan Klebold."

12

*I don't want your fuckin' thoughts and prayers you piece of worthless
shit. I want you to do your damn job and keep us safe. You're a
coward, and a whore bought and paid for by the highest political
bidder. You're paid with blood money, and you have blood on your
hands. The blood of the children you not only could have but should
have protected.*

That night I dream of Columbine.

I had spent much of the night after Anna and Taylor
and Carla and John Paul were asleep reading about the massacre
at the Littleton, Colorado high school and unwittingly took the
material into the underworld of dreamscapes and night terrors
with me.

A feeling of floating between disjointed scenes. Observing.
Unable to speak, act, influence. Powerless as the unsuspecting
victims.

A bright, sunny Monday on April 20, 1999.

The day Eric Harris and Dylan Klebold change everything

and create a blueprint for school rampage shootings still followed to this day.

The dream deteriorating into something akin to a drug-induced nightmare. Unmitigated savagery. Unimaginable horror.

Eric Harris writing his only journal entry for the year. *I hate all you people for leaving me out of so many fun things.*

6:15 A.M.

First-hour bowling class. Eric in attendance, not acting strange.

Then driving to plant diversionary explosives in a field off Wadsworth Boulevard some three miles from the school.

Later, at Eric's house. Somewhere between 10:30 A.M. and 11:00 A.M.

Videotaping final farewells.

Eric holding the camera for Dylan.

Dylan saying, *It's about half an hour before our little judgement day. Just know that I'm going to a better place than here. I didn't like life too much and I know I'll be happier wherever the fuck I go. So I'm gone.*

Dylan holding the camera for Eric.

Eric saying, *I just wanted to apologize to you guys for any crap. To everyone I love, I'm really sorry about all of this. I know my mom and dad will be fuckin' shocked beyond belief.*

11:09 A.M.

Planting duffle bag bombs in the cafeteria.

Returning to cars to wait.

Eric in a long black duster, a backpack filled with pipe bombs, a utility belt holding shotgun shells, pockets stuffed with crickets and 9mm clips.

Eric carries a 12 gauge Savage Springfield pump-action shotgun and a Hi-Point Carbine 9mm semi-automatic rifle.

Dylan in a Wrath T-shirt, black cargo pants, long black duster, backpack, cowboy boots—a single large-caliber copper-jacketed bullet in the right one.

Dylan carries a 9mm TEC-9 semi-automatic handgun and a 12 gauge Stevens double-barreled sawed-off shotgun.

Both boys wear a single glove with the fingers partially cut out to protect their shooting hands, both have a match striker for lighting explosives taped to their arms, and they have seven knives between them.

11:17 A.M.

The time Eric calculated the cafeteria will be the most crowded.

Explosives in place.

Waiting.

Eric and Dylan outside the school—one at the west entrance, one at the east, waiting, ready.

The moments before everything changes, the point just this side of the line that will forever divide before and after Columbine.

When the bombs begin to explode, those not killed or incapacitated by the blasts will run from the school—out of classrooms and the cafeteria, down the hallways, through the doors . . . and into the gunsights of Eric and Dylan, who plan to pick them off as they do.

But then . . . nothing.

Something's wrong.

Where is the HaHaHa? Where is our fun?

No explosions. No easy targets fleeing for their lives into the actual deathtrap designed for them.

What is it? What happened? Why didn't the bombs go off? *Fuck!*

Whatta we do now?

Improvise, of course. If the little sheeple won't come to us, we'll go to them.

11:18 A.M.

Diversionary explosives detonate in the Wadsworth field location. A deputy dispatched, the fire department notified.

11:19 AM.

Rachel Scott having lunch with Richard Castaldo in the grassy area next to the west entrance.

A pipe bomb launched, partially detonating.

Go! Go!

Two gunman pulling their guns from beneath their trench coats and shooting at Rachel and Richard. Rachel hit four times, killed instantly. Castaldo hit eight times in the chest, arm, and abdomen.

Eric removing his trench coat, letting it fall to the ground, aiming his 9mm carbine down the west staircase toward three students—Daniel Rohrbough, Lance Kirklin, and Sean Graves.

Then turning, firing at five students sitting on the grassy hillside opposite the west entrance. Michael Johnson hit in the face, leg, and arm. Running. Escaping. Mark Taylor shot in the chest, arms, and leg, falling to the ground, feigning death. The other three getting away uninjured.

Students at first believing it's a prank.

Business teacher Dave Sanders knowing better.

Dylan, on his way to the cafeteria to check on the explosives, encounters Lance Kirklin.

Please help me, Lance says.

Sure, I'll help you, Dylan says, and shoots him in the face.

As Dylan is doing this, Eric shoots down the steps at students sitting near the entrance to the cafeteria, wounding and partially paralyzing Anne-Marie Hochhalter.

Eric squealing, *This is what we always wanted to do. This is awesome!*

Dylan returns from the cafeteria and he and Eric fire more rounds—this time toward the soccer field. No one is hit.

They then walk into the west entrance, slinging explosives as they do.

Art teacher Patricia Nielsen, assigned to hall duty, stepping out asking, *What's all this about,* to student Brian Anderson.

Brian saying he recognizes the boys from his video production class. *They're probably making a movie.*

Nielsen approaching Eric and Dylan.

Eric leveling his carbine and firing, glass shattering, pelting Nielsen with fragments of metal and glass shards.

Her shouting, *Dear God! Dear God! Dear God!*

Inside the school now, in the main hallway, encountering teacher Dave Sanders and a student helper attempting to evacuate students and secure the school. They turn and run.

Dylan and Eric firing.

Sanders hit twice. The student gets away.

Smoke. Alarms. Gunfire. Explosions. Chaos. Pandemonium. Confusion.

A short while later, as Eric and Dylan are distracted with other things, another teacher drags Sanders into the science room where some thirty students are hiding. Sanders is severely injured, bleeding out. A handwritten note appears in the window for the cops and emergency services gathering outside—*One bleeding to death.*

Throwing bombs in the hallway, firing more rounds.

You still with me? Eric says. *We're still doing this, right?*

11:29 AM.

Eric and Dylan enter the library, Eric yelling, *Get up! All jocks stand up! We'll get the guys in the white hats!*

No one standing.

Eric saying, *Fine, I'll start shooting anyway.*

He fires his shotgun at a desk. Evan Todd, hiding beneath it, pelted with wood splinters.

Eric and Dylan walking to the opposite side of the library, shooting, reloading, killing Kyle Velasquez.

Eric saying, *Come on, let's go kill some cops.*

Dylan and Eric firing out the windows in the directions of the police. Officers returning fire. Eric and Dylan moving away from the windows.

Firing more rounds at fleeing students and cops.

Dylan firing a shotgun at a nearby table, injuring three students. Daniel Steepleton, Makai Hall, Patrick Ireland.

This is for all the shit you put us through, Dylan says.

Dylan removing his trench coat.

Eric firing under a desk, hitting and killing Steven Curnow, then doing the same under a nearby desk, hitting and wounding Kacey Ruegsegger.

Kacey, hit in the neck and shoulder, crying in pain.

Eric saying, *Quit your bitching.*

Eric stepping over to a table across the way and hitting it with his palm, kneeling, saying *Peek-a-boo* just before shooting Cassie Bernall in the head. The weapon recoiling, striking him, breaking his nose.

Momentarily dazed, Eric hesitates, then eventually turns toward the next table. Bree Pasquale sitting next to instead of under it.

You want to die? Eric asks, still woozy.

No, please.

Eric distracted, but taunting.

Dylan seeing Patrick trying to help Makai, his head rising above the table, shoots him again, twice in the head, knocking him unconscious.

Dylan moving again. Another set of tables. Seeing three athletes. Calling to Eric, *Hey, Reb. There's a nigger over here.*

Eric leaving Bree, joining Dylan, the two of them taunting Isaiah Shoels, one of sixteen black students at Columbine, with racist remarks before Eric kneels and shoots him in the chest.

Dylan kneeling, firing, killing Matthew Kechter.

Eric yelling, *Who's ready to die next?*

Eric throwing a CO_2 cartridge under the table where Daniel Steepleton, Makai Hall, and Patrick Ireland are crouching. Makai grabbing it and throwing it toward the other end of the library.

Eric then moving toward a set of bookcases, jumping up on one and shaking it, firing more rounds.

Dylan shooting a display case, then in the direction of the closest table, hitting and injuring Mark Kintgen. Turning, firing again, this time in a different direction, hitting Lisa Kreutz and Valeen Schnurr, and killing Lauren Townsend.

Valeen Schnurr screaming, *Oh my God, oh my God!*

Do you believe in God? Dylan asking.

I do.

Why? Dylan asking, then walking away.

Eric approaching a different table. Two girls crouching beneath. Bending down, looking at them. *Pathetic*, he says.

Eric then moving to another table and shooting two rounds, injuring Nicole Nowlen and John Tomlin. Tomlin attempting to get away. Dylan kicking him. Eric taunting him. Dylan shooting him several times and killing him.

Eric walking back over to where Lauren Townsend lies lifeless. Not far from her, Kelly Fleming, like Bree Pasquale had been, is sitting next to instead of under the table. Eric shooting her in the back, killing her instantly. He then shoots at the table behind her, hitting Townsend and Kreutz again, wounding Jeanna Park.

Then the two mass murderers meet in the middle of the library and reload.

Eric noticing someone hiding nearby, asking, *Who's there?*

It's me, John Savage. You know me, Dylan. What're you doing?

Oh, just killing people, Dylan responds.

You going to kill me?

What? Dylan asks.

Are you going to kill me?

Dylan hesitates, then, *Nah. Go ahead. Get out of here.*

Savage running out of the library.

As soon as he's gone, Eric fires a round toward Daniel Mauser and grazes him.

Mauser fighting back, throwing a chair at Eric, Eric firing again, hitting Mauser in the face and killing him.

Dylan and Eric moving again, randomly firing under another table, injuring Jennifer Doyle and Austin Eubanks and fatally wounding Corey DePooter.

It is now 11:35 A.M. Eric and Dylan killed ten people in the library and injured many more.

This just isn't as fun anymore, is it? Eric asks.

Maybe we should start knifing people, Dylan says.

They then move toward the main counter. Eric throws a Molotov cocktail toward one end of the library, but it doesn't explode. He then goes around the counter and Dylan joins him.

They find a student wearing a hat.

Lift your head so we can see you, Eric says.

He does. It's Evan Todd, wood splinters still embedded in his skin.

Dylan says, *Give me one good reason why we shouldn't off you right here and now.*

I don't want trouble.

Eric saying, *You don't know what trouble is.*

You used to call me a fag, Dylan says. *Who's the fag now?*

Dylan turning to Eric, *Should I kill him?*

Eric, still dazed, his nose bleeding badly, not responding.

The taunting continuing, eventually Eric and Dylan walking away.

Dylan shooting a TV. Throwing a chair at a computer station. The two boys walking out.

Seven and a half minutes in the library. Twenty-two students shot. Ten killed. Twelve wounded.

When Dylan and Eric leave the library, the survivors begin to sneak out.

For the next twenty-seven minutes or so Dylan and Eric wander around the school, aimlessly, directionless, randomly shooting, examining their undetonated bombs, talking, shouting out threats, reloading.

All the while the cops wait outside and Dave Sanders bleeds out.

Today's the day the world ends, Eric says. *Today's the day we die.*

Reentering the now mostly empty library.

After firing a few rounds through the windows at the cops below, they kill themselves, Eric firing his shotgun through the roof of his mouth, Dylan shooting himself in the head with his handgun.

White middle-class teenage boys, rampage, mass-murdering little monsters, dead now because they chose to be.

The initial attack over, the residual trauma never will be.

Columbine echoing through time, waves of insidious inspiration, ripples of rampage like radiation infecting the ill minds and imaginations of other lost, lonely boys.

13

You never really think anything like this can happen to you until it does. I will never be the same. Not ever. Am I glad to be alive? Of course. But is part of me dead? No question.

I wake the next morning feeling agitated and unrested, but knowing when the shooting will take place.

After not enough time with Anna, Taylor, Carla, and John Paul, I drive to Pottersville, through the town and to the high school.

On the drive over, I speak to Reggie by phone, receiving her permission and blessing to help Potter County with this possible shooting, being reassured that they have everything in Gulf County in hand.

Entering Potter High through the gym, I rush through the commons and over to the back corner between the stage and the bank of microwaves.

Finding Kim and LeAnn's offices empty, I walk over to Tyrese's.

There I find Tyrese, Kim, LeAnn, Chip Jeffers, Ace Bowman, and Hugh Glenn.

"John," Glenn says. "I'm glad you could join us. We were just talking about what our response should be. How far we should take this. Do we warn everyone and risk creating a panic or do we continue investigating in secret?"

"We've got to do all we can to protect the students and faculty," Tyrese says. "We can't take a chance with something like this. The potential devastation is just too great."

I'm struck again at how much Tyrese looks and sounds like Merrill. Even his mannerisms are similar. He's younger than Merrill by about ten years and weighs less than him by about seventy-five pounds, but otherwise he resembles a brother more than a cousin.

"It's true," Glenn says, "the fallout . . . if we say nothing and something happens and the parents found out we knew . . . would be . . ."

"I'm not talking about political fallout," Tyrese says. "I could give a damn about that. I'm talking about doin' our damn jobs and protecting these kids who are in our care. We're responsible for them."

"I wasn't talking about political fallout," Glenn says. "You misunderstood. But it's not like we can cancel school."

"Why not?" Chip asks.

"We cancel school and the shooter just waits until we reopen," Bowman says. "Doesn't solve anything, just kicks the can a little farther down the road."

"It's still possible there won't be a school shooting," Glenn says. "We have no definitive proof there will be. Just some notes. Hell, they could be a prank or part of some stupid lit assignment or something."

"But—" Chip begins.

"What do you think, John?" Glenn asks. "I'd really like to know."

"I think the threat is real," I say. "I think there will be a rampage shooting here. And I think I know when it will take place."

"Really?" Tyrese says.

"When?" Glenn asks.

I look over at Kim and LeAnn. "When did Tristan and Denise say their play was going to be?"

"Tomorrow," Tyrese says before they can respond. "Why? Is that when it will be?"

"What is tomorrow?" I ask.

"Friday," Kim says.

"The date," I say.

LeAnn's eyes grow wide as her mouth falls open. "Oh my God," she says.

"What?" Glenn asks. "What is it?"

"Tomorrow is April twentieth," Tyrese says. "The anniversary of Columbine."

"Fuck me," Glenn says.

"Tomorrow all over the country students plan to walk out of school in protest," Tyrese says. "Inspired by the student survivors at Parkland and to remember Columbine and to protest our inaction in protecting them."

"And someone is planning a school shooting here during a play about a school shooting while all that is going on around the country," Kim says.

"And the eyes of the world are on us," LeAnn adds. "Couldn't be a better time."

14

Reliably predicting any type of violence is nearly impossible. Predicting that an individual who has never acted out violently in the past will do so in the future is even more difficult. Accurately anticipating acts that occur as infrequently as school shootings would require a psychic with a crystal ball the likes of which we have never seen.

"If we think John is right," Glenn says. "And I take it we all do. . . I mean, there's no way to know for sure, but it's the best theory we have and it all fits, right? It still leaves us with the question *what do we do?*"

Tyrese says, "I don't think there's any question about—"

"Before we—sorry to interrupt," Glenn says. "But before we each say what we think we should do, let's go over all our options. That sound good?"

Everyone nods.

Tyrese says, "Sure. Okay. First and most obvious option is to cancel the play and close the school."

"Okay," Glenn says.

"But that only kicks the can down the road a ways," Bowman says again. "Another option would be to have school that day and catch the little bastards before they can do it. Catch them in the act and put them away."

Tyrese shakes his head. "That's way, way too risky. What if he's able to shoot someone or detonate a bomb before we catch him? If just one person got killed it wouldn't be worth doing."

"I know what you're saying," Bowman says. "I do. But if we cancel the play and close the school then all we do is stop him on that one day. He or they will still do it when we reopen. And we won't be ready and we won't know when it is. This way, we can be waiting for him or them. We can actually stop them and catch them. We can have the staff on high alert. We can have under-cover police and extra security and . . . It's our best chance—I know it's a risk, but it's our least risky option. It's our best chance of preventing the loss of life."

Tyrese shakes his head like he's not convinced. "I don't know . . . John what do you think?"

"First, whichever option you go with, we need to keep investigating the most likely suspects," I say. "If you have school tomorrow, we need to visit all the suspects tonight, see if we can't find evidence and stop him or them that way. And if you cancel the play and school, we need to keep investigating them for the same reasons—try to find them before you reopen. But Ace makes some great points. It's actually safer to have school tomorrow when you're expecting the attack and can have tactical law enforcement in place—I'd get the help of other departments and agencies and any and everybody we can find—than another random day when there's no additional security in place and you don't know what to expect or when to expect it. But it's a hell of a risk. There's no question about that."

"Yes it is," Glenn says. "But it's Tyrese's call to make. We can all have input, but ultimately the decision will fall on Tyrese—or maybe . . . I mean . . . if we need to go above your pay grade, we can let the superintendent decide. Maybe the school board."

"I spoke with the superintendent this morning," Tyrese says. "He said he'll support whatever decision we make. Says it needs to be made here on the ground, in the trenches, not from the county office where they don't know the situation like we do."

The superintendent, like the sheriff, is a political position. They both have to stand for election again soon and don't want to have been the ones to make the decision. If it goes badly they can blame Tyrese. But if it goes well and we actually prevent it from happening you can bet they will take the credit—even as they pretend not to.

I think about the weakness and lack of leadership manifest in the responses of both men, and it makes me ill.

Dad had been a very good sheriff—maybe even a great one. What Potter County has now is country miles from that.

Dad and I disagree about many things, but I never doubt where he stands or question his integrity, nor have I ever once seen him shirk a responsibility or duck accountability following difficult decisions.

"So the decision is yours," Glenn says.

Tyrese looks at me. "What do you think I should do?"

"It's an impossible situation," I say. "But I've been thinking about it and . . . while originally I was in favor of canceling the play and closing the school, I think Ace is right. It could still happen, we just won't know when. Being open, having the play . . . is a huge, huge risk, but I agree with Ace that it's less of a risk than the other way."

He nods.

"And I'll go on record now and afterward—no matter what happens—and say so."

His eyes lock onto mine. "Thank you," he says. "I really—"

"I'll go on record too," Glenn says, though he doesn't say what he'll go on record as saying.

"The thing is," I say, "if we do it, we've got to have plenty of help and cover every eventuality. Our plan has to be perfect. We've got to reduce the risks down as close to zero as we possibly can. And we've got to investigate all the suspects as thoroughly as we can between now and then. But even with all that there are no guarantees."

"No there aren't," Tyrese says.

"I think we can do it," LeAnn says. "I truly do. I think between all of us and all the help we get . . . I think we can stop him. If I'm being totally honest . . . I think John can catch him and we can help."

Kim nods and says, "Me too. I agree."

"It'll take a team effort," Glenn says, trying to insinuate himself back into the conversation.

"Yes, it will," I say. "And the truth is . . . none of us would be here if it weren't for Chip. It's his conscientious police work that has given even the possibility to prevent a massacre from happening."

15

To the Black Jack Crew. You guys are very cool. Sorry, dudes. I had to do what I had to do.

We find Mason Nickols and Dakota Emanuel where they can be found most nights—working at Sal's Pizza.

We have spent the day preparing as best we can for tomorrow —enlisting the assistance of other law enforcement agencies, going over plans, searching the school, watching security camera footage, talking to suspects—every one of them except for Mason and Dakota, who have thus far eluded us.

Sal's Pizza, a Pottersville fixture, is a small, independent storefront pizza joint on Main Street situated between an insulation place and an insurance agency. Primarily a carryout joint, there are only three small tables in the limited space between the plate glass front and the order counter.

When Kim, LeAnn, and I walk in, we find Mason and Dakota working behind the counter and a small group of teens sitting at two of the three tables, which they have shoved together.

The three of us sit at the remaining table.

"We have to order at the counter," Kim says as if we don't know. "How do you want to do this?"

"One of you go up with me to order and one stay here to keep the table. Let's try to engage them as much as possible without being too conspicuous. Depending on how that goes, we may just have to question them directly before we leave."

Kim nods. "I think it's best if you go up with LeAnn," she says. "And don't mention you're a cop."

As LeAnn and I get up and walk over to the counter, I see that DeShawn Holt and Sierra Baker are among the teens talking and eating at the other two tables.

Sierra gives us a little wave and DeShawn nods.

"You want the usual, Miss LeAnn," Dakota asks as we reach the counter.

LeAnn smiles and glances at me. "I eat here a lot."

I nod. "I did too when I lived here."

"Oh, Dakota, this is John. He's a good friend of mine. Used to live here."

"John Jordan, right?" he says. "I read about you. You're a straight-up stone killer, aren't you? Bunch of articles online about that serial killer in Atlanta, dropping bitches off Stone Mountain. Used to catch criminals, now you work with them in prison 'cause you got religion or some shit like that."

I nod, deciding not to mention I was also an investigator again.

"That's some kind of radical wicked man," he says. "Hey Mason, check this shit out. This is the dude from that serial killer site."

Mason sneers at me from the kitchen and says, "Smells like bacon to me."

"No, he like takes care of monsters in prison now," Dakota says. "He's all right."

"Take their damn order already and get your ass back here

and help me cook all this shit," he says. "And turn your pig detector back on and recalibrate that shit. He's more of a doughnut eater than she is." He nods toward Kim.

Hanging his head and revealing who the alpha is, Dakota quickly takes our order, seething as he does.

"It's okay, Dakota," LeAnn whispers. "You're right. John is one of the good guys."

He ignores her and hustles back to join Mason in the back.

When we get back to the table, Kim says, "Whatever y'all ordered, don't eat. No way Mason doesn't do something disgusting to it now."

I nod.

Sitting here inside Sal's it occurs to me that Eric Harris and Dylan Klebold worked at a pizza place together, and I wonder if that's the reason Mason and Dakota took the jobs.

Kim says, "If you're planning on blowing up the school or going on a rampage shooting tomorrow, would you be at work slinging pizza tonight?"

"Two days before Columbine, Dylan did his math homework," I say. "The day of the shooting, Eric went to his early morning bowling class and acted normally."

"They worked in a place like this, didn't they?" LeAnn says.

Kim nods. "Blackjack Pizza."

"Lots of killers are calm and stick to their routines leading up to their crimes," I say. "After Dylan did his math homework that night, he did several pages of personal writing. He wrote about the judgment that was coming in just twenty-six-and-a-half hours, but the most striking thing he put down was that knowing he was going to die gave everything a touch of triviality."

"Absolutely chilling," LeAnn says.

Kim nods and shivers a little.

I think back to what I read recently about the night before the Columbine massacre when Eric met Mark Manes to buy a hundred rounds of ammo for his TEC-9. Mark asked him if he was going shooting that night. *Nah, not tonight*, Eric had replied nonchalantly, *but I might go shooting tomorrow*.

"How can people like that be the same species as us?" LeAnn asks.

"I'm not sure they are," Kim says.

Before I can respond, Ernie, Sal's nephew and now the new owner of the place, walks in.

Ernie, who used to deliver pizza for Sal when he was a kid, had delivered a pizza to my old place at the Prairie Palm the day I first met Laura Mathers shortly after moving back here from Atlanta.

Sal, who had no children of his own and who acted as a sort of surrogate father for Ernie, had left the joint to him.

He waves and walks over when he sees us.

I stand to greet him.

"Hey, John," he says, shaking my hand. "Long time. How you been?" He then glances at and nods toward Kim and LeAnn. "Ladies."

"I sure was sorry to hear about Sal," I say. "How are you?"

"I'm fine. It was his time."

"How you like running the place?" LeAnn asks.

"It's different than I expected," he says. "Which really surprised me since I worked here for so long. Sal did far more than I realized I guess. I'll get used to it. Single hardest part is finding good help. Kids these days . . . don't want to work. Never seen such lazy, entitled, bad-attitude punks in my life."

"Careful," Kim says. "You're sounding very *get off my lawn-y*."

"You got you two fine specimens back there right now," LeAnn says.

He shakes his head in disgust. "Not for much longer," he says. "This is their last night. Thank God."

LeAnn and Kim both look at me with raised eyebrows.

"You fire them, or they quit?" I ask.

"I was about to fire them," he says. "But they beat me to the punch."

"Who decided this would be their last night?" I ask.

"They did. I needed them a little longer 'til I can train their replacements but . . . they said this was the absolute last day they would work."

"Thanks, Ernie," I say. "Good luck with everything."

He moves away, checking on the kids who are finishing up at the other table, then making his way behind the counter.

"Oh my God," LeAnn says. "It's them. It's these evil little bastards."

Kim nods. "It really seems like it could be, but we've got to resist jumping to any conclusions. It's at least possible it's just a coincidence."

"Sure," LeAnn says, "but—"

"Miss LeAnn," Sierra says. "You said to be looking and listening for anything suspicious."

As the group of teens is leaving, she and DeShawn have paused at our table.

"Yeah?"

"Well," DeShawn says, "something is going on with Mason and Dakota. They're acting even weirder than normal."

I smile at his turn of phrase.

"They're up to something," Sierra says. "I'm worried about them."

"They told us that they didn't like us," DeShawn says, "but that we weren't the biggest part of the problem so . . . not to go to school tomorrow."

16

People are so unaware . . . Well, ignorance is bliss I guess . . . That would explain my depression.

"Can't sleep?"

Anna has found me sitting at our kitchen table studying an old set of blueprints of Potter High Tyrese was able to dig out of the musty storage closet in the far back corner of the school office.

"No," I say. "Sorry if I woke you."

"You didn't. I just got up to pee and noticed you weren't there."

"I tried," I say. "I wanted to be as rested for tomorrow as I can be, but . . . every time I closed my eyes I saw the kids of Potter High being shot to death or exploding, their parents looking at us asking how we could have let this happen, so I decided to get up and try to prepare some more."

"Are you sure about doing it?" she asks.

"Not at all."

She nods but doesn't say anything else.

"I think it's the best of some really bad options, our best chance of catching him before he can do any real damage, but . . . I could be wrong and if I am . . ."

"I know it feels like it, but it's not all on you."

"No, I know. Outwardly there's nothing on me really. Unlike Tyrese or Hugh Glenn I probably won't be blamed or lose my job, but none of that matters compared to even one kid getting hurt or . . ."

She nods again and puts her hand on mine.

"If that happens . . . I'll know I'm to blame and not fit for my job, so will—"

"You won't be to blame," she says. "It wasn't your decision."

"Tyrese asked me," I say. "He went with what I said, changed what he was going to do."

"I want to be there tomorrow," she says. "I want to help. I know you've got a lot of . . . but I want to help too."

I shake my head.

"I really want to," she says.

"It's too unpredictable and volatile a situation," I say. "Anything can happen. Anything at all."

"John," she says, her tone harsh. "Are you . . . You've never been the *it's too dangerous for you, little lady* type. I can't believe you're—"

"That's not it at all," I say. "Not at all. Because there could be explosives . . . because it could be . . . I was thinking of our children, thinking we didn't both need to be there in case there was an explosion that could . . . I wanted one of us to be sure to . . . be here for Taylor and Johanna—and now Carla and John Paul."

"Oh."

"An explosives expert said that if Eric and Dylan's bombs would have worked properly at least a thousand more kids would have died at Columbine. That's nearly three times as many students as the entire student body of PHS. Because of our girls . .

. I don't think the two of us should ever be in the same dangerous situation at the same time if we can help it."

"I understand," she says.

"So why don't you go to the school in the morning, and I'll stay home with Taylor," I say.

She laughs so loud I think she's going to wake Taylor, Carla, and John Paul.

"We just need one of us to be here for them," I say, smiling at her radiant, amused face. "Doesn't matter which one."

We enjoy the joke for a moment more then she turns serious. "Is it really that dangerous?"

I shake my head. "I don't think so. I just really don't know. It will depend on how closely they follow Eric and Dylan's blueprint, how capable they are, how much work they've invested in it, how sophisticated their equipment is."

"Why don't we both stay home in the morning," she says.

"I seriously doubt they'll be that prepared and that proficient," I say. "It will be their first time, but . . . no matter what they attempt to do I believe we'll be able to stop it—hopefully, before it even starts—so what they have planned or what they're capable of is a moot point anyway."

"I vote for that," she says.

I nod and smile. "Me too."

"Think I can entice you back into bed with me?" she says.

"I know you can. No question about it. But I was thinking about getting ready and going to the school."

"At three o'clock in the morning?"

"I'd like to do another thorough search of the school before it opens," I say.

"Those are some lucky kids to have you looking out for them," she says. "Come to bed just long enough to make love to me then you can take a quick shower and be on your way to save the world."

"You're the best wife in the world," I say.

"I want to hear you say that every day for the rest of our long lives," she says. "So be sure to come home to me tomorrow evening and tell me."

"I fully intend to."

17

This morning I woke up excited to go to school. This afternoon I return home blood-splattered, ears still ringing with gunshot blasts, eyes unable to unsee exploded heads and faces, bullet-ripped and riddled bodies, and I never want to go back to school again.

Four thirty in the morning and Kim, LeAnn, Merrill, and I are walking the halls of our old alma mater.

"Searching for explosives at the ass end of morning is far more fun than I ever had when I went here," Merrill says.

"Sure," LeAnn says, "it's all fun and games until one of us gets some limbs blown off."

"We *do* need to be careful," I say. "Certain doors could be boobytrapped. If you see anything out of the ordinary, don't handle or even approach it. Just back away and we'll call the bomb squad."

The hallways are dim, the classrooms dark, and the entire building is eerily, almost unearthly quiet.

We pass beneath Pirate banners and badly decorated bulletin

boards, time intermittently folding to make it feel as if it was just a couple of years instead of decades when these hallways and classroom were filled with our friends, the lockers with our books, the days with our dreams.

"Is Tippy Lewis still the librarian?" I ask.

Kim nods. "Hard to believe, but . . . she doesn't act like she has any plans to retire anytime soon."

Tippy Lewis had been the librarian when we were here, and though she had seemed old to us then, she couldn't have been more than early thirties.

LeAnn says, "She's got no reason to retire. Only thing she does at home is read alone. At least here she's not alone—and she gets paid for it. I swear she spends her entire discretionary budget each year only on books she wants to read. Then sits in there and reads them all day. She pretty much lets Sierra and DeShawn run it. Kids don't even ask her anything anymore—just go straight to Sierra and DeShawn. Ms. Lewis does even less work than Ms. Shonda."

Shonda Saunders is the notoriously lazy janitor who makes the students relegated to in-school suspension do all her work.

I say, "Tippy Lewis helped me find a lot of great books back when we were here."

"That's 'cause she crushed on you a little," LeAnn says.

I laugh out loud. "She absolutely did not. She just—"

LeAnn looks at Kim. "Tell him."

"She definitely did," Kim says.

I shake my head. "No way. I would have picked up on something like that."

"You were completely oblivious," Kim says.

"She was just helping a student falling in love with reading find good books to read," I say.

"Sure," LeAnn says, "and she wasn't running to the back to change her moist granny panties every time you left the library either. You should stop in and see her later today. Have a little book lovers' reunion."

"Why didn't you come to our last class reunion?" Kim asks Merrill.

He shrugs. "Never crossed my mind that I should."

"Seriously, really?"

"Not really my scene."

"We missed you. You should come to the next one."

"If I'm still here, I will," he says. "Just for you."

"If you're not here," LeAnn says, "if you get shot and killed or blown up today, we'll hang a nice plaque in your honor and I'll say some words."

Her comment—even said in jest—is in poor taste, but I know she is nervous and scared and means nothing by it, so I let it go.

"Kim's right," LeAnn says, "you should come—to be seen if nothing else. You look good. I mean *real good*."

"And coming from a middle-aged white lesbian," Kim says, "that's really saying something."

"Just so big and strong and . . . How is it you and John look so much younger than us? Men are so fuckin' lucky when it comes to shit like that."

"You know what they say . . ." Merrill says. "Black don't crack. John's is genetics and clean living and happiness or some shit like that, but mine is just one of the innate privileges of being a black man in America—no stress, easy living, hidden benefits, shit like that. But who you kiddin'? Both you girls still look just the same."

"Y'all really do," I say. "Y'all look great. Must be because y'all are still in high school. Speaking of . . . where do y'all think is the most likely place for the shooter to hide explosives or extra weapons?"

It's an awkward attempt to change the subject and get our little group back on track, but no one points that out and it seems to work.

"We need to check all the mechanical and janitorial closets and the bathrooms," Kim says.

"The stage area," LeAnn says. "Especially behind it and underneath it."

"Unassigned lockers," Kim says.

"Need to pay particular attention to any loose or open grates and ceiling panels," LeAnn says.

"I think we need to split up in order to cover everything before the school opens," I say. "That okay with y'all?"

They all nod and say it is.

"Just remember not to touch anything," I say. "Just look. If you see anything suspicious at all, make a note of the location, snap a pic, and call the rest of us. Okay?"

"Okay, Dad," LeAnn says. "We'll be careful."

We each go in different directions, methodically making our way through the entirety of the main building.

I search the library at the center of the huge circle, but it, like the rest of the school, is far too large for anything but a cursory examination.

It occurs to me that this entire endeavor may very well be a waste of our time, but I don't know what else we can be doing.

After searching the library, I examine the lockers without locks in my area. I discover trash, rotting food, smelly gym clothes, blown out flip-flops, a baseball glove, tampons, discarded notebooks, abandoned art projects, cans of half-consumed soda, deodorant, antiperspirant, and an ungodly amount of AXE body sprays. I do not discover any explosives or weapons of any kind.

I next search the girls' restroom before meeting up with the others in the commons.

Together we search the kitchen, commons, and stage area.

By six thirty as the other undercover law enforcement officers start to arrive, we haven't found a single sign of a school shooting —no plans or notes, no weapons or explosives—and I can't decide if that's a good or a bad result.

18

I have no idea how we got to this place. I really don't. I've taught school for thirty years and in all that time I can't point to a single thing that could have predicted something like this. Not one. Are kids different these days? In some ways, sure, but in others they're no different than we were back in what they see as the Dark Ages.

E veryone is in place.

Undercover officers pretending to be substitutes are everywhere—in or near every classroom, at every entrance, in the commons, in the library, in the front office, in the gym, in the art building, in or near the restrooms.

Two SWAT teams are stationed in a field about half a mile from campus.

There's so much firepower in or near the school, in fact, that I felt the need to address everyone this morning before the students arrived, reminding them to use restraint and limited force and to make absolutely certain before they took any action at all. The last thing we needed was an overzealous, keyed-up cop shooting a kid pulling a handheld gaming device from his backpack.

Merrill and I are roaming the halls.

"How you feelin' about everything?" he asks.

"I think we're prepared," I say. "Given ourselves the best chance to stop him, but . . . all I can think about is all that could go wrong."

He nods. "Anything does happen . . . be a shit ton of friendly fire up in this bitch."

"We may have too many officers here," I say. "In most cases too much help is a good thing but in this situation . . ."

LeAnn and Kim are going from class to class to check in on our suspects, confirm they're here and try to get a reading on their overall state.

We run into them in the far side of the hallway on the east end of the main building.

"Anyone missing?" I ask.

"Not sure yet," Kim says. "Still working our way through them. A couple of them changed their schedules recently so what we have for them is wrong. We're trying to track them down now. Tristan and Denise are here—in the art building working on their play. Seem normal. Chase is here. He's in the gym but not dressed out like he's supposed to be, but Ace said it's not that out of the ordinary for him."

"Zach is in the media center working on the morning broadcast," LeAnn says. "Charming as ever. We're going back to the office now to see if we can find out where Evan Fowler is supposed to be and confirm he's there."

"No sign of Mason Nickols and Dakota Emanuel yet," Kim says, "but their first-period teacher says they often come in late."

"We need to let the spotters know they're not here, to be looking for them, and to let us know the moment they pull up," I say. "What do they drive?"

"Dakota doesn't have a car," LeAnn says. "Always rides with Mason in his old black Jeep Cherokee."

"Okay," I say. "We'll let the parking lot spotters know while y'all try to locate Evan."

"Take a deep breath, John," LeAnn says. "This is going to work. We've got plenty of help. This isn't all on you. Don't have a heart attack or anything."

"I'll take a nice long breath when this is over and everybody's safe and unharmed," I say. "All right. Let's go."

"Hey, I'm just trying to look out for you," she says. "Have a stroke if you want to."

We head in opposite directions down the circular hall.

As Merrill and I make our way toward the student parking lot, I'm scanning every area we pass—lockers, restroom entrances, the intermittently visible sections of library, the classrooms seen behind the long, narrow panel of glass in the closed doors.

Because today is 4/20, the high holy day of cannabis culture, we have disguised many of our activities and covert operations as if they're related to it. K-9 units roam the parking lots and hallways with what the students believe are drug dogs, but are actually bomb detection dogs. Tyrese and a small team of undercover officers are conducting supposed random searches of backpacks and lockers, ostensibly looking for weed but actually looking for weapons.

We pass Tyrese and one such team at a bank of lockers near the hallway to the commons.

"Anything?" I ask.

He shakes his head. "Not so far. But we're just getting started."

"This is bullshit," the angry young white student whose locker is being searched says. "You have no reason to search me or my locker. You're violating my civil rights."

Merrill and I continue down the hallway and out the front door.

As we walk down the long covered corridor leading to the

student parking lot, he looks at his watch and asks, "What time do most school shootings happen?"

"That's a great question," I say. "I'm not sure. It's stupid of me not to know for sure, but my sense is that more happen in the mornings than any other time. Columbine started a little before eleven thirty. What time is it?"

"Eight thirty-nine," he says.

We have approximately twenty minutes until the play starts in the commons.

When we reach the spotter at the end of the covered walkway near the flagpole, I ask him how it's going.

"It's going. K-9 is almost finished with all the cars in both lots —staff and students," he says.

He's an older officer on loan from the Bay County Sheriff's Department, gray-haired and a wrinkled, gridded face.

"Anything so far?"

He shakes his head, continuing to scan the school grounds instead of looking at me.

"Our prime suspects haven't arrived yet," I say. "Be on the lookout for an older model black Jeep Cherokee. Let us know when they arrive and tell everyone to use extreme caution."

"Do I notify you when they're here?" he says.

"Yeah."

"They're here," he says.

I follow his gaze and see Mason's faded black Cherokee slowly approaching the school from the quiet, empty street that leads to it.

"Thanks," I say, but there's not a lot of sincerity in it.

Merrill says, "Shall we?"

I nod and we begin to walk toward the lot that Mason is pulling into.

Lifting my radio, I depress the button and say, "Mason and Dakota have just arrived. Merrill and I are approaching them now."

"How you wanna play it?" Merrill asks.

"Let's hang back and see what they do," I say. "Act like we're looking at other vehicles, assisting the K-9 unit."

Mason parks his Jeep in his assigned spot and he and Dakota get out.

They are wearing normal-for-them attire and are not armed.

Mason walks directly over to us. "Knew you smelled like bacon. Got a nose for that sort of thing."

"Congratulations," I say. "Your mom must be so proud."

"What's all this shit?" Dakota asks as he walks up.

"Just a little random drug search to celebrate 4/20," I say.

Mason tosses his keys to me. "Feel free to go inside mine," he says. "Just don't plant anything or trash it in any way."

"That's very accommodating of you," I say.

His dead eyes lock with mine and he gives me a wicked, knowing smile. "I have nothing to hide. Even if I was going to do anything with . . . *drugs* . . ."

His expression and emphasis on the word *drugs* make it clear he's talking about something else.

"I'm not stupid enough to bring them to school on today of all days."

"So you were expecting us?" I say.

"You boys have yourselves a good day," he says, starting to walk away. "Just leave the keys in the front office with Miss Rose when you finish with her."

Dakota, who follows Mason, shakes his head and says, "That's some sad shit man. Dude who fought monsters in Atlanta is doin' bullshit drug searches in a high school parking lot in Patheticville, Florida."

19

I can't prove it, but I'm convinced that kids are influenced by media coverage and especially social media attention that is given to school shooters. Well, I'm not going to prop up and promote the mentally ill and sociopathic any longer. I'll never again use the name of a school shooter in any reporting I do. My focus will be exclusively on the victims and survivors.

Just before the student body begins to file into the commons for the play, Merrill, Tyrese, Kim, LeAnn, Ace Bowman, Chip Jeffers, and Hugh Glenn who just arrived are huddled together in the corner near the office to regroup.

Outside, the K-9 unit is thoroughly searching Mason's Jeep at my request. Inside, everyone remains on high alert.

"I just knew it was going to be Mason and Dakota," LeAnn says.

"Still could be," I say. "We've got to be ready. Mason couldn't've been more arrogant. Like he knew exactly what to expect."

Merrill nods. "If they were tipped off the Jeep could be

a ruse."

"Did y'all locate Evan Fowler?" I ask.

Kim shakes her head. "He's absent today."

"We need to keep an eye out for him," Ace says. "He could be planning to show up a little later and start shooting."

"We need to watch everyone and everything just like we planned," I say. "Nothing has changed. If anything . . . it's more dangerous now. We're going to be at our most vulnerable during the play. I was hoping we'd catch him before it."

"Should we cancel it?" Tyrese says.

"I still think we have everything covered," I say. "We just can't let up, can't relax for even a moment."

"If there's going to be an attack it's going to be during the play," Merrill says.

"It'll be fish in a fuckin' barrel," Ace says. "We better stop him before he starts."

A bell sounds and students begin to pour into the commons from several different directions—the gym, the back door, the two hallways that lead up to the library and classrooms.

"Here come the fish," Chip says.

"Okay, everybody," I say, "spread out. Look at everybody. Watch our suspects closely, but look at everyone in case we're wrong about who it is."

"Good work everyone," Glenn says. "Keep it up."

Dad and Reggie walk up.

Dad looks at Glenn. "Don't want to step on anybody's toes, but I have to be here helping right now. We both do."

Glenn graciously extends his hand. "Glad to have you, Sheriff. Both of you. Thanks for coming."

"Thank you," I say to them. "Okay let's spread out."

We disperse and disappear within the throng of caged teenagers.

As I'm making my way through the crowd toward the back of the stage, someone grabs my arm.

I turn to see DeShawn Holt and Sierra Baker standing there.

"Where is Miss LeAnn?" he asks.

"In here somewhere. Why?"

"There's talk," he says. "Lots of kids whispering about there being a big surprise at the end of the play."

"Thought y'all weren't coming today?" I ask.

"Had to be here to help if we could," Sierra says.

"They say what kind of surprise?" I ask.

"Just a big one—something no one will ever forget."

"Okay, thanks," I say. "I'll let Miss LeAnn know."

When I reach the back of the stage, I look around, inspecting the actors and their props, then send a text to LeAnn, Kim, Tyrese, Ace, and Merrill to let them know what DeShawn and Sierra said.

Across the stage I see a Potter County deputy inspecting the gun props, ensuring they are all in fact props and have the small orange tips on the ends of the barrels. Denise and Tristan had argued to have the orange tips removed, claiming they take away from the power of their production, but received a hard *no* from Tyrese.

I nod to the deputy, take one more look around then walk back out front.

As I'm about halfway up the side, the curtains open and the play begins. To my surprise, within a few minutes most of the students have stopped talking and are actually watching the play.

I pause and look around from this vantage point closer to the rows of seated students.

The play proceeds. If possible it's even worse than it was in rehearsal. Bad writing. Overacting. Poor staging. Heavy-handed. Idiotic and incomprehensible. Yet the student body watching it is transfixed.

Among the kids strutting and fretting their hour upon the stage are the Dupree twins, their every movement an exercise in overdramatic, insincere, exaggerated effeteness.

Not far from me on a small portable riser, Zach Griffith is videoing the play with the same enthusiasm he had at the baseball game.

Eventually, I turn and continue toward the back, my eyes scanning the crowd, the room, the hallway, the teachers' lounge.

Joining Tyrese at the center back, I turn to take in the entire area.

There are undercover cops everywhere—at every door, on each side of the stage, along the aisles, mixed in within the seated students.

"I can still stop it if you think I need to," Tyrese says.

"It looks like we've got nearly as many cops as we do students," I say. "I think we're okay. I guess it's possible we missed something, but . . ."

"Okay," he says.

As I continue to look around the large open room, he seems to turn his attention to the play for a moment.

"Took a creative writing class in college," he says. "We studied all forms of fiction—novels, screenplays, stage plays, short stories. This play reminds me of something the professor said. She said story's not the place for making an overt point. The truths revealed in story are far more subtle than that. Said if you have a message to share send a telegram."

I smile. "Hopefully, if he continues to pursue writing, Tristan will have that same professor someday."

"Ironically," he says, "this is a ripoff of a bad community college play his older brother was in last year. This is unabashed stage plagiarism."

LeAnn rushes up to us, Kim not far behind her.

"I just spoke with Evan's mom," LeAnn says. "She's at their house. He's not there. She said she thought he went to school today. Doesn't know where else he could be."

Kim nods. "Two different kids said they saw him here this

morning," she says. "But we've looked everywhere and can't find him."

"Okay," I say. "Let everyone you can know to be looking for him, but remind them not to so focus on him that they miss someone else."

Tyrese says, "Remember . . . Just because his mama doesn't know where he is and we can't find him doesn't mean he's the shooter."

"Exactly," I say. "Has anyone checked the baseball field?"

"I'll send someone now," Tyrese says.

The tension in the commons is palpable. I can feel the high-strung energy of dread and expectation like an overtightened guitar string about to snap.

I scan the crowd again. Dad and Reggie are up near the front, one on each side, pretending to watch the play. Hugh Glenn has disappeared. He's probably out in his vehicle or hiding some-where else. DeShawn and Sierra in the back row on the left side give me a little wave as I look in their direction. Mason is glaring at me from where he sits on the opposite side toward the middle. When our eyes lock, he gives me a cold smile and forms a gun with his thumb and forefinger and pretends to shoot me.

Merrill walks up and shakes his head at Tyrese. "Look here, Cuz. I ain't about tellin' you how to do your damn job, but . . . this fuckin' play man . . . They's got to be a law against torturing kids with shit like this. It's like you tryin' to drive one of 'em to shoot up this bitch."

As Merrill talks he continues to scan the commons.

Tyrese smiles. "It is bad," he says. "But it could be worse."

"How?" Merrill says. "If they's in blackface?"

"I actually had to stop them from doing that," he says. "No, it would be worse if they weren't doing it at all. This shit's givin' marginalized kids a voice, a creative outlet. Might just change their lives. We can sit through an hour of almost anything for that."

"Well, shit, Principal Joe Clark," Merrill says, referring to the character Morgan Freeman played in *Lean on Me*, "my bad. Didn't realize you's changing lives up in here. Hats off."

Tyrese shakes his head.

"Seriously," Merrill says, his voice changing, softening, growing sincere, "that's some of the most commendable shit I've heard in quite a while."

"You think I'm gonna waste an opportunity like this?" Tyrese says. "First black principal in this little backwoods town? I'm doin' my best to Obama this shit. No other principal I know would let the kids put on a production like this."

Merrill nods. "You right about that. I'm very proud of you little cuz. Very proud."

"You just help me keep any of these kids from gettin' killed," he says. His words and tone are meant to sound dismissive but his voice is thick with appreciation and pride.

The K-9 sergeant from Potter Correctional Institution walks in from out front with the FDLE bomb detection K-9 officer and motions me over.

I walk over to meet them near the front office.

"We did a thorough search of the Cherokee," he says. "It's clean. I mean real clean."

"Like someone-just-cleaned-it *clean*?" I ask.

"Exactly like that," he says.

I nod and think about it.

"But," the FDLE officer says, "it hasn't always been. At some point it's had explosive material in it."

The sergeant holds up the keys, but I'm so lost in thought already it takes a moment for me to take them.

"Hope that helps," he says.

They turn to walk back outside.

They turn again and reach for their guns as the explosions and gunfire starts.

20

I realize on some level that some of the semiautomatic guns my company manufactures will be used in school shootings, but am I responsible for that? Are beer brewers and automakers responsible for the people drunk drivers kill? How you gonna put that on us?

As I turn back toward the commons I can see that most of the other law enforcement officers in the room are responding in a similar manner—jumping up, spinning around, reaching for their weapons.

"Wait," I say. "Don't shoot."

I say it to the two men behind me and into my radio at the same time.

"They're just sound effects from the play," I say. "No one is really shooting. Don't fire. I repeat, don't fire."

On the stage, the teen gunman has started shooting his fellow classmates, each in turn confessing to his or her crime before falling to the floor dead—just like they had in rehearsal. Only now the sound effects are several decibels higher and sound even more authentic—an authenticity that's going to get innocent kids shot and killed by the police there to protect them unless we're very, very lucky.

I repeat what I said into the radio again. As soon as I'm finished I hear Tyrese and Kim yelling similar sentiments.

The teenage rampage killer on stage shoots himself in the head and falls dead not far from his victims, and I wonder why he didn't make the suspect list.

For a few moments there is complete and utter silence.

If anyone is breathing it can't be heard.

No movement. No sound. Nothing.

Then one by one the victims and eventually the gunman stand and walk to the front of the stage.

The first victim says, "We now invite you to join us and millions of other students around the world, including the survivors of the recent Parkland school shooting, to mark the nineteenth anniversary of the Columbine shooting, and walk out to protest the inaction of our leaders to protect us. All around the world right now students are participating in a walkout. Will you join us?"

She then steps off the stage and walks down the center aisle, followed by the other actors, then the crew.

"Whatta we do?" someone asks on the radio.

"Do we let them go?" another voice says.

"How do we proceed?" still another voice asks.

Tyrese says, "Let them go."

I picture the students walking outside into an ambush—not unlike what Eric and Dylan planned to do.

"We need to look for shooters outside," I say. "Everyone be alert. This isn't over. If you're guarding a door or a certain location stay in position. If you were sitting or standing near the student body go outside with them. Stay with them. Spotters, search the area for shooters, Check the roofs, the woods across the street, vehicles driving by. Everyone try to form a barrier around the kids."

The cast and crew walk through the commons, down the hallway next to the main office, and out the front door.

Many of the students from the audience join them, but more than I expect remain behind.

Merrill and Tyrese run up to me.

Merrill says, "We just lost all control of this situation. If there's a shooter waiting on them outside, the casualties will be catastrophic."

"Come on," I say.

We run outside ahead of the students, searching for shooters.

I can feel the tension in my body as I expect to be shot at any moment.

Now in addition to the spotter, two other cops have binoculars and are scanning the parking lot and area around the school.

"Anything?" I ask the original spotter.

He's the closest to us. The others are out in the parking lot.

"Nothing so far," he says, continuing to look.

The rigid students are resigned and sincere, seeming to sense the import of both the moment and the movement they're joining.

"Who has eyes on our suspects?" I ask.

"I'm right behind Mason and Dakota," Kim says. "They're just walking out like everyone else."

"Tristan and Denise are still backstage," LeAnn says. "I'm going to see why. I figured they'd be leading the procession."

"Still no sign of Evan," Chip says, "but Zach is videoing the walkout."

"Chase has just stepped out the front door," Ace says.

I turn and look back down the corridor.

I can see Ace Bowman standing next to the front door, watching the students closely as they exit the building.

About five feet in front of him, heading this way, I see Chase Dailey, a guitar case strapped to his back, his long, thick, curly hair bouncing a bit as he tries to maneuver around the other students moving more slowly than he'd prefer.

I rush toward him, scenes from *El Mariachi* and *Desperado* flickering on the movie screen of my mind as I do.

"Hey Chase," I say. "Step over here with me for a minute."

I can tell he's trying to figure out where he knows me from, but he complies and joins me next to the narrow flower bed beside the walkway.

"What kind of guitar do you have today?" I ask.

"Same as always," he says. "I only have one."

"Can I take a look at it?"

"*Now*?" he asks, his voice rising in surprise as he glances at all the activity around us. "Sure, I guess," he says.

He removed the strap from over his shoulder and carefully sets the case on the ground. Kneeling next to it, he slowly begins to unhasp the holders, his hands trembling as he does.

Just before he opens it, he hesitates.

"There some reason you don't want to open it?" I ask.

"Just don't want anything to happen to it," he says. "It's all I got."

He slowly lifts the lid of the case but only enough to give me the slightest view of the instrument.

"Take it out and let me see it better," I say.

"Really? Here? Like this? Why?"

"Hurry," I say.

He does as he's told.

It's just an acoustic guitar and there's nothing else in the case.

"Thank you," I say, and rush off to the rejoin the other cops out where the students are congregating.

"We got nothing," the spotter says. "No glint from the woods or on the roof. No movement. No nothing."

"Always nothin' until there's somethin'," Merrill says.

"Unless . . ." the spotter says, "there's just more nothin'."

Which is all we have—both while the students are outside and once they re-enter the school and return to class.

Nothing during lunch. Nothing in the afternoon. And after the last bus delivers its last student safely home for the day still nothing. Just more nothing.

21

We are ALL impacted by gun violence. You're never too young to make your voice heard! #NationalSchoolWalkout #NeverAgain

"How could we have been that wrong?" Kim asks.

Kim, LeAnn, Merrill, and I are at a table in The Oasis.

Once The Sports Oasis, Pottersville's premiere drinkery had devolved from a sports bar into a dive since the last time I had been inside. Now just The Oasis, the large, second-story bar is dim and dingy and in disrepair.

Of the three worn and warped pool tables in need of re-felting and restoration, only one is lit by the light hanging above it. Of the four dart machines, only one is plugged in and illuminated—but there doesn't seem to be even a single set of matching darts.

"It's sweet of you to say *we*," I say, "but the question is *how could I have been so wrong?*"

On the jukebox, Little Big Town's "Better Man" is ending, "Drunk Girl" by Chris Janson beginning.

Though there's not much in the way of country music I seek out, I'm constantly surrounded by it. It's the soundtrack of small Southern town life. I've heard both songs before, and though I appreciate the sentiment behind both, I believe that "Drunk Girl" had the potential to be a great song, but needed more work before it was released.

"I was so sure it was going to happen today," LeAnn says.

"We all were," Kim says, looking at me and adding, "You weren't any more wrong than the rest of us."

On the small, round table between us are three empty Bud Lights and a nearly full glass of flat fountain Diet Coke.

"It's my round," LeAnn says. "John, you want something else besides that disgusting Diet Coke? Janna keeps O'Doul's in stock for a friend of mine. Want one of those?"

I nod. "Sure. Thanks."

Beside me Merrill tenses ever so slightly. It's only the hint of a physical reaction really but the energy emanating from it is palpable. I ignore it.

LeAnn steps over to the bar and buys another round from Janna Todd, the new art teacher at the high school who works here part time.

"Wonder why she works here?" I ask.

"'Cause teachers are so poorly paid," Kim says.

"I get that," I say, "but it's—it can't be much money. Nobody's ever in here, are they?"

"May be to display those," Merrill says, nodding toward Janna's big fake breasts, most of which are visible in her bright, too-tight sweetheart T-shirt.

"Not exactly dress code, is it?" Kim says.

"I don't know . . ." Merrill says. "I saw a movie online about some naughty school girls and there was a teacher in it that dressed like that."

She laughs. "That's a very different school."

LeAnn returns with our drinks and distributes them. We all clink the bottles and take a drink.

The near-beer tastes far better than I expect and feels good going down.

I'm surprised by how much I like it—especially since I've never cared much for beer. I'm also surprised by how much it makes me want a real drink.

Kim looks at LeAnn. "Why do you think Janna works here? Can't be for the money, can it?"

"I think she does all right a couple of nights a week—Thirsty Thursday and Saturdays when they have a band—but I think it's more for the company and socialization. New in town. Doesn't know anyone. Tryin' to find a man, maybe."

"Then she's wookin' pa nub in all da wong places," Merrill says.

We all laugh.

We're still laughing a moment later when Chip Jeffers walks in and over to the table.

We offer him room at the table and tell him to pull up a chair, but he says he can't stay, just doing his rounds and saw us.

"What the hell happened today?" he asks.

"We were just talking about that," Kim says.

"Question is," Merrill says, "did he not go through with it—lost his nerve or because we were there—or was there never going to be a shooting to begin with?"

"*That is* the question," I say.

"What's the answer?" LeAnn asks.

I shrug. "I don't know."

"I thought for sure we were going to catch him today," Chip says.

"Am I the only one feels foolish?" Kim asks.

I shake my head. "I feel a right prize idiot, now don't I?" I say in my best British accent, which isn't very good. "I'm the reason we were there today. The reason there were so many of us there."

"We had to be," Merrill says. "It all fit. We couldn't take a chance on something like that. There's not a one of us who wouldn't do it again tomorrow."

"That's true," LeAnn says.

"Absolutely," Chip says. "Well, I've got to go. Keep me posted if anything comes up."

"Will do," Kim says.

He walks away, pausing to speak to Janna and her Barbie Doll breasts before leaving. As he leaves, a few other small groups arrive—an older woman with a cast who walks like she's already buzzed, two youngish men who look like they just finished shooting an episode of *Swamp People*, and a handful of football coaches. Ace Bowman, who's with the coaches, waves when he sees us and walks over.

"Long day," he says. "We all deserve a drink or two after that."

"No doubt," LeAnn says.

Patting Kim on the back, he says, "We're gonna have a quick one then I've got to get back to the school for a Pirate Booty meeting. Call you when I get home?"

She nods.

"Wait," Merrill says. "We can't just let that pass. You've got to get back for a what now?"

"Athletic supporters meeting," he says. "I didn't come up with the name, but the donors think it's cute and they're payin' the bills."

Merrill shakes his head.

"Thank you for everything you guys did today," Ace says. "I can't tell you how much I appreciate it."

"We're not done," I say. "We're gonna stay with it until we figure it out."

"Glad to hear it," he says. "Our little school is lucky to have y'all."

When he drifts back over to rejoin his party, LeAnn looks at

Kim. "Sounds like someone's gonna get a Pirate booty call later tonight."

We laugh again and I stand and declare it's my turn to get the next round, though I'm the only one finished.

"Not for me," Merrill says. "I've got to go in a few."

"I've got nowhere to be," LeAnn says. "And Kim doesn't until she has to shiver Ace's timber later, so set us up."

I move over toward the bar, purposefully positioning myself so that the older lady with the cast on is between me and our table.

Janna, just returning from delivering the coaches' drinks to their table, comes up behind the bar and says, "Give me just a minute, sweetie."

"Take your time," I say.

She then serves the two *Swamp People* men and the older woman without having to ask what they'd like. Using my finely honed detective skills, I deduce that they are regulars who are very regular.

While she's doing this, I glance back at our table to see if any of them are looking over here or could see me if they did.

"Okay, sweetheart," Jann says, stepping up to me, "what can I get you?"

"Two Bud Lights, an O'Doul's, and a shot of vodka."

"What kind of vodka would you like?"

"Whatever's closest," I say. "I'm not picky."

She smiles and locks eyes with me. "I like that in a man. Coming right up."

When she returns with the drinks, I have the cash waiting for her. While she turns to the register behind her to make change, I quickly knock back the shot of well vodka.

22

Most of the seniors at Marjory Stoneman Douglas weren't alive when the Columbine massacre happened. How is it that nineteen years later nothing has changed?

My body responds to the vodka like the old friend it is, nearly overwhelmed it has been so long.

When Janna gives me my change, I leave several dollars and the shot glass on the bar and return to the table with the three beers.

"Thank you, kind sir," LeAnn says.

"My pleasure," I say.

"I noticed she delivered the coaches' drinks," LeAnn says.

"They're in here all the time and tip well," Kim says, "and, well, they're coaches."

As I talk I try to stay as far back as possible so none of them will smell the liquor on my breath, hoping that the near beer will help mask it.

"Hey," Merrill says, "I thought I remembered that O'Doul's

has a small amount of alcohol in it. I just Googled it and it does. It's a very, very small amount, but it's there."

I shake my head. "Then it shouldn't be called non-alcoholic beer." I place the bottle down on the table and slide it away from me.

"I'm sorry," LeAnn says. "I didn't know."

"It's no big deal," I say. "No problem at all."

"You good?" Merrill asks.

I nod. "All good."

He studies me for a moment. I look away.

A forty-something woman with longish black hair and dark circles beneath her black eyes walks in and sits at the bar, giving a little wave in our direction as she does.

"You recognize her, don't you, John?" LeAnn says.

I shake my head. "No, don't think so."

"Do you, Merrill?" she asks.

He shakes his head.

"Sure y'all do," Kim says. "That's Inez Abanes."

"Who?" I ask.

"You know," LeAnn says, "Inez Abanes. She's our biology teacher."

"Okay," I say, not knowing where they're going with this.

"She swears up and down that she went to school with us," LeAnn says. "But we don't recognize her. Do either of you?"

We both shake our heads.

"She acts like we hung out and shit, but we have no idea who she is," LeAnn says.

"You're feeling bad for her, aren't you?" Kim asks.

"Well," I say, "I'm sure she's just trying to—"

"I've searched through every yearbook of our era," she says. "She's not in them. Not in one."

"It's bizarre," LeAnn says. "She's so earnest and convincing but she did not go to school with us. Anyway . . . just wanted to see if either of you recognized her. Okay, back to shit that matters."

"Let's figure out what happened today," I say. "And what we're going to do about it."

"It's impossible to prove a negative," Merrill says, "so we'll never know, but . . . what we did may be the reason there wasn't a shooting today."

Kim nods. "That's true. Very true. No cop gets credit for the crime she prevents from happening. How much media coverage do our intelligence and law enforcement agencies get for stopping a terrorist act before it happens?"

"If we stopped it today," I say. "If that's what happened . . . did we stop it or just delay it? And if we delayed it . . . by how long?"

"We need to keep the school on high alert," LeAnn says.

"Yes, we do," Kim says.

"Do you know even after all the shootings we've had . . ." LeAnn says, "our school still doesn't have a real plan and has never done a drill?"

"*Really*?" I ask.

"The only thing that's been done," she says, "is Tyrese had each teacher submit to him what they would do in the event of an active shooter situation—like three possible plans. That's it. That's all the superintendent asked for. Tyrese has tried to get them to do more, but so far . . . they haven't."

"Unbelievable," I say.

"No one ever thinks it's going to happen to their school," Kim says. "*We're a small school in a small town. We know these kids and their families. No one would do something like that here.*"

"Exactly," LeAnn says.

"And statistically," Kim says, "they have a good chance of being right—or lucky. But . . . That wouldn't be enough for me."

I nod. "Me either."

We fall quiet a moment.

"I keep hearing about students and teachers sleeping together," I say. "How pervasive is that?"

"Not very," LeAnn says. "Probably about like it was back when we were in school—an occasional, pretty rare kind of thing. There are lots of rumors, of course, but actual sex between teachers and students is rare. And actually, there's a downward trend in teen sexuality now anyway. Teens are having less sex. They have more anxiety and depression, but less sex."

"I ain't no psychiatrist or nothing," Merrill says, "but that shit could be related."

"I hear a lot of different teachers' names," I say, "including the buxom bartender, but—"

"Was I one of them?" LeAnn says.

"Sorry, no," I say.

"Damn," she says. "Gots to work on my rep."

"Lots of teachers," I continue, "but the same few students come up over and over—including the Dupree twins."

"Well, with them you never know," Kim says. "I wouldn't be too quick to dismiss anything you hear about them."

"That's because you've got the suspicious mind of a cop," LeAnn says.

"Doesn't make me wrong," Kim says.

"Hate to be the asshole who points this out," Merrill says. "but did any of you notice how similar some of what was in the play was to the journal fragments the custodian found?"

"I worked real hard not to see or hear any of that dreadful drivel," LeAnn says.

"I was blocking it out too," Kim says. "Why?"

"I just wonder if the notes the custodian found were part of the play—either from research or an earlier draft or something."

I shake my head and let out an exasperated sigh. "I can't believe I didn't think of that," I say.

"Can't think of everything," Kim says.

"It would've been easy enough to ask Tristan or Denise," I say, still shaking my head at my amateurish mistake. "I just didn't think about it. If I had everyone do all that we did today over some discarded pages from a play . . . I need to retire right now."

"Look," Kim says. "I hope it is. I'd rather us have done all we did for nothing than . . . the alternative. Right?"

We all express our agreement.

"Okay," Merrill says, standing. "Got to go."

"Thanks for everything today," I say.

"You good?" he asks me, his eyes locking onto mine.

I nod. "I am. Thanks."

"Y'all figure out what's next and I can help, let me know," he says.

Kim and LeAnn both stand and give Merrill a hug.

"I'm gonna step over to see Ace," Kim says. "Be back in a minute. Next round's on me."

She and Merrill leave and LeAnn and I are left alone.

Neither of us says anything for a moment.

Eventually she says, "I know the circumstances have been . . . but it's been nice getting to hang out with you. Don't see many of our old class very often. Except Kimmy and a couple of others."

I nod. "I've really enjoyed hanging with you too."

"I think this calls for some eighties music," she says, withdrawing a few dollars from her phone case. "Hold my beer. I'll be right back."

When she stumbles over to the jukebox, I reach for the O'Doul's.

In another moment "I Melt with You" by Modern English begins to play. Before the song is over, the bottle is empty.

The Call's "Everywhere I Go" is next and "Fascination Street" by The Cure is playing when LeAnn and Kim make it back to the table.

"Great choices," I say to LeAnn. "Appreciate you playing some lesser-known songs."

"Of course, honey," she says. "This big girl's still got a few moves."

"One more round," Kim says. "John, what can I get you?"

"How was Ace?" LeAnn asks, then turning to me explains, "He can get a little jealous sometimes."

"He's okay. He knows we're all old friends. And I reminded him that unlike Janna, John and Merrill didn't have their dicks hanging out."

LeAnn's laugh is loud and borders on being obnoxious.

"You ever get jealous of Anna?" Kim asks me.

"I'm ashamed to say there have been times."

"But it's not all the time I bet," LeAnn says.

I shake my head. "Only a few times over the years. Mostly back before we got together."

"Oh, you mean all the years," LeAnn says. "That's a long damn time, going all the way back to high school."

I nod.

"Just a few times in all that time?" she says.

"Still a few too many," I say.

"You work real hard at trying to be perfect, don't you?" she says.

"So last drink of the night," Kim says, and I can tell she's trying to change the subject. "What can I get you, John? It's not like Janna's gonna bring it over to us."

"If LeAnn's going to analyze me, I want a real drink," I say. "Get me a vodka and cranberry."

"Really?" Kim says.

"Really. Just one won't be a . . . Besides, we're celebrating. No kids got killed today."

"Are you sure?" LeAnn asks.

"I am," I say. "Just because I choose not to drink doesn't meant I can't. It's fine. Really. Besides, it'll prove to you I'm not working too hard to be perfect."

"Well, alrighty then," Kim says. "Drinks for the class of eighty-six coming up."

While she is at the bar, Tyrese comes in, looks around, and then walks over and joins us.

By the time Kim returns with our drinks, including one for Tyrese, Quarterflash's "Find Another Fool" is playing.

"What now?" Tyrese asks.

"We were just about to talk about that," Kim says.

"Did we dodge a bullet today or was there never gonna be one fired?" he asks.

"We're not sure," I say.

"I think until we know definitively differently," Kim says, "we should keep acting as if the bullet is still going to be fired."

"*Definitively differently*?" LeAnn says.

"Shut up," she says. "I'm a little buzzed."

"Buzzed or not, she's right," I say.

"So how do we do that?" Tyrese asks.

"We need to find out where Evan Fowler was today," I say. "Read Tristan's play and compare it to the notes we found. Keep watching our primary suspects. Keep the school on high alert. Get Kim some backup. Continue to investigate and try to figure out what's going on or what we missed. And we do all this until we know definitively differently."

23

School shootings, almost a uniquely American phenomenon, aren't a price associated with freedom. Doing nothing will change nothing. The lack of leadership and action by Congress leaves blood on their hands and ensures that history will record them as cowards and prostitutes who put money and politics over the lives of our children.

By the time we hang around long enough to make sure we're good and sobered up and I follow Kim and LeAnn to their places, then drive back to Wewa, it's late when I get home.

Our home is dim and quiet, its occupants fast asleep.

As badly as I want, even need to see Anna, I'm glad she's not seeing me in my current condition.

Stepping through the mudroom, I pause in the kitchen to empty my pockets, double checking to make sure I threw away all the receipts with alcohol on them before leaving Pottersville.

After placing my wallet, phone, gun, and badge on the kitchen counter, I stumble back through the mudroom and out into the garage where our washer and dryer are, unsteadily undressing and dropping my booze and cigarette smoke-smelling clothes into the washing machine and starting it.

Back in the kitchen gathering my things I notice John Paul's bottle, formula mix, and diaper bag and feel guilty for not being here to help Anna more with him and Carla.

Quickly but quietly I pad down the hallway and into the guest bathroom, ostensibly showering in here instead of our bathroom in an attempt not to disturb Anna.

I can never get the water temperature in here adjusted just right, but the too-hot drops cascading from the high shower head are sobering and begin to calm the raw nerves jangling just beneath my skin.

The soap and shampoo suds seem to strip away a film of smoke but are powerless against the residue of guilt that clings to me like bad karma.

As I'm rinsing the shampoo from my hair, I hear the door open.

"John?" Anna asks, whispering in an attempt not to wake Taylor in the next room.

"Yeah. Hey. I was trying not to wake you."

"Really?" she asks, gently closing the door behind her. "Why? You always wake me. We always talk. No matter what time it is."

"I meant until I crawled into bed beside you," I say.

"Oh."

"I'm almost out," I say.

"Stay in," she says.

In another moment, she is pulling back the curtain and stepping in with me, her naked body by far the most extraordinary thing I've seen all day.

I grab her, pulling her under the water with me, and kiss her hard on the mouth, hoping the massive amounts of gum I've been chewing for the past couple of hours will do its job.

As I kiss her, my hands move all over her body, rubbing, caressing, lingering at my favorite spots.

When we break from our kiss, breathless and intoxicated, she says, "Are you okay?"

"Yeah. Why?"

"Just seem like you might not be."

"I am," I say. "I'm exhausted and frustrated and feel foolish, but I'm okay."

She takes a little step back and her eyes lock onto mine.

"I'm probably projecting," she says. "Sorry if I am. But finding you in here like this . . . has me a little . . . Chris used to always shower in the guest bathroom downstairs before coming to bed. I realized later it was to wash the woman he had been with off of him, the scent of sex and perfume. I think finding you in here like this reminds me of that . . . has brought up some painful and embarrassing moments."

"Oh God, Anna, I'm so, so sorry," I say. "I had no idea."

"How could you? You haven't done anything wrong. I was just explaining why I'm . . . how I'm feeling."

"I'm an insensitive idiot," I say. "I'm so sorry."

"No, you're being way too hard on yourself," she says. "You couldn't have known."

"I would *never* cheat on you," I say. "Not ever. No matter what."

"I know that. I wasn't thinking you had. Truly."

"I stayed out later than I should have," I say. "I haven't been helping with Taylor or John Paul like I should. I'm truly sorry."

"Stop apologizing," she says. "There's no need. I'm sorry today went the way it did."

"It could've been so much worse," I say. "I'll take a day like today over an actual school shooting any day. I just wish we could've caught him so we don't have to worry about it happening when we're not there, but that's enough about that for tonight. I want to hear about your day."

"The only thing I have to say is . . . You wanna make love in here or in our bedroom?"

I laugh. "You already know the answer."

Though we've successfully had sex in a few showers in our time, we both agree that for all their steamy sexiness, the bed is far better for quality and quantity.

We quietly steal into our bedroom like teenagers trying not to wake their parents, and it strikes me how ironic it is that we go from kids trying not to wake our parents to parents trying not to wake our kids.

As we enter our room, the room that is of all the rooms in the world the most *ours*, a line of Rumi's comes to mind. *Lovers find secret places inside this violent world where they make transactions with beauty.*

Our lovemaking is passionate and intense, leading me to conclude that I had just the right amount of alcohol the right amount of time ago to only enhance and not detract from our intimacy.

Afterwards, she falls asleep in my arms.

All I can think about is wriggling my arm and chest out from beneath her, slipping out of the bed, sneaking down the hallway, through the kitchen and mudroom, out the side door, and to my car and the bottle of vodka hidden there, waiting for me like a patient, secret lover.

And the only reason I just think about it instead of actually doing it is because of her earlier reaction to me being late and showering before she saw me and the old feelings of being deceived and cheated on that it reminded her of. It might be only for tonight, but there's no way I'm sneaking out of bed and leaving her for my other lover waiting for me in the car.

24

The ugly truth is we're infatuated with guns. Gun culture isn't something separate from or inside American culture. American culture is gun culture.

On the morning of the rampage shooting at Potter High School I awake late with my first hangover in over a decade.

I figured I'd wake up Saturday morning paying for my sins, but I guess I hadn't had as much to drink as I thought I had. For the rest of the weekend, during our sacred family time, I had drank very little, but last night after Johanna had been safely delivered home and everyone else was asleep I had quickly found my way to the bottom of my end-of-weekend bottle.

After a quick shower and rushing to get ready, I spend the precious few extra minutes I have with my family in the kitchen. Anna and Taylor are on one side of the table, Carla and John Paul on the other. Everyone is eating something.

Johanna, who spent the weekend with us, has returned to her mother's, and her empty seat makes me sad.

"How're you feeling?" Anna asks. "You had another restless night, didn't you?"

"I'm okay," I say. "Hope I didn't keep you up."

"Well," Carla says tilting John's bottle up a bit, "this little one let me have the best night of sleep I've had since he arrived."

"That was very nice of you, little man," I say, bending down to kiss his forehead. "Very, very thoughtful of you. Yes it was."

"I slept good too," Taylor says. "And I let you and Mommy sleep all night too, didn't I?"

"You sure did, big girl," I say, making my way over to her and, to her delight, lavishing her with excessive hugs and kisses—if hugs and kisses could be given in excess.

"Which direction are you headed in?" Anna asks. "St. Joe or Pottersville?"

"Reggie, good, generous soul that she is, is giving me another day at PHS," I say. "We're gonna do some follow-up with our suspects and make a plan for going forward."

"Take an extra close look at Mason Nickols and Dakota Emanuel," Carla says. "They come into the diner sometimes late at night when they finish up over at Sal's. That's two sick, creepy, psycho . . ." she glances at Taylor, ". . . so and so's."

"Mommy, what's a so and so?" Taylor asks.

"It's not good," Anna says.

"We are," I say to Carla. "They are at the top of our list. You ever hear them say anything about the school or the other students?"

She nods. "All the time. They're world-class haters. And not just of the other students. I've heard them use the N-word about Tyrese and all kind of sexist . . . stuff about the new art teacher that tends bar nights at The Oasis. Others too. They hate all the coaches and jocks. Even the janitor. I truly believe they're . . . evil."

"Any other kids ever come in acting like that or anyone else you'd suspect of something like this?"

She nods. "There are a couple of kids that fit the . . . type or whatever, but . . . I don't know their names. I could probably pick them out of a yearbook."

"Then I'll bring one home tonight," I say. "Thank you."

"It's no problem, dude, just don't let them be shootin' up my school."

25

I cannot stop hearing the sounds of guns and explosives as I walk down my hallway. I cannot unsee my classmates being carried out on stretchers heading to the hospital or the morgue. I cannot unsee the bodies on the hallway and classroom floors.

Potter High School.
7:55 A.M.

First bell rings.

Students leaving the commons for their first class, lumbering up and around the halls like a slow-moving herd of zombies.

8:00 A.M.

First period begins.

The commons and main hallways now empty, appearing suddenly and inexplicably abandoned, eerily quiet after being so busy and noisy moments before.

8:07 A.M.

First shots fired or first explosions detonated. Later there will be debate about which.

Tyrese on the radio. "Were those gunshots?"

Kim and LeAnn rushing out of their offices.

"Go look at the monitors and radio me where he is," Kim says, withdrawing her weapon. "And tell Tyrese to put the school on lockdown. Go. Hurry."

As LeAnn enters the back door to the main office, Kim runs through the commons, gun drawn, head moving about, scanning, searching, scouring.

Kim pulling her sheriff's department radio, calling dispatch. "Active shooter at Potter High School. I repeat, active shooter at Potter High School. SRO in pursuit."

Alarms blaring.

Tyrese on the intercom, telling teachers there's an active shooter situation, the school's on lockdown, it's not a drill.

More shots.

Explosions.

Smoke.

Fire.

Loud, concussive bangs rattling the school, raining down debris.

The explosions rocking the building make the earlier shots sound smaller somehow—popguns by comparison, or Fourth of July firecrackers.

The big bangs of the bombs are deafening, jarring, overwhelming.

The high school has become a combat zone.

"Where are they?" Kim says into her school radio.

"Can't see," LeAnn says, studying the monitor of the security camera feeds. "Too much smoke. Okay wait. I see you. Oh God, be careful Kim. I can't . . . I can't tell where they are. They could be right around you."

More explosions.

"*Shit*," LeAnn says. "Explosions have taken out three of our cameras."

"Are you fuckin' *kiddin'* me?" Kim says.

"Damnit, make that four. I'm going blind up here."

"Just find them," Kim says. "Look for any movement at all, even whirls in the smoke."

Next to LeAnn, Tyrese is studying the monitor.

"*Anything?*" she asks him.

"Kim, this is Tyrese, use extreme precaution. Backup is on the way."

Tyrese wonders if he should have said *caution* instead of *precaution*, but the thought is gone as quickly as it came when he sees the shooter in one of the small squares on the bottom of the large monitor.

"*There,*" he yells.

He points to the feed, LeAnn leaning in, glancing down, seeing the figure not believing what she's seeing.

The gunman is wearing what could be considered the school shooter's uniform—long black duster, the collar up, black boots, black fatigues, black gloves, a black military-style cap—but with one significant addition. Unlike in any previous school rampage shootings, this time the shooter is wearing a mask.

26

We as students can't understand why it's so much harder to get a driver's license or a job or a pet or an old clunker car than it is to buy semiautomatic weapons.

"Kim, Kim," LeAnn yells into the radio. "He's coming up behind you."

"Where?" Kim asks.

"He's— Wait. Where'd he go?"

The dark, disquieting figure is gone.

LeAnn turns to Tyrese. "Where'd he go?"

"It looks like he went into the library," Tyrese says. "But I can't tell for sure. He's definitely behind you back this direction— between you and the hallway that leads back down to the commons."

"Okay," Kim says. "Who is it?"

"We're not sure," LeAnn says.

"He's wearing a mask," Tyrese says.

"Really?"

"Yeah."

"What kind?"

"It's a . . . It's just a blank white mask."

LeAnn shivers as she thinks about the cold, expressionless, anonymous white mask and the sheer impersonal terror that can be projected onto the cruel, uncaring canvas of its blankness. It's a mask of absence, a face that has stared into the abyss and seen the crippling void of nothingness, the emotionless, expressionless face responding to a godless universe devoid of love and meaning.

"How many are there?" Kim asks. "Is it just the one?"

"That's all we've seen so far," LeAnn says, "but it's really hard to see. Please be careful. Or better yet come . . . back down here with us and wait for backup."

27

Our school is splattered with our blood. What level of callousness and self-involvement and simple inhumane not giving a fuck is required for you not to stop everything you're doing and work together to make sure this never happens at another high school ever again?

Potter High School library.

8:07 A.M.

"Was that gunfire?" Mrs. Lewis the librarian asks. "That sounded like gunfire."

"Sounded like firecrackers to me," Slow Stevie says.

"Everyone, get down," Mrs. Lewis says. "Just in case. Get under the tables."

Before the students are on the floor—especially Slow Stevie—Principal Monroe is on the intercom telling them there's an active shooter in the school.

This makes Slow Stevie move a little faster. But only a little. And it's not like he'll be able to fit under one of the tables anyway.

The library, which is located in the center of the circular main building of the school, has four entrances—each consisting of double glass doors with glass sidelights around them.

Locking down the library is futile. Still, Mrs. Lewis intends to try. Or at least she did until the explosions begin.

"Stay down," she yells to the fifteen or so students in what is sometimes referred to as the media center.

She yells it from where she cowers behind the counter.

Semi-automatic rifle fire. Louder. Closer.

Glass shattering.

The glass doors to Mrs. Lewis's right, the first set on the south side of the school, are being shot to shit.

Students screaming.

Alarms blaring.

Someone crying.

From her hidden position beneath the main counter where she mostly stands all day, Mrs. Lewis can't see anything that's going on. She can only hear it.

She can hear the rounds ricocheting around the room. She can hear doors slamming and people screaming. She can hear glass shards falling like heavy rain or light hail on the library floor. And she can hear someone crying—maybe more than one person—but she can't make out if the sobs are cries of fear or pain.

She wants to crawl around the counter and check on the students or at least yell to ask if they're all right, but she's too scared to do either. She doesn't want to be, but she is.

Mrs. Lewis doesn't want the kids in her care to die, but more than that she doesn't want to die herself.

If she's completely honest, she knew deep down that this would be the way she'd react if ever put in this situation. She had just never fathomed she'd ever be put in this situation.

Mrs. Lewis hears what sounds like the way her father and

other old-timers around these parts used to thump watermelons to check to see if they were ripe.

More screams.

"*Motherfucker*," Slow Stevie yells. "Son of a . . . *motherfucker*."

Somebody yells, "Slow Stevie's shot."

"Are you okay?" someone else yells.

"Somebody help Slow Stevie," someone else yells.

More screams. More crying. More gunshots. More explosions.

Mrs. Lewis thinks that Potter High School sounds like an urban war zone. It's not a thought she'd ever imagined she'd think, but here she is crouched behind the library counter thinking that very thing.

28

It seems like a bad dream. It is, isn't it? A nightmare we're going to wake up from soon. It can't be something that really happened in the real world, can it? That can't be real blood. Those can't be the actual dead bodies of kids. It can't be that our reality is worse than any nightmare we could have, can it?

The classroom doors of Potter High School can only be locked from the outside with a key.

During a lockdown each teacher has to open his or her door far enough to reach out, insert and turn the key with one hand while holding the handle still with the other, then pull it closed.

When coach and athletic director and Social Studies teacher Ace Bowman had asked why this was at a faculty meeting last year where lockdown procedures were being discussed, he was told it was to prevent a student from being able to lock the door from the inside and barricade himself in the room in a hostage situation.

The answer wasn't satisfactory to Ace but he didn't say anything at the time.

Right about now he's really wishing he had.

His first-period remedial Social Studies class is small—something he's always glad for, but never so much as at this moment.

When the gunshots and explosions begin, Ace stands and quietly and calmly instructs his students to get inside his office.

His office, like all the offices in all the classrooms, is essentially a large wooden box built in the front corner of the room.

Though about the size of a prison cell, he believes he'll be able to fit the thirteen remedial Social Studies students inside.

As the frightened kids rush into the small office, he runs over to the classroom door to lock it.

Reaching his beefy hands and hairy forearms through as narrow an opening as will accommodate them, he fumbles with his keys, trying to fit the right one in the lock, as the Pottersville Pirate on his lanyard appears to be dancing down below.

The first round pierces the pinky of his right hand and rips more than a third of it off, bone and all.

The second round penetrates his left hand, leaving a black and bloody hole not unlike a Renaissance painting of the crucified Christ's nail-pierced palm.

He screams in pain. Drops the keys. Falls back into the classroom.

Lying on the floor just a few feet from the office door where the last few screaming students are running, he rolls over and begins to crawl on his knees and elbows, holding his shot-up hands aloft as he does.

Two of his football players push past the students running into the office and step out to help him, but step back as the gunman appears at the classroom door and starts firing.

Stumbling into the office, they slam the door as rounds pierce and pock it.

The bigger of the two then motions to a huge, old metal filing cabinet and they each drag a side of it and half-carry, half-slide it over in front of the door.

It means, of course, they're leaving Coach Bowman on his own on the other side, but somehow they both know, though they haven't had time to even think it, that it's what he would want them to do.

"Everybody get down low and push on the filing cabinet," the kid most everyone calls Big Cup says.

Though the old filing cabinet is tall, it's not as tall as the door or the narrow pane of glass that runs nearly to the top. They've got to stay down.

They could still get shot, but it would require the gunman dragging over a chair, climbing up on it, and shooting down at an angle through the small strip of glass at the top not blocked by the cabinet.

"Somebody get the lights," Rester Stokes says.

Someone does.

Now they are thirteen students piled on top of each other in the dark on the floor of a small office that smells like socks and cheap cologne, pressing a rusting old filing cabinet against a wooden door as if their lives depend on it.

They only hear what happens next and later they won't all remember hearing it the same way, but most will report the gunman saying some form of the phrase, "Any last words?"

Some of the students think they hear Coach Bowman say, "Tell—" while others think they hear "hell," but whether he's about to leave a message for a loved one or telling the shooter to *Go to hell*, there is no disagreement on the sound of rapid gunfire that comes next and the cries and screams of Coach Bowman. Nor of the rounds then shot at them through the office door, the shatters of glass, the pings of the bullets striking the filing cabinet.

Several of the kids huddled in the dark office are injured, but the only fatality is that of Coach Ace Bowman, whose long, big-hipped body lies bloody and bullet-riddled on the thin, industrial carpet of the classroom floor.

29

A text I thought I'd never send: Someone is shooting people at my school.

When all the shooting starts, Josh Stewart is in the boys' restroom on the east side of the school. At first he's not sure what he's hearing, but then he hears someone scream and guesses it's gunfire.

Today is Josh's fifteenth birthday.

To celebrate, his mom had gotten up early and made him a big birthday breakfast for him, which included his favorite— breakfast burritos.

His mom's efforts made him feel loved and celebrated, but also a little nauseated, and by the time he walked into his first-period class—Biology with Mrs. Abanes—he had to walk right back out again, and by the time he rounded the final curve before the boys' bathroom he was running.

A school shooting at Potter High and he's caught with his fuckin' pants down.

Finishing as fast as he can, doing only a decent at best job wiping, and not bothering to wash his hands, he decides to make a run for it.

He decides this in the split second he has to decide and he does so because he thinks that the gunfire sounds far away and that he'll be far safer in the classroom with Mrs. Abanes, who seems far too solid and stern to get shot or let any of her students get shot, than he would out here by himself.

Picturing himself as a vulnerable, young gazelle separated from the herd, Josh runs as fast as he ever has around the empty hallway toward Mrs. Abanes's classroom.

Explosions rocking the school.

Smoke beginning to fill the hallway.

Obnoxious alarm bleating.

And the gunfire sounding closer now.

Am I actually running toward the shots? he wonders.

It's hard to tell.

So many sounds. All of them ricocheting around the hard surfaces of the circular hallway.

For the briefest of moments, he thinks of turning back, but figures he can still make it.

Long, skinny teen legs stretched out, arms and heart pumping, little gazelle running for his life.

As he rounds the final curve before Mrs. Abanes's room, flailing as if death itself is chasing him, something out of a horror movie is standing there in the smoke.

Long black leather duster. White expressionless face. Rifle rising. Firing.

The first round shatters his ankle and brings him down hard, head first into the cinderblock wall, knocking him unconscious so that he's unaware of what the subsequent rounds do.

30

Guns don't kill people. People kill people. Guns just make it easier and quicker for people to kill people.

Frannie Schultz cowers in the back corner of the science lab between a bookshelf and a discarded chemistry table surrounded by people she would not have chosen to die with.

Beyond the classroom door out in the hallway, gunfire continues to ring out at a rapid rate, punctuated by explosions that rattle the specimen jars on the shelves along the far wall and trays of glass beakers on the tables beneath them.

For all the noise outside, inside the room is eerily silent.

No one is talking or even whispering. No one is moving.

Beyond the barrier of the classroom door, there are only the shocking sounds of gunfire and explosions, alarms and screams, and the occasional intercom instruction. Inside the science lab, inside Frannie's own head, there is only the mental dissonance involved in trying to reconcile the sights and sounds of school with those of war.

Frannie is seventeen, neither a goody-goody nor a popular party girl. When she is thought of at all by her classmates, it is as *a nice girl, sort of quiet, sort of plain.*

She's aware of this on some level, and wonders if she's going to die today and only ever have been a plain, quiet, nice enough girl.

She doesn't want that to have been her life.

She doesn't want to die like this, hiding in the dark.

She doesn't want to die surrounded by so many virtual strangers.

But most of all she doesn't want to die a virgin.

She wants to have been a different sort of girl. Not radically different. Just different enough.

And as the gunshots get closer and the glass from the library doors begins to shatter, she decides to start being a different sort of girl right now.

Pushing herself up and pressing through the other kids huddled around her on her hands and knees, she crawls over to where Derek Burrell, her secret crush and the most decent guy in their class, is leaning against the wall behind a desk looking out the window.

"Hey," she says.

"Hey," he says, his large pale face blushing crimson beneath his blond curls.

He makes room for her behind the desk, though to do so exposes him more. Of course, given his enormous size, one desk alone was never going to be enough to shield him.

"You mind if I stay over here with you?" she asks.

"*No,*" he says, his voice rising in surprise. "Not at all, but . . ."

Here we go, she thinks.

"I think I'm about to break this window open and go get my gun out of my truck," he says. "It's just right there. I can be back inside of two minutes. Maybe less."

Once he's free, will he really come back? she wonders. *Should he? Would I?*

"That way if those whack jobs come in here tryin' to shoot us," he continues, "I'll be able to shoot back. See how they like that."

He's big and a bit goofy and *whack job* sounds funny coming out of his mouth, but he's charming and evidently heroic.

"What if one of them's outside?" she asks.

"I been watching. Haven't seen anyone so far."

"It's so cool of you to even want to."

"You mind watching for me?" he says. "Yell if you see anyone."

She shakes her head. "No, not at all. But would you do something for me?"

"'Course. What's that?"

"Will you take me out if we survive this?"

"*Really?*" he asks. "I'll survive this just so I can."

31

It was just like any other Monday morning. Until it wasn't. It made me want a gun. Maybe we all should just start carrying a gun. Go back to the Wild West and just shoot the shit out of each other. You think you don't want a gun until someone has one shooting at you.

Janna Todd's first-period study hall is the only class she has inside the main building. All her other classes, her art classes, take place in the art building.

If the shooting had happened during any other period she wouldn't even be up here for it. She'd be safely tucked away in the art building where she should be.

She's an art teacher for fuck sake, not a study hall monitor. The only reason she has to cover a study hall is that she's teaching at Podunk High. Ironically, the only reason she's teaching at Podunk High is she thought it would be safe.

When the first shots were fired, there was some debate about what exactly they were, with a couple of the boys who hunt swearing they weren't gunshots. But she knew. Knew instantly that the day she had dreaded had arrived.

Fuckin' Monday mornings, man, she thinks.

At first she tells the students to get under their desks, but soon realizes how little good that's going to do.

Think. Whatta we do?

With only six students she has more options than most teachers, but what does that mean?

It means you can either hide or move them more easily. Fight or flight? Hide or run?

She wants to grab them and run to Ace's room and hide in there with him. He'll know what to do. But she can't do that. He's half a school away and it sounds like some of the shooting and screaming is coming from that direction.

Lock the outside door. Put everyone in the office and barricade both doors.

When the bombs begin to explode something inside her shifts, and she knows she's got to get out of here.

Got to get the kids out of here and into the art building.

The exit door leading to the covered walkway out to the art building is only thirty feet from the study hall classroom door.

We make a break. Run for it. We do it now before it gets any worse in here. Before these fuckin' bombs bring down this building on top of us.

"Okay, listen up everybody," she says. "We're going to go to the art building. I can lock us inside there. We'll be safe. Okay?"

None of the scared students respond.

"We need to get out of here before the shooters get down here or before one of their bombs brings down the school. Okay?"

They nod.

She holds up her keys. "Line up. When I open the door, run as fast as you can around to the exit closest to the art building. Careful not to trip each other. Don't run faster than the person in front of you. But run as fast as you can. Got it?"

They nod again and line up.

As they do she tries to decide if it's best for her to be in the front or the back of the line. In the front, she can lead them. She can take the risk that a shooter is already out there in this side of the hallway and will start shooting as soon as they step out. But what if she goes first and they don't follow? In the rear, she can make sure they all go and can direct them from the back.

She decides to do both.

She'll be the first to step out, but as soon as she does, assuming she doesn't get shot, she'll stand to the side and let the students out and then follow them.

She explains what she's going to do.

"Ready?"

Another bomb explodes. This one far closer.

"Let's go. Come on. Now. We have to go now."

She shoves open the door and steps out. Quickly glances around. Is tempted to run to the right, toward Ace's room, but makes herself stand firm.

"Go. Go. Go."

The students do as she says, filing out of the classroom, running as fast as they can.

She follows.

So far so good.

More explosions. More gunfire. And that fuckin' deafenin' fire alarm.

They reach the alcove that leads to the exit.

As they round the corner, she thinks *We made it. We're safe.*

Just fifteen feet from the double glass doors that lead out of the danger and chaos of this apocalypse.

She feels such relief. She made the right decision.

But when they reach the doors, and push on them, they only give a little.

Looking down she sees that the bars to the door have been zip-tied together.

Several large, thick zip ties have the two doors strapped together.

"*Shit*! Who's got a knife?" she asks.

Everyone shakes their heads.

"None of you rednecks have a pocket knife on you? Are you fuckin' kiddin' me?"

Some of the kids continue to shove on the door, but it's no use. The ties aren't going to give, the doors aren't going to open.

"We could try to break the glass," one of the kids says.

"With what? Your hard head? Back to the classroom. Now. Hurry."

They begin to run back in the direction of all the explosions and alarms and screams and gunfire.

But as they're about halfway down the alcove, a figure appears out of the smoke in the main hallway. Looking like something out of a comic book, he's in all black, including a long black leather duster, fatigues, and gloves, and has on a white mask beneath a black military-style hat.

Raising his rifle, he begins to fire, spraying bullets like windswept hail throughout the alcove.

Within seconds all seven people—six students and one teacher—are sprawled across the floor, their life's blood leaking out of them.

32

People say he just went crazy like it could happen to anyone or it's as random as getting struck by lightning, but I don't think so. He didn't just go crazy. There were signs to see if anyone was looking.

I arrive at Potter High School around a quarter after—just eight minutes into the attack.

As I run through the main entrance, I can hear sirens in the distance. Backup is on the way.

Inside, Tyrese and LeAnn quickly tell me what they know and toss me a radio.

"Hurry, John," LeAnn says. "Kim is up there by herself."

"Radio her," I say. "Let her know I'm coming up. Not to shoot me. Find out her position. I'll be monitoring. And be sure to tell the Potter County deputies that we're up there."

Tyrese says, "We think Kim has been shot. We don't know how bad. Want me to come with you?"

I shake my head as I'm running away.

Withdrawing my weapon, I make my way up the hallway that leads to the main, circular one beyond.

The acrid air is thick with smoke and the smell of burned gunpowder. Visibility is very low.

Through the fog, I can hear the dissonant sounds of disembodied screams, the arrhythmic bursts of semi-automatic gunfire, the intermittent explosions of bombs, and the incessant blare of the fire alarm.

As I reach the main hallway, it gets worse—the smoke thicker, the racket louder, the terrified screams more piercing.

Unable to determine where exactly the shots are coming from, I take a right and head south in the main hallway.

Even if it wasn't dim and filled with smoke, the circularness of the hallway would make it difficult to see very far in either direction, its hard surfaces bouncing noises around, making it impossible to isolate or pin down the direction of any single sound.

"Any word on Kim's position yet?" I ask into the radio.

"Not yet. Where are you?"

"You can't see me," I say, looking up, searching for security cameras.

"Most of them are out because of the explosions."

"Have somebody cut the fire alarm," I say. "It's handicapping us."

"I'll go do it now," Tyrese says.

Reaching the first set of library doors, I see that they are shot up and shattered, large shards of glass hanging precariously over the jagged opening.

I pause and glance in. There is no movement, and though I'm sure there are students hiding inside, no one is visible.

As I round the first arching curve of the hallway, I can hear the live gunfire better and believe I'm getting close.

Another loud explosion close by, though I can't be certain exactly where, leaves my ears ringing.

Up ahead I hear shots being fired, and as I get closer, I can see

Kim sitting on the floor in a pool of blood, leaning against the wall of a small alcove that leads to a dark, empty classroom, returning fire. On the floor a few feet away is her shot-up radio.

I rush over to her, crouching behind the same wall.

"You okay?" I ask. "Where are you hit?"

"Don't worry about me," she says. "Just get that evil fuck before he gets anyone else."

"How many are there?" I ask.

"Just one as far as I know."

"Who is it?"

"Don't know. Coward's wearing a mask."

"Backup is coming," I say. "And an ambulance for you."

"Okay, but just get him."

A round blasts above us, chipping off the corner of a cinderblock.

"Shit," she says. "What the— That was close. Are the other deputies already up here with us?"

"I'm not sure. Why?"

"That was a different weapon than he was using before."

I radio Tyrese. "Is SWAT or any Potter County deputies up here with us yet?"

"No, they're pulling up onto the property now."

"Okay," I say. "I've got a message for them. I'll radio you back in a second."

I return my attention to Kim. "Can you keep firing at him from here while I run around and come up on him from the other side?"

She nods. "Yeah."

"You sure?"

"Go."

I do.

I dart out from the alcove and back down the hall in the direction I have just come.

As I do, I radio Tyrese, let him know Kim's position and

condition, and what I'm doing, asking him to convey that to anyone else entering this part of the building.

Eyes stinging, throat burning, I begin coughing and hacking.

I run fast and carelessly. If there's a second shooter I'm making myself an easy target for him.

Thankfully, mercifully, the fire alarm stops.

Visibility is still low, especially with the way my eyes are watering, but I can hear a little better now—only a little better, though. My ears continue to ring.

I try to run as quietly as possible, not drawing any attention to myself as I make my way toward the shooter, but the smoke and smell of nitroglycerin have me coughing.

My old alma mater looks like a bombed out building from a war-torn town in the Middle East, lights shot out and dangling by shorting electrical wires, glass shards crunching beneath my shoes, huge chunks of walls missing.

I pass by another shot-out library door, then an open classroom with a dead body crumpled on the floor, but the most horrific scene by far is the blood-covered side hallway leading out to the art building and the pile of bodies lying dead or dying in it.

As I near the place I estimate the shooter to be, I can hear the blasts of his shotgun and the return bangs of Kim's sidearm.

I slow down, hoping to be able to sneak up behind him and take him alive, but as I round the curving hallway, he spins toward me, levels the barrel of his shotgun in my direction and fires.

The round whizzes by my head. I can hear and feel it.

In the split second before I fire back, I can see that not only is the boy not wearing a mask, but he's not one of the suspects we've been investigating.

He's big and blond and sort of soft looking, dressed in jeans, boots, and a T-shirt, and I don't think I've ever seen him before.

He fires another round.

I aim at the shotgun, attempting to knock it out of his hands, but his head is leaning down on the stock, sighting, and I'm afraid the round will hit him in the face.

Lowering my gun, I squeeze off two quick rounds. One aimed at his left hip, the other his left knee.

He spins around and goes down, his shotgun thudding heavily on the hard hallway floor as he does.

33

These aren't random shootings. They're school shootings. They're not happening at libraries or malls or churches or fast-food restaurants. They're happening at school. The school part is as significant as the shooting part.

Ears still ringing, I run over to him, kick the shotgun away from, pat him down, and cuff him.

Leaving him there bleeding on the floor, I rush over to check on Kim—but not before letting her know that's what I'm doing.

"You hanging in?" I ask, continuing to glance around in case there's another shooter.

She nods. "Still here. Who was under the mask?"

"I didn't recognize him," I say. "He wasn't wearing a mask."

"What?" she asks. "Help me up. Take me over to see him."

"You sure?" I ask, but she is already trying to pull herself up.

"Where are you hit?" I ask.

She holsters her gun and reaches up with her right hand.

"Pull me up by my right. My left arm and left thigh are . . . wounded."

Getting her up is obviously painful for her, but she's determined.

I duck down and she drapes her right arm over my shoulder, and I help her sort of limp and hop on one leg down the hallway.

"Oh my God," she says. "That's not him. That's Derek Burrell. He's a good kid. He wasn't the shooter."

"He was shooting at you and at me," I say.

"I can't . . ." she says, shaking her head. "I don't know why he would be . . . but . . . the shooter we're looking for is smaller than Derek, dressed in all black, wearing a mask. Help me down."

"Derek?" she asks. "Derek? Can you hear me?"

He mumbles something as I help her down beside him.

As she talks to him, I continue to search the area around us for other shooters or backup.

Tyrese on the radio. "Kim, John, Potter deputies and EMT are on the way up to you. Where are you?"

I tell him. "Tell everyone to use extreme caution. We believe we still have an active shooter situation."

"I was . . ." Derek says, "trying . . . to help. Did I . . . get him before . . . he got me?"

Kim looks up at me. "Uncuff him, John."

"Are you sure?" I say. "Let's wait and—"

"I'm positive," she says. "No way he was a part of this. He's too hurt to do anything now anyway. Please."

"Okay," I say.

Continuing to search all around us for the shooter, I kneel down beside him and quickly remove the cuffs. Standing, I return them to my belt and withdraw my gun.

A classroom door opens about ten feet away and a teacher and two students lean out.

"Is it safe to come out?" the teacher asks.

"No," I say. "Not yet. Stay in—"

"Is that— Did he get Derek?"

"Derek," one of the female students says. "Is he okay?"

"I tried to get him not to," the teacher says, "but I couldn't stop him. He went to his truck and got his gun and went out to stop the shooters."

The bottom drops out inside me and my heart plunges into my stomach.

Kim says, "He was in there when the shooting started?"

"He was in here for most of it," the teacher says. "Just went out into the hallway a couple of minutes ago."

"Oh, no," Kim says. "No. Derek, hang in there. Help is on the way. You're a very brave young man. You're going to be okay. Hang in there."

Another explosion goes off somewhere else in the building.

"Back in the room, now," I yell, but the teacher and students have already disappeared inside.

I can hear the approach of the deputies from both sides of the hallway.

"We're over here," I yell. "It's John Jordan and Deputy Kimberly Miller. We have a student here who needs immediate medical attention."

Eventually, flashlight beams find us and Potter County deputies step out of the smoke.

They are followed by EMTs who begin to work on Kim and Derek as I fill them in on what we know.

"So we've still got a shooter roaming the hallways?" a deputy says.

"He must not be in the main hallway since y'all just came from both directions and didn't see him," I say, "but yeah, somewhere in the school. When we have enough personnel, we need to get the kids in the classrooms out and do a thorough search of the building."

"Our SWAT team will be on site any minute now," he says. "All available officers are rolling, and we've got FDLE and other agencies on their way. Before long we'll have more help than we'll know what to do with."

"Until then, let's guard the EMTs while they help the wounded and get them out of the building—all while looking for the shooter."

"Hopefully," another deputy says, "he's holed up in some small space somewhere blowing his brainpan all over the wall."

"I don't think so," I say.

"Oh yeah, why's that?"

"If he was planning on killing himself," I say, "he wouldn't have needed to wear a mask."

"He's got a mask on?" he says. "We hadn't heard that."

"Yeah," I say, "and my guess is he plans to discard it and the rest of his attire and weaponry to blend in with the other students."

"Oh, my God," Kim says, "that's ..."

"He probably already has," I say. "Now just waiting to walk out of the building with the rest of them."

Kim shakes her head. "Wow. Oh my God. If that's ... true ... If he's able to pull that off he'll ..."

"Live to do it again," the deputy says.

34

Face it, there are two sets of rules. The ones for the popular and pretty kids, the jocks and prom queens, and the ones for the rest of us.

As the smoke begins to dissipate some I realize it has been a few minutes since we've heard either gunshots or explosions.

While two deputies guard Kim and Derek and the EMTs working on them, two others search the halls.

I'm about to start a search of my own when I see LeAnn and Tyrese approaching.

"It's still not safe," I say.

LeAnn rushes over to Kim.

Tyrese says, "Safe enough for y'all, it's safe enough for us. We're not doing any good down in the office. We need to evacuate the school."

"We have no idea where the shooter is," I say.

"But he's stopped shooting," he says.

"For now," I say. "Could be more to come. Need to act as if there is."

"We've got parents outside wanting their kids," he says. "We don't get them out soon, they'll be coming in here to get them."

I nod. "Okay. When more officers arrive, we can begin an orderly evacuation. Have each class escorted by a couple of officers, while SWAT sweeps the building."

"That'll work," he says.

Over by Kim, LeAnn is saying, "I should've been up here with you. I'm so sorry you got shot."

"I'm okay," she says. "But I'm worried about Derek. He needs to get to a hospital."

"They're working on it," LeAnn says.

"Have you heard from Ace?" Kim asks. "Is he safe? I'm surprised he's not out here barkin' orders at everybody."

The body in the classroom I passed as I ran over here flashes in my mind. Whether it's what I actually saw or not, I now see the dead body of Ace Bowman lying on the floor.

"I'll check on him in a minute. I'm sure he's fine. Just hunkered down with his class. You just lay back and let them take care of you. We'll take care of everything else."

"We need more EMTs and ambulances," I say to the deputy nearest to me. "They'll probably need to send them out of Gulf, Bay, and Calhoun Counties."

He nods and radios it in.

"Okay," the EMT working on Derek says, "we need to go now."

I turn to the deputy. "Let the others know we're coming out with wounded. You two lead them. Tyrese and I'll guard them from the back."

Tyrese says, "We should just take them out of the back exit. Have the ambulances pick them up by the art building."

I shake my head. "The hallway to that door is blocked. We

need to go there to search for survivors next. There, the library, and a classroom on the northeast side."

The first EMT nods to himself and starts pushing the stretcher around the hallway toward the commons and main entrance. We follow.

"Why there?" Kim asks. "That's where Ace's room is. Unless he was in the gym or the front office. He was probably in the gym. Did anything happen in the gym?"

"No," Tyrese says. "Everything in the gym is fine."

"Come on everyone," the EMT with Derek says. "Pick up the pace. We need to move."

Not for the first time I say a prayer for Derek, pleading for his recovery, begging God not to have let me killed a kid.

The wheels of the gurneys are hindered by debris, shards of glass, chunks of cement, rubble, and shell casings, but we make steady progress.

LeAnn, who walks beside Kim's gurney holding her hand, is more exposed than I would like but refuses to be anywhere else.

As we near the short hallway that leads down to the commons, Hugh Glenn is there with additional deputies and his small SWAT team.

He gives me a look like *what do we do?*

I say, "Can you send two of the deputies with you to help escort these two patients to ambulances while I brief you on what we're dealing with and we begin a sweep and evacuation of the building?"

"Stan, Rob, with them," he says. "Everyone else follow me. And as soon as y'all have them safely loaded in the ambulances get back in here and help. Escort the other EMTs in if they've arrived."

The EMTs and four deputies, along with Kim, Derek, and LeAnn continue down the hallway.

I watch after them as I brief Glenn on what's going on and

make subtle suggestions about what to do, Tyrese jumping in with information and suggestions as I do.

He agrees with what Tyrese and I suggest, ordering SWAT to sweep the building while the deputies escort the classes from the school.

"Everyone talk to each other," he says. "Overcommunicate. Let everyone know exactly where you are and what you're doing so we don't shoot each other. And find the little fucker who did this to our school."

They rush off to start their respective jobs.

Tyrese says, "I'll go announce what we're doing on the intercom so the teachers and students will be ready. And let them know to stay together and close to their escorts since we haven't apprehended the shooter yet."

When he rushed off to do that, Glenn turns to me and says, "Why the hell didn't the bastard do this Friday when we were ready for him?"

Believing his answer is in his question, I don't respond.

"How many fatalities?" Glenn asks.

"No idea yet," I say.

"Well, let's go find out."

"You might want to have SWAT start their sweep in the library," I say. "It's open. Be easy for him to access and offers lots of places to hide."

He radios his SWAT team and tells them.

"Remind them there are mostly other students in there so to use extreme caution."

He does.

When he's done, we head to the northeast section of the circle to assess injuries and fatalities.

"Can you imagine if we shot a kid?" he says. "I mean besides the shooter. We'd be . . . brought before a firing squad and shot ourselves."

I don't mention me shooting Derek and the evidence that

indicates he wasn't one of the shooters but just a brave boy trying to help. As soon as I do or he finds out, I'm out. Kicked off the case, placed on administrative leave while undergoing a use of deadly force review. Until then I want to do all I can to help find the shooter, secure the scene, and get help to the wounded.

"Say a prayer that that doesn't happen," he says. "That's not something we could recover from."

35

I heard someone say that we've gotten to the point that every year more Americans are killed by firearms than in the entire Korean War. Every two years more Americans are killed than in all of the eight years of the Vietnam War. That can't be right, can it? Hell, even if it's close it's fuckin' staggering.

Hugh Glenn, two deputies who have just rejoined us, and I approach the open classroom with the body on the floor I saw when running by earlier.

We all have our weapons drawn—even Glenn, something I've never seen before.

When we reach the doorway, we stand on either side, entering two by two, and sweep the room before we do anything else.

Once we're satisfied the room is clear, we confirm my suspicions about who is lying dead on the floor and identify ourselves to the students hiding in his barricaded office.

My heart hurts for Kim, but as with my shooting of Derek, I have no time to grieve or process any of it right now.

"Coach Bowman was so brave," one of the girls says as she exits the office and glances down at him.

"He saved our lives," another student says.

The students are frightened and in shock and have a few minor injuries—mostly self-inflicted as they scrambled to get away from the gunman—but they're okay and there are no other fatalities in here besides Bowman.

"Did any of you see where the shooter went or anything that might help us catch him?"

"You haven't caught him yet?"

"He was wearing all black with a mask."

None of them saw where he went or anything that might help us catch him.

As one of the deputies escorts the class around the hallway, down to the commons, and out of the school, I take Bowman's keys and lock the door. I'd like to do more for him—for Kim, but I can't even cover him until we get forensics in to process the scene.

"We need to go to the library next," I say to Glenn, "and then the back exit that leads out to the art room, but I need to make a call first."

As I call LeAnn, Glenn and the deputy step down to the next classroom door and look in.

"John," LeAnn says.

"Are you still with Kim?" I ask.

"Yeah. They're loading her in the ambulance now. Not sure what I should do. I want to go with her, but feel like I'm needed here."

"You have to stay," Kim says in the background. "I'm okay. Really."

"You probably should go with her after you hear what I have to say."

"What? What is it?"

"Ace was shot and killed," I say. "I'm so sorry. I just wanted her to hear it from you instead of a stranger or on TV."

"Oh, God, no, John," she says. "Are you sure?"

In the background I can hear Kim saying, "What is it? What happened? Is John all right?"

"I'm very sorry. I know he was your friend too. I've got to go. I'll call and check on you both when I can."

"Just be careful, John."

When I end the call, I see that Glenn is having the deputy escort the next class out instead of going with us to the library.

"Ready?" I ask.

Glenn nods and we walk in the opposite direction as the deputy and students, toward the nearest library entrance.

By the time we enter the library through the still-locked door frame, glass crunching under our shoes as we do, SWAT is completing its sweep.

"All clear," one of the officers says.

"Y'all can come out now," another adds.

Slowly, the students begin to crawl out from beneath desks and tables, the librarian slowly rising from behind the counter.

"Anyone hurt?" Glenn asks.

One of the SWAT guys emerges from the TV production room with Zach Griffith.

"I didn't know you were back there, Zach," the librarian says in surprise. "You were in there the entire time?"

He nods. "Yes, ma'am."

A student on the far side of the library near a shelf of bullet-riddled books says, "Slow Stevie got shot. He needs help."

Another student says, "Somebody help Slow Stevie."

The SWAT leader radios for a deputy and EMTs.

"Anyone else injured?" Glenn asks.

"Mason is," one of the girls says.

Everyone glances at her and then at Mason Nickols not far from her.

"I'm fine," he says.

"You're bleeding," she says.

"It's just a scratch."

The librarian says, "When did you come in here?"

"You're shot," the girl says.

"Just as all of it started," he says. "Y'all were already hiding. I came in to check out a book and just dove under a desk. Didn't know what else to do."

I look at Mason closely. He's wearing all black—pants, shirt, boots. But no duster and no mask.

Two EMTs and a deputy arrive.

As the EMTs examine Stevie and Mason, I motion for the deputy and tell him that Mason is a suspect and to keep a close eye on him.

I then step over to take a closer look at Mason's wound.

The EMT has cut the sleeve of his shirt and exposed a gunshot wound in the inside of his left arm.

"You're very lucky," she says. "Just a few inches over and it would've hit your heart."

"Don't have one," he says. "'Sides, a few inches the other way and it wouldn't've hit me at all."

"When did you get hit?" I ask. "Where were you?"

He shrugs. "Not sure. Either running in here or when I was cowering under the desk with the rest of the cowards."

"Where is Dakota?" I ask. "Thought y'all were inseparable?"

"You thought wrong. And I don't know. Not even sure if he came to school today."

My phone vibrates. I pull it out and see that it's Anna.

I step away, answer it, ask her to hold for a second, and tell the deputy to stay with Mason and let the doctors know we need detailed notes on his injuries and the slug for ballistics.

"Hey," I say into the phone.

"You okay? Kids are posting video clips of the shooting all over social media."

"I'm fine, but we're still in the middle of it. Can I call you back as soon as we finish evacuating the school and—"

"Of course. Sorry. Just be careful. Come home to us safely tonight."

"Promise," I say. "I love you."

"Love you more," she says.

Before I can get out my usual response of "Not possible" she is gone.

I remind the SWAT team that in addition to searching for a shooter we're looking for weapons, discarded clothing, and a mask also, then Glenn and I meet another deputy and two new EMTs in the hallway and head around to the back exit and the massacre I saw there when running toward Derek Burrell.

36

Everyone is looking for someone or something to blame. As long as it's not them or something they're in favor of. They like guns, they blame video games or movies or music. They blame bullies and the parents and legal and illegal drugs. They blame the media. They blame their political opponent. But have you ever heard anyone stand up and say we're all to blame? We've all built this country where this happens. All of us. We all contribute to it. And it only happens here.

The blood-splattered carnage of the back hallway exit is even worse than I had been able to take in as I ran by earlier.

Shocking. Horrific. Unsettling. As visually appalling as any scene dreamed up by the most demented of torture porn directors.

Blood-soaked bullet holes pock the walls. Red Rorschach against white cinderblock.

Acoustic ceiling tiles hanging from warped frames.

Bodies on the floor in an expanding pool of blood, its outer edges tacky and dark. Pile of kids partially obscuring the bloody Pottersville Pirate.

After we identify ourselves, we can perceive movement in the pile of what we thought were all dead bodies.

The first person to stand is Dakota Emanuel. Wet blood drips from his right cheek and raised hands. Like Mason and not unlike the shooter, he's in all black.

"We pretended to be dead," he says.

"Are you hit?" one of the EMTs asks.

He shakes his head.

Others begin to stand, slowly, hesitantly, like Dakota their hands raised.

I start to ask why their hands are raised and realize I'm pointing my gun in their direction.

I quickly lower it, but not too far in case the shooter is hidden among the bloody bodies.

Eventually, all the bodies but three are upright. Of them, four are wounded, their open gunshot holes contributing to the bloodbath they've all just been lying in.

Many within the pitiful group stand before us shaking, crying, whimpering, moaning. All of them, with the possible exception of Dakota, in shock.

Among the three bodies remaining, unmoving, unresponsive on the floor, are two male students—the twin foster kids named Hayden and Hunter Dupree—and Janna Todd, the art teacher and sometime barmaid with the big breasts. All three of them are deceased.

"We tried to get out," one of the girls not crying says. "But the door was locked."

"When we turned around the gunman was there. Just started shooting at us."

"Is the door normally locked?" I ask.

"It's not locked, it's zip-tied," one of the guys in the back says. "Fucker didn't want any of us escaping."

"Or anyone coming in to help us."

"I can't believe Miss Janna is dead," a female student says. "And poor Hayden and Hunter, as if their lives weren't bad enough. I mean, *fuck*."

"Where did you come from, Dakota?" the same guy from the back asks.

"You weren't with them?" I ask.

He gives me a sinister smile without warmth or humor, merely annoyance and mild amusement at being caught.

Shaking his head, he says, "I'm . . . I wasn't in their class. I came up after it had all happened. I had planned to sneak out of the building, but when I saw the doors were locked, I laid down with them and pretended to be dead."

"What class were you in?" I ask. "How'd you get out?"

"Algebra. Ms. Candace. I was running late. Was headed to class when all this shit started."

"So you really weren't in class," I say.

"Not technically, no. I was headed to it. Almost in it. Almost but not quite."

"Did you see the shooter?" I ask. "Any of you?"

"Just before he shot us," one of the girls says. "He was like something out of a movie."

"I never saw him," Dakota says. "But I heard the hell out of him. Sounded like he has a real big gun. Very impressive the way he was spraying his loads all over the place."

"We only saw him a second before he started shooting," one of the large, athletic-looking boys says. "But when I saw him my first thought was it was either Mason or Dakota."

Dakota laughs. "Guess we shoulda shot you first."

"That's not funny," one of the girls says. "Not in the least bit funny."

"Chill, man, fuck," Dakota says. "I's just playin. I got shot at like the rest of you. Shit, Mason did too. Hell, he got shot."

"How do you know that?" I ask.

He hesitates. "I . . . I heard him scream as he ran into the library. I just assumed."

The outspoken girl who told Dakota he wasn't funny glances down at Janna Todd and the two students. "Can we get away from the . . . dead bodies on the floor? Can we please get out of here?"

"Sorry," I say. "Of course. Deputy Lancaster is going to escort you out of the building. Stay with him and close together."

"But you haven't caught the shooter yet," Dakota says, his voice full of insincere feeling. "What if he gets us?"

"You'll be safe," I say.

"You can't know that," he says. "I'm scared."

"If you'd rather stay here . . ." I say.

"Fuck that."

"You can stay with me," I say. "I have more questions for you anyway."

"I'll take my chances with the shooter," he says.

"Then I'll catch you later," I say.

"Okay," Lancaster says. "Let's go."

As he begins to lead them away, another deputy runs up from the other direction.

"Sheriff," he says. "Got something you need to see."

37

*Killing was both easier and more difficult than I thought it would be.
And in different ways than I expected.*

The deputy leads us over to a set of lockers along the northeast wall.

All around us, the shredded school is busy with activity.

In the wispy, dwindling smoke, deputies are escorting classes out of the building, EMTs are working on and transporting the wounded, and the SWAT team is conducting a thorough, methodical sweep.

There hasn't been any more gunfire since Derek went down, and only one explosion since then—none in the last several minutes.

The deputy's name is Markson. He's young and tall and has skin the color of hot chocolate.

"I was on my way to get the next class," he is saying, "when I passed this slightly open locker. I could see something hanging out. I'm not sure what I thought it was and I know I probably should've just left it for forensics or the bomb squad, but . . . I paused for a minute and looked at all the lockers. Only two in this section don't have locks on them and those are the only two slightly open with something hanging out of them."

I study the bank of lockers as he tells his story.

"I know I shouldn't've opened them with all the . . . explosives going off and without gloves on, but . . . I couldn't help myself. I had to know and . . . look what I found."

He swings open the first locker door and steps aside for us to see.

A white mask lies atop a pile of black clothes, including gloves and a duster. Behind them an AR-15 style rifle leans against the back corner. In contrast to the attire worn by other school shooters, the black gloves here are not fingerless.

"You were right," Glenn says. "He's just walking around looking like any other student right now."

"Not just one of them," Markson says, opening the other locker.

The same white mask on the same pile of black clothes, but instead of a rifle this locker holds a handgun—a 9mm Luger.

"There were two," Glenn says. "And we'll never find them now. They're probably already out of the building, mixed in with all the other kids. This is just . . . what a nightmare."

I withdraw a pair of latex gloves from my pocket and snap them on. Very carefully I begin to search through the items.

"No boots," I say. "In either locker. We need to get out front and see which students are wearing black paramilitary-style boots."

38

I heard a Russian video game maker created a first-person shooter game that takes place in a high school and that they market it and sell it in the US, where we have school shootings, not in Russia where they don't. That's fucked up. A video game where you can actually be a school shooter shooting at other students. Don't tell me our enemies don't love it that we're killing each other—doing their job for them.

Students stumble out of the front doors and down the covered walkway like a huge herd of cows coming through a cattle chute into a livestock sale.

Dazed, their stunned, thousand-yard stares not unlike those of war veterans or terrorist attack survivors.

Parents waiting behind barriers, worried expressions on their searching faces.

Cop cars everywhere.

Students and teachers and parents and law enforcement and EMTs all frantically moving about like angry ants scattered around a toppled ant bed.

Media trucks and vans in the side field, more arriving every moment, reporters in front of cameras pointing at a soon-to-be-infamous high school where nothing will ever be the same.

Flashing lights of emergency vehicles strobing the scene, their effectiveness greatly diminished by the morning sun, like a club when someone turns the house lights on.

Several of us scurrying through the crowd, searching the shoes of students, bumping into the already traumatized kids because we're looking down.

A deputy at the door, pulling aside kids with black boots on like a zealous TSA agent, Tyrese beside him identifying them, making a list to go with the pictures he's taking.

As we search the shoes of the student and faculty exodus taking place, it occurs to me that just because witnesses described the shooter as having black boots on doesn't mean he couldn't be wearing dark shoes.

I radio the others. "Don't just check for boots, but any dark shoe—especially those that could be mistaken for boots. Also, don't just focus on our suspects. Look at everyone closely and carefully."

Scanning the footwear all around me, I move with the herd—mostly in the same direction, but at a slower pace.

All around me all the feet have one thing in common—they are moving.

For as far as I can see, all the feet I can see are moving—except for two pair.

In the distance, just at the end of the covered walkway, two pairs of feet are not only not moving, they are facing the wrong direction.

Like a tree in the middle of a stream, the two pairs of unmoving feet facing the wrong direction make the flow of fleeing students divert around them.

As I get closer I can see that one pair of feet have on black paramilitary-style boots like the ones we're looking for, while the other has on no shoes at all, only socks.

Long before I look up for confirmation, I know who the feet belong to, know who is facing the traumatized crowd, taking in the dazed and devastated children whose lives will never be the same again.

Everyone else is putting as much distance between them and the scene of the crime as they can—everyone except Mason Nickols and Dakota Emanuel.

"What're y'all doing?" I ask as I reach them.

"Question is," Mason says. "What're y'all doing? Y'all look like bloodhounds, all running around with your heads down like you're sniffing the ground."

"Why aren't you two moving?" I ask. "Exiting the area."

"Just wanted to see everyone's faces," Dakota says.

"Who comes out on a stretcher," Mason says. "Who doesn't come out at all."

"That's sweet," I say, then looking at Dakota, "Where are your shoes?"

"Must have come off when I was running for my life," he says. "Not sure. I wasn't thinking too much about my shoes."

"What kind were you wearing?"

He hesitates. "Huh? What kind of shoes?" He shrugs. "I don't know, just some old boots."

"Black?" I ask.

"Yeah, why? D'you find 'em?"

"We will."

"Well, don't worry about returning them," he says. "So much blood in that back hallway, I'm sure they look like the fuckin' brogans Michael Myers wears."

Mason smiles and shakes his head. "Dude, can you imagine if Michael Myers was in fuckin' high school during the age of rampage?"

"Oh boy, that would be *si-ick*," Dakota says. "Carnage City, bitches."

"Someone needs to do one of these with a knife," Mason says.

"Sure as shit do."

A knowing look passes between them like *next time*.

"Have y'all caught the shooter yet?" Mason asks.

"We heard he got away," Dakota says. "That he upped Eric and Dylan's game so he could do it again."

"We're very close," I say. "Some of us closer than others."

Mason's mouth contorts into a cold, creepy smile. "Well, good luck with that," he says. "Sounds like you're going to need it. Guess we'll be goin' now . . .'less you have some reason we shouldn't."

"Yeah," Dakota says. "You wanna deputize us or somethin'? We could blow this bitch wide open."

"You've done enough for today," I say. "We'll be in touch soon."

"No need," Mason says. "He tol' you he doesn't want the boots back."

As they slowly step away, taking it all in one more time before they do, DeShawn and Sierra rush up to me.

"Have you seen Ms. LeAnn and Ms. Kim?" Sierra asks. "They didn't get . . . did they?"

"We can't find them anywhere," DeShawn says.

"They're at the hospital," I say.

"Oh no," Sierra says. "Are they going to be okay?"

I nod. "They'll be fine."

"Is this what y'all wanted our help with?" DeShawn asks.

"Still can't believe it happened," Sierra says. "Wish we could'a helped prevent it."

"We might can still help," DeShawn says. "Y'all haven't caught them yet, have you?"

"Do y'all know anything that could be helpful?" I ask.

They shrug. "I'm sure we do. We just don't know what it is yet. We need to know more about what happened to know for sure."

"If you think of anything," I say, "let Mr. Monroe or Ms. Miller or Ms. Dunne know."

They are unsatisfied with this response, but as I move off to examine more shoes and try to locate the other suspects, I try not to be too broken up about it.

I haven't gotten far before I see Dad and Merrill walking up the circular drive toward me.

39

Most school shooters show signs of clinical depression and other psychological issues, but schools don't have enough mental health counselors to pick up on such signs, let alone do something about them.

"Y ou okay?" Dad asks.

I nod.

"How can we help?"

I look around to see who might be close enough to us to hear. "Let's step over here for a minute."

They follow me to a spot a few feet away from the throng.

I give them a brief rundown of what has happened and where we're at.

"Is Kimmy going to be okay?" Dad asks.

"I don't know," I say. "Have no idea of her condition or how she's doing. Hoping LeAnn will let us know when she knows."

"So the shooter's somewhere out here with everybody else?"

Merrill says. "We need to be searching for black boots, that right?"

I tell them about shooting Derek Burrell.

"Oh, Son, I'm so sorry," Dad says. "That's . . . Are you okay?"

I shake my head.

"What condition is the kid in?" Merrill asks.

"Don't know that either," I say.

"All you did was return fire," Dad says. "He was shooting at Kimmy and you."

"I shot a kid," I say. "But I can't even think about that right now. Right now all I'm thinking about is that I'm about to be taken off this, put on administrative leave while my use of deadly force is investigated. Hugh Glenn hasn't mentioned it yet—probably doesn't even know to do it, but as soon as FDLE arrives I'll be sidelined. I'd like to get as much done before then as possible. I really want to know which of these sick, twisted little psychos put Derek and me in that position to begin with."

"My money's on the two fringe fuckers you's talkin' to when we pulled up," Merrill says.

I nod. "It's a good bet. They definitely get voted most likely to Columbine in my yearbook, but we need to look at all our suspects and anyone we may have missed."

They nod.

"We can help look for them, see what kind of shoes they're wearing, and get a good read on them," Dad says. "Think we remember all of them from Friday."

"If y'all could do that, I'd like to go look at the security camera footage," I say.

"Go," Merrill says. "We got this."

"Thanks."

I rush back toward the building, grabbing Tyrese as I do.

"Can you help me look at the security camera footage?" I ask.

"Yeah," he says, walking next to me in the opposite direction as everyone else. "Of course. There's just not much of it. Not just 'cause it all happened so fast, but the bombs blew out a lot of the feeds." He shakes his head. "Still can't believe this happened. Still don't know how it could have—especially the explosives. Know how y'all searched the school before it opened on Friday? We did the same thing this morning. How the hell'd we miss that many bombs?"

"Maybe you didn't," I say. "Maybe he brought them in when he came in this morning."

"Guess he had to," he says. "There were just so many and they were so spread out."

"Not really," I say. "All but two or three were in the same area in the hallway where he was. He could've planted the others just before or just after first bell."

He nods. "Makes sense. Maybe the cameras caught him doing it."

As we near the entrance, we pass Tristan Ward and Denise Royal, two of the very last students to exit the building.

"Can you believe this?" Tristan says, an undeniable excitement in his voice. "I was telling Denise this is a prime example of life imitating art. I'm sure people will blame my play, say I inspired all this, but . . ."

"They're not going to silence our voices," Denise adds. "Art is too important to be . . ." she searches for something profound but comes up short, ". . . silenced."

"Actually," I say, "this was a prime example of life imitating life. Columbine, not your play, is the inspiration and pattern here."

"But surely—"

"Where have y'all been?" I ask. "Why so late getting out of the building?"

"We were in the process of moving props and lighting from the main stage in the commons back out to the art building."

That really doesn't answer my question.

"Where were you during the shooting?" I ask.

"On our way back from the art building to get another load?" Denise says.

"Where exactly?" I ask, glancing at their shoes.

They both have on black boots and though neither are para-military-style they both could be mistaken for them pretty easily. Especially as they moved by during a stressful and intense situation.

"Not sure exactly," she says. "I guess just about to come back into the main building."

"Through which door?" I ask.

"The back door out by the art building."

"Couldn't have been," I say. "The shooter zip-tied it so it wouldn't open."

"Oh, well, then, I guess we were already back inside the main building."

"We were already backstage," Tristan says. "Behind the curtain. Remember?"

"Oh yeah," she says. "That's right."

"So you were backstage during the entire shooting?" I ask.

"Yeah," he says.

She nods her agreement.

"And exited the building from there?" I ask.

"Yeah," Tristan says. "Why?"

"Because that would have put you in the commons, closer to this main exit than virtually all the other students, and would have meant that you would be among the first to exit the building, not the last."

"Oh," Denise says, and looks to Tristan for help. "Well . . ."

"We stayed where we were until an officer came and told us to leave, they were evacuating the building. We had just been on the stage making art about this very type of incident and now it was happening . . . We wanted to linger at that intersection where life and art meet as long as we could."

A member of the SWAT team opens one of the front doors and motions us over.

"We've got to go," I say. "We'll talk to you again soon, get your official statements then."

Tristan says, "My play is my statement. There is nothing else to be said."

"Oh," I say, "there's plenty left to be said—about your play and your movements during the shooting, but we'll get to that a little later."

40

We could stop school shootings in America right now if we really wanted to. And we wouldn't have to violate anyone's civil rights to do it. But we're not willing to spend the money and effort required to do it. Mostly the money. Don't kid yourself, we care more about money than we do kids. Especially the old rich bastards buying most of the elections and many of the politicians. They may care about their kids —though even that's in doubt—but they sure as shit don't care about your poor public school children and you're a fool if you think they do.

"We finished evacuating the building," the SWAT leader says. "We're still doing our sweep and we need to get a bomb squad in here as soon as possible, but everybody's out. Every *living* person anyway."

"Great," I say. "Thank you."

"Have you seen Sheriff Glenn?" he asks.

"Not in the last little while," I say as Tyrese shakes his head.

"Wanted to give him a report but we can't find him and he's not answering his radio."

"I'll locate him after we review the security camera footage and let him know," I say.

Tyrese and I continue into and through the main office and into the first room to the right which serves as a kind of catchall that includes the principal designee's desk and the security monitor.

The security monitor is a huge TV mounted to the wall, seventy inches or more, filled with the images of the security camera feeds.

Divided into small blocks showing single-camera feeds, the monitor displays rows, six high and eight across, of scenes from the school, many of which are now blank.

In some of the images the school looks normal. In others it appears to have suffered a terrorist attack. In most of the frames nothing is happening. In a few the SWAT team can be seen continuing their sweep of the building.

Tyrese shakes his head as he looks at his school. "I still can't believe any of this is real," he says. "And under my watch. I really loved being the principal here."

"And you will again," I say.

"No way they let me keep my job after this," he says. "It was tenuous to begin with. Now . . . the first black principal will be blamed for the first school shooting."

"We'll make sure everyone knows all that you did," I say. "How hard you worked to prevent it. It'll work out."

He nods, but I can tell he's resigned to the reality of life in a small town in the Deep South where racism is rampant and *nigger* rolls as easily off the tongues of a certain type of self-identified white patriotic Christians as *Jesus*.

"Anyway . . ." he says with a sigh, "I can make any single image the size of the full screen by double-clicking on it."

"Cool," I say. "We'll definitely need to do that. For now, though, let's just scan all of them."

"How far back do you want to go?" he asks.

I think about it. As much as I'd like to watch the entire weekend, I can't right now. Someone would have to eventually, but I
don't have the time right now—and wouldn't even if I wasn't
about to be asked to leave.

"Let's start at five this morning," I say. "Can you speed it up
until we see someone?"

"Sure. Why don't I watch the ones on this side and you watch
the ones on that side?"

"Sounds good," I say. "Stop it if you see anything at all. Even a
shadow."

"Will do."

I pull out my phone, open the camera, switch it to video, and
start recording. Holding it back and in between us, I attempt to
record the entire monitor, getting all the feeds at once.

We quickly scan the footage, him looking at the left side
feeds, me the right, beginning at five this morning and going
until about twenty after six when the group Tyrese mentioned
before begins to search the building. The group of teachers and
administrators is mostly made up of those who helped us on
Friday—without the law enforcement officers and includes Ace
Bowman.

Tyrese says, "This was his sometime office. 'Course he had
three. Rarely used this one, but . . . Can't believe he was just here
helping us and now he's . . . gone. This was just like a half hour
before he was killed."

It is surreal to see him and know that he's now lying dead on
his classroom floor some fifty feet away from where we stand
right now.

Before the staff began searching the school, there was no one
else on the footage—not a single soul, not a janitor, not another
teacher, not a student sneaking in to plant pipe bombs.

Following the uneventful search of the school by the group,
no one else is seen on the camera feeds until the groups of
people begin arriving to start the school day—lunch ladies to

cook and serve breakfast, energetic early bird teachers, the first busloads of children, the younger teens who can't drive insisting on getting dropped off early for extra time with friends.

During this time, there is a lot of movement and activity in the parking lots and main office and the commons, but very little where the shooting took place—only the random teacher opening and entering his or her classroom a few minutes early instead of stopping by the teachers' lounge.

Not in any of it is there anything suspicious. No one goes near the places where the bombs would explode less than half an hour later.

We continue to watch as the commons fills and then empties again as the first bell rings and the sleepy student body mass migrates up to the lockers, classrooms, and library.

Even in this there is nothing suspicious, nothing that makes us pause or rewind the footage.

And then just minutes after filling, the hallways are empty again.

Classroom doors closed, teachers and students safely tucked away inside.

A couple of stragglers arriving late to class. A couple of students checking out of class to rush to the restroom. None of them doing anything remotely resembling planting a bomb or preparing for a rampage shooting.

And then the calm before the storm. A few minutes where nothing seems to happen.

And then the first explosion.

"Pause it," I say. "Run it back a couple of minutes."

He does.

As he's rewinding it and as it begins to play again, we both study the school for the shooter.

"Where is he?" Tyrese asks. "I don't see him."

"I'm not—"

As soon as the first explosion takes place the first two cameras go out.

"Look," I say, pointing to the area where we lost the feeds, "the first two cameras they took out are just inside and outside of the back door. I bet that's where they entered from. They take them out first so they're not seen coming in, then once they're inside, they zip-tie the door and begin their rampage."

"You think they did this entire thing without being seen by the cameras?" he asks.

"We're about to find out."

After the first explosions, Tyrese runs out of the main office, says something in his radio, then runs back in. Kim and LeAnn run out of their offices, say something to each other, then Kim crosses the commons and up to the main hallway as LeAnn runs into the back door of the main office.

The two janitors rush out of their room in the opposite hallway and out the front door as the lunchroom ladies run out of the back door of the kitchen. Neither group stops—all of them get in their cars and drive off.

Various teachers open their classroom doors and look out briefly before locking them and going back inside.

Kim makes her way up the south side of the hallway.

More explosions. More camera feeds blinking off.

The librarian steps out of the north entrance, looking around, starting to run, then stopping and returning to the library and locking the door behind her.

Other teachers and students make similar calculations.

Then several more explosions. More camera feeds dying. Smoke and debris filling the hallway.

"There," Tyrese says. "There's one of them."

41

Not only is violence not the solution, it's not even the problem. It's just the symptom.

"Right there," Tyrese says, pausing the system.

I move over and focus on the feed he's pointing to.

There, in the southwest section of the hallway, just as witnesses described, is one of the shooters, dressed in black, with a leather duster, boots, military-style black hat, and blank white expressionless mask.

The collar of his duster is turned up, he's hunched over some, and both the quality and angle of the video are not ideal, but he appears to be one of the smaller, slighter members on our suspects list. Of course, that's most of the skinny, undeveloped kids on our list.

As he stalks his way around the hall, he seems to be firing randomly—putting rounds into the ceiling, walls, doors, and floor. Occasionally he takes aim at the security cameras tracking his movement but rarely hits one.

"Not a very good shot, is he?" Tyrese says.

"Most school shooters aren't," I say. "And don't have to be to do a lot of damage."

More explosions occur back over in the south section of the hallway, more camera feeds are lost.

"The other shooter must be over there where the cameras are out," Tyrese says. "Maybe he's headed east and they plan to meet up on the other end of the circle."

I nod.

Another feed shows Ace Bowman attempting to lock his classroom door.

In the feed next to it, the shooter takes aim at something outside the frame. A moment later, back in the other feed, Ace's hand explodes and he lets go and falls back, leaving the key in the door, the white, now blood-splattered cord holding his keys and lanyard dangling.

Eventually, the shooter steps into the frame that Ace's hands had been in and then into the classroom and out of view.

After just a few moments, the shooter steps into the hallway again and heads back in the direction he has just come from.

As he passes the northwest library entrance he fires several rounds into the glass doors without slowing his pace.

Continuing east, the shooter begins to try the doorknobs of the classrooms he comes to, finding them locked, moving on, occasionally firing into the rooms through the narrow glass pane.

More explosions rocking the school.

More smoke in the hallways.

Another feed shows a young, skinny, long-legged boy running out of the upper boys' bathroom and in the direction of the shooter, his bony arms pumping feverishly through the smoke.

He doesn't make it far.

Rounding the north curve, he comes face-to-face with the shooter and tries to lock it up and turn directions.

In the other frame, the shooter in the long black leather duster and expressionless white mask raises his rifle and fires.

Back in the boy's frame, his left ankle appears to be hit, his leg flying out from underneath him as he stumbles and falls head-first into the cinderblock wall.

And though the boy doesn't move, the shooter fires more rounds at him before continuing on in the direction the boy has just come from.

When the shooter reaches Janna Todd's room and finds the door open, he goes inside, but quickly comes back out again.

As he's doing this, another feed shows Janna and her small class running down the short hallway toward the back exit.

Finding the doors locked, they turn and begin to run back down the short hallway toward the main circular one.

Like witnessing a horrific car collision in slow motion, we can see the shooter moving southwest, steadily approaching the area where the back hallway splits off the main one.

Looking back and forth from frame to frame, we can see Janna and the students running down the back hall, getting to a little past the halfway point, as the shooter curves around and reaches the opening. The shooter stopping, turning. The students stopping, turning. The shooter raising his rifle. The students trying to run in the opposite direction though there is nowhere to go, tripping over each other, stumbling, flailing, falling. The shooter firing. Janna being struck in the head, crumpling to the floor, students collapsing around her.

Even on the small, low-quality videos it's as horrific as anything I've ever seen.

With all the students on the blood-covered floor, dead or dying, the shooter continues west, disappearing as the hallway curves south and he reaches the section where most of the cameras have been destroyed.

In other areas of the hallway where the security cameras are still functioning, more explosions, more smoke, more gunfire, more debris.

We continue to watch the feeds but don't see anyone else until I arrive and run through the commons and up toward the south side of the main hallway.

I'm picked up on various security cameras as I jog through the smoke until I vanish into the southeast area of the hall where the cameras have been bombed.

During this time we've not seen either shooter on any feed again.

One has been in the southeast section the entire time and the other disappeared into it after the back exit hallway massacre.

"Both shooters were in the part of the building that you ran into," Tyrese says.

"Yeah, but by the time I got there I think they had already changed clothes and joined the other students."

"Why didn't they shoot Derek Burrell?" he asks.

"They were probably already changed and hiding among the students when he came out," I say, "but it could have been that they saw him and hid from him, hoping he would get blamed for the shooting or shoot someone or get shot by someone else, which is what happened."

"Is it possible he was in on it?" Tyrese asks. "He doesn't seem like the type of kid who would be involved in something like this, but . . . I never figured any of our kids would really go through with something like this so I just don't know anymore."

"It's possible," I say. "Right now we have to assume anything is."

"If he's not . . . and was just trying to help . . ."

"I know," I say, frowning and shaking my head, as the hole inside me becomes a little more cavernous.

"Did the shooters shoot Kim or did Derek?" he asks.

"I think it was one of the shooters—probably the one who

stayed on the south side of the hallway, but it'll take ballistics for us to know for sure."

"I wish we knew how she and Derek are doing," he says.

"LeAnn's supposed to call us as soon as she knows something."

"I hope it's good news," he says. "And I know you—"

Before he can finish what he's saying, one of the SWAT guys runs into the office and yells, "We've found undetonated explosives. We've got to get out of the building now."

42

A lot of us go to school in daily fear of physical violence. It's the cruelest of caste systems. Everybody has his place and once you're in it you can't leave it. Once you're a slut or a faggot or poor white trash or slow or stupid or smelly or fat or a nerd or geek or a big ol' mother-loving, thumb-sucking titty-baby. And don't even get me started on the blacks, Mexicans, Jews, or Muslims.

"They used a lot of explosives, but a bunch of 'em didn't go off," Kenneth Lee, the scruffy-bearded, Einstein-haired, middle-aged bomb squad tech is saying.

"Thankfully," Hugh Glenn says.

He and Chip Jeffers, who have been missing for most of the morning, have joined our small group, consisting of Tyrese, myself, the SWAT team leader, the patrol lieutenant, a sheriff's department investigator, a medical examiner investigator, and an FDLE crime scene tech.

It's early afternoon. We're standing out in front of the high school. Students, teachers, parents, and staff have all gone home, taking their trauma with them.

When the additional undetonated explosives were found, the entire area had been evacuated. The school campus is now mostly vacant, the parking lots empty except for a few random vehicles—most likely those belonging to the victims, some of whom are at the hospital, some of whom are still lying dead inside the school.

The emergency vehicles now form a perimeter at the farthest edges of the school property, the massive media presence, local onlookers, and the few grief-stricken parents still waiting for word about their missing children are all on the other side of it.

Unable to do anything more here, Dad and Merrill are out following up leads and gathering more information about our suspects and the kids who wore black boots today.

While waiting for the bomb squad to finish searching and clearing the buildings, I interviewed as many teachers and students and staff as I could before they left, gathered as much information about every aspect of the attack as I could, and called LeAnn for updates far too many times—particularly considering all she could tell me each time was both Kim and Derek were still in surgery and she'd call me the moment either of them came out and she learned anything at all.

"Most of 'em were pretty crude," Lee says. "Simple, basic design, not very powerful. Not surprised so many didn't go off. More surprised at how many did. Since Columbine a lot of rampage shooters try to use some explosives as part of their attack, but most of the time they don't work. There were probably more that worked at this shooting than most."

He pauses, presumably to see if any of us have any questions, but continues before we'd be able to ask them.

"We're talkin' mostly pipe bombs and a few IEDs on timers. Simple but effective stuff."

"How much more damage would've been done if they had all detonated?" I ask.

"Hard to say. Nothing catastrophic. In terms of the building at least. Wouldn't've brought it down or anything. But we'd be looking at more injuries, possibly fatalities, but only if the kids were close to them. I'd say the devices used were either deployed to be used mainly as diversionary tactics or more likely they didn't know what they were doing and made big firecrackers more than anything else."

"Once we identify our suspects," the sheriff's investigator says, "can you let us know what kind of supplies they would need to build with, so we can look for them at their houses?"

"'Course," Lee says.

"Is it safe for forensics, ME, and investigators to go in?" Hugh Glenn asks.

Lee nods.

"Okay," the FDLE tech says, "let's get in there and get to work."

As the FDLE crime scene techs and the ME investigators enter the building, the leader of the SWAT team walks over to me.

"We looked for what you asked us to," he says. "Wanna see what we found?"

I nod. "Absolutely."

So far no one has taken my weapon, put me on administrative leave, or asked me to go home. I plan to keep investigating until they do.

We follow the techs inside but head in the opposite direction.

He leads me through the commons, behind the curtain and backstage.

There among the costumes and props from Tristan and Denise's play is a pair of black paramilitary style boots. They are partially hidden behind the box of guns used in the play.

"We haven't touched them," he says.

I slip on a pair of latex gloves and lift the boots to examine the bottoms, as I make a mental note to make sure forensics and ballistics check to make sure none of the guns are real. There appear to be traces of blood on the bottoms of the boots.

"Great work," I say.

"There's more," he says.

I replace the boots where he found them and say, "I'm ready whenever you are."

"Follow me."

He leads me back through the commons, up the hallway to the library.

Carefully stepping through the shattered glass of the doors, he leads me behind the counter, past the back office, to the media department where Zach Griffith works and the room he came out of following the shooting.

"We found another pair under the desk in here," he says. "Under there."

He points to a desk with a computer and camera on it.

I walk around it, kneel down, and look beneath.

There on the carpet beside the plastic chair mat is another pair of black boots not unlike the ones they found behind the stage.

I lift and examine them.

There are no obvious signs of blood, but they look like they've been cleaned recently.

"Great work," I say, standing up. "We need to get the crime scene techs in here to process them."

When we exit the library, I thank him again, and he goes in one direction and I go in the other. Instead of walking back outside with him, I walk around the hallway to take another look at the scene and see how the FDLE techs and ME investigators are proceeding.

As I pass Ace Bowman's classroom, I see one of the ME investigators examining his body.

In the classroom and all through the hallway, crime scene photographers and videographers are documenting every aspect of the surreal site.

Most of the smoke is long gone from the building but the acrid odor remains.

Passing the back hallway exit and seeing the bodies of the teacher and two students being processed by an ME investigator I realize we had far fewer fatalities than we might have had. There are many who are wounded and I have no idea if any of them have potential life-threatening injuries, but as of this moment only two teachers and two students have been killed.

Nearing the place where I shot Derek Burrell my heart begins to beat arrhythmically and a cold, sweaty sheen begins to cover my clammy skin.

I pause roughly where I had fired from and look over to where he had been standing. Even without the smoke and gunfire, pandemonium and adrenaline, the curve of the hallway wall and the little alcove he was in make it difficult to see.

It's no wonder, given everything that was going on that from his position and limited visibility, he shot at both Kim and me.

I continue around the hall, avoiding the debris and blood and working crime scene techs, toward the lockers where the shooters' things had been found.

As I reach them, I can see that FDLE techs are already processing the lockers and the things in them.

After examining the lockers and their relative position to everything else, I stand beside them and look in both directions.

From where the lockers are located, Mason could have quickly jogged over and entered the library and Dakota could have run around the corner to join the bodies on the back hallway floor. And they could've done it without being seen by Kim or Derek—probably before Derek even came out into the hallway with his gun.

"Look at this," one of the techs says, holding up the outfit from the locker with the rifle in it.

In the crime scene suit and mask, it's difficult to tell if the blobish figure is male or female, and the small voice coming from behind the mask doesn't help.

I turn to study the clothes. And am surprised by what I see.

The shirt, pants, and duster have all been sewn together to form one garment. They've also been cut down the middle in the back the way funeral homes do the clothes of dead people, but unlike the duds of the dead, these have velcro sewn in them.

"Made it easy to get in and out of, didn't they?" the tech says.

"Yes it did," I say. "They planned all along to discard their gear and hide among the other students."

"It's ingenious," the tech says. "Like a costume for an actor who has to be able to change quickly backstage."

"Both outfits are like that?" I ask.

Another tech holds up the other one from the locker with the handgun inside it and nods.

"They're the same except for size and soil," she says. "This one is shorter and smaller and, unlike the bigger one, has less damage to it, less blood on it."

A ballistic tech about five feet away examining the two guns used by the shooters says, "That fits with what I'm seeing here. The rifle has lots of empty magazines and was fired at an extremely high rate, but the nine wasn't used nearly as much. Only has one clip—the one that's in it—and looks to have only been fired about seven or eight times. Of course both weapons have the serial numbers filed off so they'll be impossible to trace."

"So the little guy did less," the tech holding the smaller outfit says.

"A lot less," the ballistics tech says.

"Interesting," I say. "I wonder if the bigger gunman knows and how he feels about it? If the smaller guy lost his nerve, didn't do his part, that may be a wedge we can drive between them."

"That's going to have to be something you let us do," Hugh Glenn says, walking up beside me.

I turn to face him, wondering again where he disappeared to earlier. The best I can figure is that he and Jeffers, if they hadn't just been hiding out of fear, had been huddled somewhere planning a media strategy or actually talking to the media.

An FDLE investigator wearing gloves and holding an evidence bag is standing next to him.

"I've spoken with Reggie and as of right now you are on administrative leave pending the investigation into your use of deadly force."

I nod.

"Will you lift your arms and let me remove your sidearm?" the FDLE investigator asks.

"Of course," I say. Then do.

"Is this the weapon you used?" she asks.

I nod. "Yes."

"Do you have any others on you?"

"I have a Glock .40 caliber in an ankle holster on my right leg."

"I'll need to take that too," she says.

I bend down and lift my pants leg but let her remove the weapon with her gloved hands.

"We're gonna need you to go to the station and write your report about exactly what happened here," Glenn says. "Fill out some more paperwork. We'll wait to interview you until tomorrow."

"I know your sheriff is going to reiterate it," the FDLE investigator says, "but I can't stress enough how absolutely vital it is that you don't intervene or interfere in either case—the one involving what happened here at the school and the one related to your use of deadly force. Come on, we'll walk you out."

43

Sooner or later, no matter what subculture you identify with—high school students, church attendees, movie theatergoers, country music concert fans, mall shoppers—a gunman is going to kill members of your group.

I pull out of the Potter High School parking lot feeling sad and frustrated and anxious and knowing the location and hours of every package store in the area.

As I pass the media vans and trucks, the camera crews and reporters all working near them, I am shocked at how many there already are. Local, regional, national, and even international news outlets have already descended onto our little town to broadcast to the world what has happened here in this tiny place that the rest of the world had never before even heard of.

On my way to the Potter County Sheriff's Department, I make a series of calls.

The first is to Anna.

"Are you okay?" she's saying. "I'm worried."

"Right now I'm just trying not to think about it," I say. "I've got several things I have to get through first."

"Will you be questioned this afternoon?"

"Not officially, no. I'll be interviewed formally tomorrow. If they have a question about something at the scene or a quick clarification, they'll ask it, but today I just have to fill out paperwork and write my initial report. Allegedly it gives me time for the shock to wear off, but it's also a way of comparing what I write in my statement to what I say in the interview."

"You think they're really going to try to trip you up or—"

"I'm just saying it's a criminal investigation. And it's conducted like one. We don't have a union so it's not like I have a union rep or anything."

"We need to hire you a good attorney," she says.

"We can't afford that."

"We can't afford *not* to," she says.

"It'll be okay," I say. "I'll be careful. I . . . I might be able to get one from the Police Benevolence Association, but even then we . . . truly . . . we have zero money for a lawyer."

"If only you were sleeping with a great attorney," she says.

"You could . . . Could *you* represent me?"

"Of course."

"It's not a conflict of interest or—"

"Of course not," she says.

"What about Taylor and Johanna and— Would you have the time to . . ."

"*John*," she says, her voice emphatic, both firm and loving. "*Honey*, I'm representing you. End of discussion. I got this. Don't worry about anything else. Okay?"

"Okay," I say, and sigh as I feel an enormous relief and comfort wash over me. "Thank you."

"Are you okay to write your report?" she asks. "You seem out of it."

"I'm messed up about what happened," I say, "but I also

haven't had anything to drink or eat since first thing this morning. What time is it?"

"Almost four. Stop at the first place you come to and drink and eat something," she says, adding with a laugh, "unless it's a liquor store."

A fter I end my conversation with Anna, I call the sheriff of Gulf County and my boss, Reggie Summers.

"You okay?" Reggie asks.

I shrug.

"John?"

"Sorry," I say. "I shrugged."

"Giving me a shrug on the phone without saying anything does not inspire confidence."

"I'm okay," I lied. "Just tired and drained. Need to eat something."

"Well, make sure you do that before you try to write your report," she says.

I nod.

"What're you doing now?" she asks. "Nodding?"

"Sorry."

"Dude, you're worrying me."

"I'm okay. Really. Just . . . a little out of it."

"Well, get back in it long enough to hear me loud and clear on this," she says. "Be careful. Take this seriously. Stop on your way and eat and drink something, then take a little time to breathe and think and prepare your report before you go in and write it. Okay?"

I make sure my response is verbal. "Okay. Will do."

"And listen very, very carefully to me on this, John," she says. "No matter how much you want to, don't keep investigating this case—not for one moment. That's grounds for immediate dismissal. I have no wiggle room on this. You'll be under criminal investigation by FDLE. They'll be looking at you very closely. I know you're going to want to work this thing. I know you're going to want to know who put you and that kid in the position to shoot at each other, but you can't. You have to let it go. Or you'll never get to work another case again. Understand? Please tell me you do and not by nodding your damn head."

"I understand," I say. "I do."

"I seriously doubt you do," she says. "You're my best investigator. The best I've ever seen. You've got a real gift. Don't throw it away. Don't work the one case you can't and not be able to work the hundreds of others you can as soon as you're cleared. I mean it, John. Get your head right in a hurry or you're gonna fuck up your future and I don't want to see that happen. And . . . let me know what I can do to help you."

44

I read in the paper that the guns most of these kids use are pretty much military weaponry. They're not for hunting or protecting your family and property or even for target practice. They're created to kill as many people as fast as possible. How can weapons like that even be sold?

"How is she?" I ask.

LeAnn jumps up from her seat in the surgical waiting room of Gulf Coast Medical Center in Panama City and violently and enthusiastically hugs me.

"Oh John," she says, starting to cry. "I'm so glad to see you. I'm so . . . I've been so . . . just . . ."

"I'm sorry," I say, "I should've asked how you were first."

We hold each other for a long moment, then release and take a step back as LeAnn wipes at her tears.

"I guess I've got some kind of post-traumatic stress going on and haven't been able to do anything with it but sit here and worry and relive it all and . . . I'm just so glad you're here."

"Wish I could've been sooner."

I had gone to the sheriff's department that for most of my life had been my dad's and written my report. It had taken a while. I was not thinking clearly and everything took me twice as long to do, but I got it done.

And then I found the nearest package store.

I haven't taken a single drink yet—that will come later—but it's amazing how much more at ease, how much less anxious, knowing it's in my car makes me.

"It's actually perfect timing," she says. "They told me I could go in in just a few minutes. I thought her mom would be here by now, but ... she's ... such a ... mess."

I remember Kim's mom from back in school. What I remember most is a series of men and a lack of sobriety. I remember always being grateful that though my mom suffered from the latter, she never made me or my siblings suffer through the former.

"Any word on how she's doing?" I ask.

"I'm assuming you mean Kim and not her crazy mom," she says. "She's okay. She's going to be okay. We'll know more once we get back there."

"How about Derek?"

"He survived the surgery but is still listed in critical condition. How are *you*? You don't look so good, pal."

"I'll be okay if he is," I say.

She shakes her head, her frizzy blond hair waving about, and forms a frown with her clown-red lips. "I'm so sorry that happened, buddy, but it wasn't your fault. You can't blame yourself for . . . Kim said he fired at you first, that he had been shooting at her. You didn't do anything wrong. Come on now."

I shake my head and look away.

"Let's go see Kimmy," she says. "That'll cheer you up."

She leads me back to Kim's room.

We find Kim propped up on pillows in her bed, her bandaged

right wrist stationary on another pillow positioned for that purpose.

She smiles faintly when we walk in.

"Hey," she says. "I'm so glad y'all came. I didn't think they were ever going to let me see anyone."

"Came?" LeAnn says. "Bitch, I been here all day. Haven't left."

"Ah, thank you so much. Who's got the best best friend ever?"

"Obviously you do," LeAnn says.

"Yes I do," Kim says.

"And I do too," LeAnn says. "I'm so glad you're still here with us so you can keep being my best best friend."

"Little bastards didn't manage to kill me but they got me good enough. How are you, John?"

I nod. "I'm okay. Just glad you are."

She starts to say something else but bursts into tears instead.

LeAnn and I move closer to her, LeAnn starting to shed tears of her own again.

"I . . . still can't believe it's real," Kim says. "None of it. The shooting itself. Getting shot. Ace. Derek. None of it seems real."

"We're all still in shock," LeAnn says. "It's not supposed to feel real."

"Did y'all catch him?" Kim asks. "Who was it? Who did all this to us?"

I shake my head. "We think there were two shooters—one with a rifle and one with a handgun."

"Really?" she says, squinting and looking into the distance. "I only saw one. And he had a handgun. But I have no idea how . . . It doesn't make sense at all. One minute I was shooting back at something out of a horror movie with a handgun and the next it's Derek falling down on the floor with a shotgun, bleeding out. Was he involved?"

"We think he was trying to help," I say. "Students in his class say he was in there with them from the beginning and at some point went out to his truck and got his shotgun, came back in with it to shoot the shooters."

"But he didn't?"

I shake my head again. "At this point it appears he only shot at you and me."

"Where the hell'd the shooters go?" she asks.

"The one with the rifle stayed mostly on the north side of the hallway and did the most damage—"

"Is he the one who shot Ace?"

I nod.

Fresh tears fall.

"Among others. The one with the handgun stayed mostly on the south side in the section near you. At some point, they both took off their outfits and stuffed them and their guns into lockers then blended in with the other students."

"Oh my God," she says. "So they're still out there and we don't have any idea who they are?"

"Well," I say, "we have some ideas."

"Please tell me you're going to find them, John," LeAnn says. "How can we possibly go back to school knowing there are such brutal, coldblooded killers among us?"

"Actually," I say, "I'm off the case."

"What?" she says.

"Suspended while the investigation into my shooting of Derek Burrell is conducted," I say.

"Oh my God, John," Kim says. "That's so—but it was a clean shoot. You'll be— You saved my life. He shot at both of us."

"You can still find out who did it for us, can't you?" LeAnn says. "Unofficially. Make sure they get the right kids."

"Go anywhere near it and I'll be fired."

"So we're dependent on fuckin' Chip Fife and Clueless Glenn?" LeAnn says.

"Several agencies and top law enforcement officers will be involved," I say. "Including FDLE and the FBI."

"The FBI?" LeAnn says.

"In a school shooting like this?" I say. "Absolutely."

Kim looks at LeAnn. "It'll be a long time before the school opens again. And they're not going to send us back in until the killers are caught. Promise you that. Tell her, John."

I start to, but before I can my phone vibrates in my pocket and I pull it out to see that Anna's calling.

"Sorry," I tell them, holding up my phone. "It's Anna. I need to take it. Give me just a second."

"Of course," Kim says.

LeAnn nods.

"Hey," I say into the phone.

"Where are you?" she asks.

I can tell something is wrong.

"At the hospital," I say. "LeAnn and I are with Kim in her room. Her mom's gonna be here soon, but we're—"

"I need you to come home now," she says. "Don't watch TV or listen to the radio. Don't even answer your phone. Just come home."

45

I know people want us to have less guns or less of a certain type of gun, but a gun can't be evil. Only a person can. Evil is in the mind of mankind not the chamber of a gun. What good is taking away guns going to do?

Rushing into our home, I ask, "What's wrong?"

Anna pauses the TV playing in the living room.

Quickly crossing through the kitchen I find that she is alone. "Where are the—"

"Carla is playing with the kids in their room so we can talk," she says.

"About what?"

She nods toward the TV. "I didn't want you to be blindsided by this while you were out there on your own."

"Okay."

"It's bad," she says. "Take a breath and brace yourself for it."

I do. When I nod, she lifts the remote, points it at the TV, and pushes a button.

The screen is filled with images of the pandemonium outside Potter High School earlier today—kids and teachers running out, cops and EMTs running in, parents waiting anxiously, what looks to be hundreds of patrol cars and emergency vehicles, all with their lights flashing.

And then a shot of me as I rush through the crowd searching the students' feet for black boots.

"WMKG with an update to the breaking story we've been bringing you all day of a school shooting in the small town of Pottersville in the Panhandle of Florida," an unseen reporter is saying. "We're receiving reports that an off-duty officer from neighboring Gulf County, this man shown here, was in the school when the shooting occurred and that he shot an unarmed student who had nothing to do with the attack being perpetrated on the school."

I glance over at her and frown. "I wasn't off-duty and he wasn't unarmed."

"The officer is believed to be John Jordan, an investigator with the Gulf County Sheriff's Department with quite a checkered past. We have as yet no idea why Investigator Jordan was even at the school outside of his jurisdiction or why he opened fire on an unarmed kid."

The footage of the front of the school is replaced by a studio shot and a female news anchor wearing an ill-advised sleeveless red dress.

"Tom, do I understand correctly that this Officer Jordan attended high school at Potter High?"

"Yes, Christy, that is what we've been told."

"Maybe he was there for some sort of alumni event or to speak at a career day or something like that," she says.

"It's possible," Tom says. "We just don't know. But whatever it was . . . this off-duty officer's visit to Potter High has turned tragic."

"Wait, hey Tom," Christy says as they cut back to her. "I've just received word that . . . Mr. . . ah . . . Jordan was recently released from prison, that he actually did part of his time at the state facility near the town of Pottersville. How can that be right? Please tell me we don't have an ex-con carrying a gun and a badge. How could that be possible?"

"The only way I can think of, Christy," Tom says, "is if he had been pardoned by the governor. We'll have to look into it more and see what's really going on."

"Can you imagine the political fallout of pardoning a convicted felon, only to have him then kill an unarmed kid?"

"Now, Christy, the minor in question, whose name we haven't released yet, is not deceased. He's in critical condition, fighting for his life at this very moment."

"Oh, yes, sorry. I was just speaking hypothetically. No, I didn't mean that the young man in question isn't very much alive and that we aren't praying for him as he fights for his life at this very moment."

Anna lifts the remote and pauses the TV again.

"You okay?" she asks.

I shake my head. "No, but I wasn't long before that."

She turns to me, and hugs me, dropping the remote as she does.

I hug her back, clinging to her a little more than makes me comfortable but enough to comfort me nonetheless.

We hold each other for a long, wordless moment, and though it seems as if we're both giving and receiving affection, I am doing most or all of the receiving and she is doing most or all of the giving.

Eventually, we release each other.

"There's plenty more where that came from," she says. "Don't be shy about getting what you need."

"Thanks."

I glance at the TV.

"Do all their inaccuracies make it less of a blow?" she asks.

I let out a harsh little laugh. "No, I wish they did, but . . ."

"I'm so sorry, baby. What can I do?"

"Just get me through tomorrow," I say.

"I've already been preparing for it," she says. "It's going to be fine. I promise."

I nod, unconvinced. "Thank you."

"In light of what they're reporting," she says, "I think we need to release a statement. Just a short one to correct the inaccuracies."

"I don't know . . ."

"Tell you what," she says. "I'll draft one and let you look at it. If you still don't want to release it . . . we won't."

I nod. "Thanks."

"Okay, what do you need first?" she says. "Food? Shower? Hugs from the kids? Call Johanna?"

"I wonder what Johanna has heard—or will hear before this is all over?" I say. "I need to call her and Susan first. Then hugs from Taylor and John and then a long hot shower."

46

It's a disorder not a decision. Don't you get it? People don't choose to be crazy. A homicidal maniac is just that. Why are we not watching each other more closely? Why aren't we treating mental illness?

"What the hell happened, John?" Susan says.

I always dread talking to my ex-wife. Even when everything seems as idyllic as a day at the beach. In the best of conditions, when the sky appears clear and the waters calm, there's always a dangerous undertow swirling just beneath the salt-foam surface of the Gulf between us.

"What has she heard?" I ask.

"Nothing," she says. "So far. But it's just a matter of time. It's everywhere. I'm getting calls from the parents of her friends wanting to know if the cop on the news is her dad."

"Sorry."

"I'm already getting calls from news agencies requesting interviews," she says. "Apparently they want to talk about violent behavior in your past. Asked if you had ever pulled a gun on me, ever hit me—that sort of thing."

My mouth grows dry and I find it difficult to swallow, as my thudding heart feels like it has been placed in a cold, dark echo chamber.

"You should know . . ." she says. "Dad is planning to talk to them."

Tom Daniels, her father and my onetime colleague, had once been the Inspector General of the Florida Department of Corrections. Never much of a fan of mine, we had nonetheless been forced to work a couple of cases together. At a certain point I had accused him of committing a crime, but was unable to prove it because he had destroyed evidence and tampered with witnesses. As bad as what I imagine he'll say is, I know it will be worse.

"I've begged him not to," she says. "For Johanna's sake, but he says he's doing it for her and that this is my best chance of getting sole custody."

I'm filled with such rage that I seem to black out a moment.

I find it infuriating that a disgraced, bitter old bent cop is going to have the opportunity to pile on with lies and vitriol to the biggest audience possible in an attempt to not only destroy me but take my daughter away from me.

"John?" Susan is saying. "John? John, are you there?"

"All I did was my job," I say. "Tried to keep kids from getting killed."

"I'm sure you did," she says, "but if you killed one in the process . . ."

"I didn't. I haven't. It wasn't like that and he's not dead."

"I'm not saying what it was like," she says. "I have no idea. I'm telling you how it looks and why someone like Dad has an opening. That's all."

"Can I speak to Johanna?" I say.

"I think you need to calm down first," she says. "Think you

need to get your head right, your anger under control before you do, don't you?"

"I'm fine, but even if I wasn't, you know I don't let anything affect how I am with her. I wouldn't—"

"I was just about to feed and bathe her," she says. "Use that time to try and pull yourself together. I'll call you after that and we'll see what kind of shape you're in."

"I'm together," I say. "I'm fine to talk to her now and I need—"

I stop as I realize the only person I'm talking to is myself.

Consumed with anger and frustration, I decide the best thing for me to do is go for a run, then come back and try to meditate.

"You sure that's a good idea?" Anna asks when I tell her.

I nod.

"Want me to go with you?"

"I'm okay," I say. "Really, I'll be fine."

"Want to see Taylor before you go?" she asks. "I can tell she senses something is going on."

The truth is I want to wait until I get back, don't want to do anything but run as fast and as far as I can with hard, driving music being pumped into my brain through my earbuds, but I say, "Absolutely. Of course."

Following a quick visit with Carla, John, and Taylor, and lots and lots of hugs and love from Taylor, I'm stepping out our side door to go running when I see them.

Descending onto our lawn like a swarm of pestilence are members of the media.

As I stumble back into the mudroom and realize I'm now a prisoner here in my own home, the first thought I have is how I'm going to get the vodka from my car into the house later tonight without being seen.

Coming up behind me, Anna says, "I'll call Reggie and have her send some deputies over to get them off our property. Why don't you go ahead and take a shower and I'll fix you something to eat? I'll also finish the statement I've been working on in my head and let you read it. If you approve it, I'll walk out there and give it to them tonight. Be a lot better tonight in terms of the news cycle anyway."

While I'm in the shower, I get the text I've been expecting from Susan. *She fell asleep. We can try again tomorrow night if you're in a better way.*

I'm overcome with an intense urge to break something but manage to refrain from hurling my phone at the hardest surface I can find.

After slowly drying off and getting dressed, I walk into the kitchen to find my dinner on the table, the media out of our yard, and Anna dressed in her best gray skirt and white blouse, anxious to get my approval on the statement she has crafted so she can go out and read it to the reporters now blocking our road.

She couldn't look any sharper or more confidently competent. She has been a stay-at-home mom for so long I had forgotten just how incredibly professional and badass beautiful she can be in her official capacity as an officer of the court.

I listen attentively as she reads the statement and give her my unreserved and instantaneous approval to go and drop it on the unsuspecting, outmatched members of the media—something I would have done anyway, even if the statement hadn't been as perfect as a poem—because while the reporters are distracted by my beautiful and brilliant wife, I sneak out to my car and bring in the various size bottles I plan to strategically hide all over the house.

47

Do you have any idea how hard it is to have to fight a war inside your own head every single second of every single day? Of course I want to put a bullet in my brain.

The next morning a little hungover, I am interviewed by FDLE about my use of deadly force.

Anna is with me, and though the rules don't allow for her to say anything, her presence has a huge impact on the entire proceeding. She radiates confidence and reassures me just by the way she sits beside me. She is assertive without being aggressive, forceful without exerting any overt force, persistent without being pushy—and all of this before the interview even begins.

"This is a first for me," the middle-aged male FDLE agent conducting the interview says. "Never interviewed an officer represented by his wife."

With his salt-and-pepper high-and-tight haircut, white shirt, black tie, and black slacks, he looks more 60s era FBI than modern FDLE.

"If the man who represents himself has a fool for a client," he says, "what is the man who's represented by his wife?"

"In my case," I say, "a genius."

"Before we begin," he says, "I just want to say how sorry I am that this happened, that you were ever even put in a position like this. I'm not here to trip you up, not out to get you. I'll be square with you all the way through. You can count on that. I also want to say before we start recording that I've had a number of FDLE agents who have worked with you over the years step to me and tell me what an outstanding investigator and human being you are. These are people I'd go through a door with—hell, some of 'em I have. Their words carry water with me. Oceans of it."

"I appreciate you sharing that with me," I say. "I know you didn't have to."

"Okay," he says. "Shall we begin?"

I nod and Anna pats my leg in support.

"Why don't we begin by you taking me through everything you can recall about yesterday from the time you woke up until the time Derek Burrell was shot."

I do, being as specific and detailed as I can, and not consciously holding anything back.

When I finish I receive several affirming nods and pats from Anna.

"You're saying Derek definitely swung around with a shotgun and fired at you?"

"Yes, sir," I say, and though I know he did, I'm less sure in that moment than I have been at any other time since it happened.

"And you're sure you fired just two rounds at him?" he asks.

"Yes, sir."

"Do you recall where you aimed?"

"I believe I do. He was holding a shotgun in a shooter's stance, so at first I thought I would shoot to hit the shotgun or his hand holding it, but his head was leaning on the stock to sight down the barrel, so I decided to aim for his left hip and left knee since they were the closest to me. But it all happened so fast—in far less time than it takes to tell you. I just remember thinking about the officers at Columbine and Parkland who didn't act quickly enough. I wasn't going to hesitate, wasn't going to wait in a safe place for backup. So it's possible that the first round was higher than I thought, maybe I did try for the gun itself after all. But I think I aimed both rounds at his upper left leg and knee. My thinking was to either knock the gun out of his hands or knock him off his feet. And I think I went with the latter."

"Did you shoot to kill?"

"Absolutely not," I say. "I had a headshot. I didn't take it."

He nods. "Okay. We'll see what ballistics shows. Now, can we go back to why you were there to begin with?"

I tell him again.

"So you were assisting the Potter County Sheriff's Department in the investigation into the possible school shooting threat? Were you on loan from your department?"

"Not, officially, no."

"And you say Sheriff Glenn knew you were involved but didn't specifically ask you to be?"

"He may have asked . . . I'm just saying I wasn't in an official capacity."

"Why you?" he asks. "Why were you involved instead of an investigator from the Potter department?"

"I was asked by the deputy who found the notes—Chip Jeffers, who used to work for my dad when he was sheriff here—and the SRO and guidance counselor, who're friends from high school."

"But that still doesn't explain why, does it?" he says. "Do you know why they asked you?"

"The sense I got was that no one was really taking Deputy Jeffers seriously and he felt like he needed to take action. He asked to meet with my father, who sent me when he couldn't make it."

"And you took the threat seriously?"

"To be honest, I took a bit of convincing," I say. "But yes, I came to."

"And it was your idea to guard the school on the twentieth during the play because it was the anniversary of Columbine?"

That's something I haven't told him and that's not in my report. He's being very thorough.

"Yes, sir, it was."

"Do you think the actions y'all took stopped the shooting on Friday or that it was planned for Monday all along?"

"I have no idea."

"Please don't take this the wrong way," he says. "I'm not trying to provoke you. I'm truly not. But . . . do you see yourself as a super cop?"

I shake my head.

"Do you think others see you that way?"

"No, sir," I say.

"Well, they do. Sorry to use that term. I don't mean it in the worst way it sounds. But it conveys some of what I'm asking. Anyway . . . many of those who know you do see you like that— some even use that term. Does that surprise you?"

I shrug.

"Verbally for the recording, please," he says.

"Yeah, I guess it would."

"Many of your colleagues and officers you've worked with in other agencies say you're a truly great investigator—relentless with a keen mind for making connections."

I don't respond.

"Would you say that you try to do too much?" he asks.

"I'm sure I have on occasion," I say. "I don't think I'd say in general."

"Did you on this occasion?"

"I don't believe so, no, sir," I say. "I was just on my way to a meeting about how to regroup after Friday. The shooting had already started when I reached the school. The SRO was the only one responding and needed backup. At that point all I did was what any other cop would do and—"

"Sadly, that's not the case," he says. "We've seen numerous instances of cops waiting outside the school for backup while kids are being killed inside."

"Well, I doubt many would now that we have a better understanding of how these rampage shootings work and that there's no tactical advantage to waiting outside because it's not a hostage situation."

"Well, we still have some that do—that *have* very recently. What you and Deputy Miller did was heroic, which is why I hate that you're in this situation, hate that I have to be asking you these questions—especially this next one."

I brace myself for what's about to come and I can feel Anna next to me doing the same.

"Do you drink?" he asks.

My heart sinks into my stomach and begins to bang around down there.

I nod. "I'm a recovering alcoholic," I say. "I have issues with addiction. I was not drunk nor did I have anything to drink the day of the shooting. Not a single drop. I was not impaired in any way. Alcohol is not an issue here, was not involved in any way."

Though she can't say anything, I can tell Anna is surprised by my response. I'm sure she expected me to say that I have over a decade of sobriety, but of course I can't say that now.

"What about the night before?" he asks. "Did you drink then? Were you hungover from the night before?"

I don't respond.

"I'm not trying to trip you up," he says. "I'm sorry to have to even be asking, but . . . it's our understanding that you and some of the others involved in Friday's . . . exercise went out for drinks afterwards."

I nod. "A few of us got together at The Oasis to discuss what happened and what to do going forward. Some of them drank. No one got drunk. I had two non-alcoholic beers."

He nods as if he already knows all this.

"Okay, but what about after that?" he asks. "We have a receipt from a purchase you made at Top Shelf, the package store out on Highway 84. We have two others from the weekend—one from a Good Spirits on Saturday and the Salt Shaker on Sunday."

48

Life's tough. Boo-hoo. Get over it. My life's no picnic bud, but you don't see me walking into a school with an assault rifle and shooting the place to shit, do you?

"Why didn't you tell me?" Anna asks.

"That I'm drinking again?" I say. "That I randomly and with no good reason threw away over a decade of sobriety? That I'm weaker than I thought I was? That I was hungover on Monday morning and I can't be absolutely certain that it didn't contribute to me shooting a kid? You know why. I haven't felt this much shame and embarrassment in a long, long time."

She reaches over and takes my hand.

We are in the car, heading home. I'm driving. She's in the seat next to me.

"I wish you had felt like you could tell me," she says. "Wish I had picked up on it without you having to."

"The only reason you didn't is because you attributed everything to the school stuff—the frustration and fatigue from Friday and the guilt and post-traumatic stress from yesterday."

"Still . . ."

"And I would've told you," I say. "It would've just been when I was ready to get sober again."

"That mean you're not ready to stop?"

I frown and nod.

She hesitates a moment, seeming to let that in, then nods.

"How does that make you feel?" I ask.

"I'm feeling an awful lot right now," she says.

"I'm sorry," I say.

But not sorry enough not to do it, the critic inside my head says.

"Well, at least now it's out in the open," she says. "No more sneaking around, no more deception, no more hiding it."

I nod.

"I don't want to be lied to, John," she says. "I can deal with a lot of things but not that. I love you. I want you, want what we have, but I won't be lied to or cheated on."

I nod again.

Neither of us says anything else and we ride along in silence on the long, flat, rural highway between Pottersville and Wewa, the planted pines on either side of us vibrantly green in the morning sun.

Our silence isn't exactly awkward, but it is fraught, resonant with both the echoes of what we've said and the vacuity of what we haven't.

"Like last night," I say, "you were incredible in there today. A powerful force, a calming presence. Thank you for what you've done for me. Sorry you were blindsided by my drinking."

She nods but doesn't say anything and when I glance over at her I can see tears streaming down her cheeks.

"I'm so sorry, Anna," I say.

She shakes her head. "You don't need to keep saying that."

"But—"

"Tell you what," she says. "Why don't you tell me one more time, but only after you've stopped drinking."

"Okay," I say, and we retreat back into our silences—this time they seem more like two separate ones, as if we're each inhabiting our own.

We ride like this for several miles and countless rows of slash pines.

Eventually my phone vibrates and I pull it out to glance at it. It's LeAnn.

"You mind if I take this?" I ask. "It's—"

"No," she says. "Take it."

"Hey," I say.

"How are you holding up, pal?" she asks.

"Not so great," I say. "Could really use some good news."

I had asked her to see what she could find out about Derek's condition.

"Afraid I don't have any of that," she says. "Sorry. Wish I did."

"What's his condition?" I ask, hoping he still has one.

"He's still listed as critical," she says, "but he's alive. That's something."

"Yes it is."

"Did you aim for the barrel of the gun?" she asks.

"Yeah. I'm . . . I think I did. Why?"

"They're saying the bullet hit the barrel and sort of skittered down it and went into his head and lodged in his brain."

Fuck.

"They've put him in a medical-induced coma and are trying to get the swelling in his brain to go down so they can go in and operate, try to remove the bullet."

I try to say something but nothing comes out.

"He lost a lot of blood from the bullet hole in his left leg. It went clean through but severed a major artery and . . . well, losing blood the way he did impacts everything else."

"I guarantee she got LeAnn to help her write it."

As she starts to say something my phone vibrates. It's LeAnn. I smile and show her.

"Hey," I say.

"She did good, didn't she?"

"She did great. Thanks for helping her put it together."

"Ah, you noticed. It's the least we could do, try to get those rat bastards off you. They gonna vilify a genuine hero like that. Not as long as this big-mouth blonde's around."

"Thank you."

"Plus it did her good to do it," she says. "Gets her mind off Ace. He was no prize, but he was hers."

"Has she been interviewed yet?" I ask.

"They tried to do it in her hospital room, but her mom kept interjecting herself into the conversation. Think she's headed to do it now."

"Any word on Derek?"

"Sorry, but no change. 'Course, I guess that's better than a change for the worse, right?"

50

My gun is a tool, an in-case-of-emergency, last resort, there-if-I-need-it defense. It's not my identity, my culture, my religion.

"How you?" Merrill asks.

"Been better."

He and Tyrese have found me down by the lake in my backyard in early evening, the soft hazy glow of sunset lightly touching everything with a muted magnificence that seems almost transcendent.

I came out here to pray and meditate after realizing the media trucks were gone.

"Some brutal shit they been sayin' about you on the six and ten," he says.

"Seems better after what Kim Miller said to them," Tyrese adds.

I nod.

"My cuz here has some concerns he wants to go over with you," Merrill says.

"Okay."

"First," Tyrese says, "I want to thank you for all you did for our school. I haven't had a chance to do that yet, and I wanted to tell you in person. Everything you did is greatly appreciated. There's no doubt it saved lives and I'm sorry it's takin' the toll on you that it is."

I don't say anything, just give him an expression of appreciation and a small nod.

"Secondly, I wanted to say that I have grave concerns about the Potter County investigator they assigned to the case. I went to school with him and he's . . . Let's just say he's not the smartest person I ever met. Kim confirmed he's pretty inept. I'm afraid he's not gonna catch the killers and—"

"It's not just down to him," I say. "FDLE has investigators working it. And the FBI does or will too."

"But he's the lead," he says. "He keeps emphasizing that. He's in charge. He's the kind of ignorant that has no idea just how ignorant he is and his insecurities make him defensive, arrogant, and unteachable. No way he'll take the help he's being offered. We've decided not to reopen the school during this school year. We only have five weeks left and there was so much damage done to the buildings . . . but I don't want to start the school year next year without having caught the shooters."

"I understand," I say. "I'd suggest you talk to the sheriff about your concerns and—"

"He's the one who assigned the moron to head up the investigation. He's not going to do anything."

"I think you can have more influence on him than you imagine," I say. "Hugh's a political animal and he wants to look good and get reelected, so be sure to point out to him the political upside to getting it right. Tell him to let FDLE handle the investigation. That they'll let him make the arrest and give his department all the credit and if anything goes wrong he can blame them."

"He's hopin' you'd help with it," Merrill says.

"I'm under investigation for the shooting," I say. "If I go anywhere near it I'll be fired. But even if I wasn't, there's nothing I could do anyway since it's not my county."

"I've asked Merrill to look into it as much as he can as a PI," Tyrese says. "And I wondered if you'd help him."

"I would if I could. You both know that. But I can't even look like I'm talking to a witness."

"Here's what I was thinkin'," Merrill says. "We just have conversations—you know, like we do—and in these conversations I might share with you what I'm working on, what I'm uncovering and what I'm thinkin' I should do next. And bein' the good friend you are, you listen to me and you maybe even offer me suggestions 'cause you don't want to see your friend waste his time or do somethin' stupid."

"Conversations," I say.

"Just like we're having right now," he says. "And in these conversations I may have occasion to share with you information another cousin of mine who works for the sheriff's department might be sharin' with me. Such as ballistics are back."

"Oh yeah?"

"Yeah. And just like you thought. Most of the shots and all the fatalities came from the rifle. The nine was used very little. Fired into a classroom or two and in the library. Hit Kim twice and . . . are you ready for this? Hit Derek in his foot. Bullet was still in his boot."

I think about it. "So that's why he was firing at us," I say. "He had been fired on first—actually hit. The handgun shooter fires at him from the same direction Kim was in, so when he fires back he's firing at her. The gunman disappears and leaves them shooting at each other."

"Then you show up and join in," Merrill says. "All y'all victims of the shooter with the nine. Didn't shoot much, but he made 'em count."

"Interesting conversation," I say.

"Figured you might like it, maybe even want to have more."

"I just might," I say.

"What other kinds of things would you like to talk about?"

"I'd be interested in discussing things like the victims, the forensics, the movements of the suspects, what kinds of things the kids are saying since the shooting, who was wearing black paramilitary-style boots, what was found on the boots that were found on the stage and in the video production room, more about the explosives and if any of the kids have a history of making them. Things like that."

"It's interesting," Merrill says, "I's actually wondering and wantin' to talk about some of those very things."

51

It's simple. If you see something, say something. If you see a dude devolving into a bad place, do something—intervene, report it to someone who can help. Do something. Everybody's waiting for someone else to do something but we can't do that anymore.

It's late and I've been drinking for a while when I hear a knock at the front door.

Stumbling out of the comfortable chair in my library where I have been alternating between studying the information Merrill has gathered on the case and dozing, I unsteadily rush over to answer it before it wakes Taylor, John Paul, or their mothers.

Glancing through the darkened, beveled glass, I can see that the local, vaguely familiar man on my front stoop is not a reporter.

I unlock and open the door and start to whisper for him to—

He's shoving his way in, the door smacking the wall and the library door behind it loudly.

Grabbing me, he slings me back against the wall behind me.

As I bounce off it, he grabs me again and throws me back into the corner of the foyer, his left forearm against my throat, pinning me there, his right hand pressing the barrel of an old Taurus .357 into my left temple.

"You sorry piece of shit," he's saying. "You—"

I'm trying to reason with him but the words aren't coming out right.

"Are you drunk?" he says. "You pathetic piece of shit, you're drunk as fuck."

I can hear John Paul crying upstairs. A moment later, the light in the guest bedroom comes on, and Carla appears on the upstairs landing.

"John?"

"Go back in your room," I say. "It's okay."

"It's not okay. He's—"

"'Less you want to see this motherfucker's pickled brains all over this wall," the man says, "get back in there and close the goddamn door."

"Go," I say. "It's okay. Just go inside and lock your door."

Reluctantly, hesitantly, she does just that.

"How could you . . ." the man is saying. "Were you drunk when you shot him?"

"What? Who? No."

"The fuck you mean *who*?" he says. "How many unarmed kids you shot, you son of a bitch? My sister's kid, that's who. Derek. How could you shoot a good kid like that? Never in any trouble. Took care of his mama. Worked hard to help her. Made good grades in school."

"I'm sorry," I say. "I . . . didn't mean . . . It was an accident . . . a—"

"Well, I'm about to have the same kind of accident with your fuckin' head."

And then Anna is there behind him, the small, slim 9mm from the drawer beside her bed pressed into the back of his head.

"Lower the gun," she says. "Now."

She's standing too close to him and I want to tell her but to do so would tip him off to something that might not have crossed his mind.

Suddenly, faster than he seems capable, he brings his left arm down off my neck and throws a vicious elbow into the side of Anna's head, knocking her into the door to my library and to the ground, the little nine skittering across the laminate flooring and into the corner opposite us.

I bring up my hands, grabbing his right wrist with my left and pushing his gun hand away from my head and grabbing him by the throat with my right.

I shove him back, and he falls out the front door, tripping on the step and falling partially on the little brick stoop and partially on the damp grass of the front yard beyond.

I fall with him, on top of him.

But the moment we hit the ground, he is rolling, maneuvering out from underneath me, twisting his way on top of me.

And then he's pounding on me—mostly with the bottoms of his fists.

As I try to fend off his attack I can't tell if the gun is still in his hand but don't think it can be given the way that hand has formed a fist and is striking my face.

Anna is behind him again. This time too far away for him to reach.

"I will shoot you," she says. "Get off him. Now."

"Okay, okay," he says, raising his hands and climbing off me.

The moment he's on his feet, he takes off running—out of our yard, into our neighbors', across the road, and disappearing into the night.

"Are you okay?" she asks.

"Help me up," I say.

She tries to.

Eventually, with her help, I sit up, roll over on my hands and knees and push up from there.

She grabs the .357 Derek's uncle left on our lawn and helps me back inside and locks the door behind us.

Leading me straight into the downstairs guest bathroom, she eases me down on the side of the tub and begins to clean the cuts on my face with peroxide, evaluating the damage done as she wipes the blood and dirt away.

"Do you wish you hadn't married me?" I ask.

"*What*? Of course not. Why would you say something like that?"

"He's right. I'm pathetic. You didn't sign up to be with a . . . with . . . for all this. Drunk . . . child . . . killer. No one would . . . blame you for finding the nearest . . . exit. Hell, I think . . . you should."

She shakes her head. "I guess I never realized you're such a maudlin drunk," she says.

I actually start laughing out loud at that, though to do so hurts my face.

"I hope you're not too drunk to hear this now and remember it tomorrow," she says. "You're the love of my life and the best man I've ever known and wild horses couldn't drag me away."

Later that night I fall asleep with The Sundays' cover of "Wild Horses" playing in my head, and when I wake the next morning I still remember what Anna said.

52

Everybody gets bullied—even bullies. Especially bullies. What do you think turned them into bullies? What, so you can't take a little bullying without blowing up your fuckin' school?

I t's the evening of the next day. Merrill and I are at Lake Alice Park watching Johanna and Taylor climb on the playground equipment from a nearby wooden bench.

"You said you wanted to know what the kids are sayin' since it happened," he says. "Most all of 'em think Mason Nickols and Dakota Emanuel did it. A few have said they've heard them brag about doing it and about how they're going to be the only ones in history who get to do it again."

I nod, continuing to keep an eye on the girls.

"Lots of crazy shit bein' talked too," he says. "Conspiracy theory shit. Pizzagate government child-sex-ring type shit. Some talkin' 'bout this whole thing a ploy to make the first black principal look bad. Others sayin' a contractor in town did it so he can build a new school. Somebody said that kid Zach Griffith is making a movie and did it all for it. That he and Tristan and Denise were in on it together, that the play and protest were part of it. Just inane shit. Tell me this. Why do people believe crazy conspiracy theories? Especially about dramatic or traumatic events."

"Research says it comes down to three main reasons," I say. "Desire for understanding and or certainty, desire for security and or control, and for a positive self-image."

"Care to elaborate a little?"

"Uncertainty is uncomfortable," I say. "We crave answers and avoid ambiguity. And answers that fit our worldview, confirm our biases, or that we have some emotional investment in are particularly appealing. Some people would rather have wrong answers than no answers at all. The more powerless or out of control or socially marginalized a person is, the more attractive conspiracy theories become. Believing in them can cause a person to feel more secure because it explains why the deck is stacked against them, it gives them what they see as secret knowledge, and it provides a community of sorts for them, a place to belong."

"Explains a lot about our political culture these days," he says.

"Sure," I say. "Corrupt and manipulative politicians and their pundits prey on the most vulnerable in order to keep their money and power. The black man or the brown man or the gay man or the woman or the person with different beliefs, philosophies, or customs than you is conspiring against you. It's their fault you don't have the life you want and they're coming to take the little that you do have."

His nodding head transitions into shaking. "Damn. Damn. Damn."

"And teenagers are some of the most powerless and vulnerable people on the planet," I say. "It's not surprising so many of them are grasping for explanations for the trauma they've just gone through."

"It's funny," he says. "The jocks are sayin' it was an attack on them while the art kids and nerds are sayin' it was an attack on them."

I nod. "What did you find out about the victims?"

"Kids that got injured run the gamut," he says. "Seems to be equal number of each tribe—jocks, popular, nerds, artists, druggies, goths, et cetera. The two students who got killed were foster kids—twin brothers, Hayden and Hunter Dupree. Had the kind of lives that'd make you believe in conspiracy theories. Emotional, verbal, physical, and sexual abuse—by their parents, then by their first set of foster parents. They were relatively new to town. The two teachers or the coach and the teacher were well liked and respected. They were viewed as good at their jobs and known for treating all the kids the same. More than one non-athletic kid said Bowman treated them just as well as he did his football players."

"That's nice to hear," I say.

"And it relates to something else I keep hearing," he says. "Everybody and I mean everybody I've talked to says Potter High doesn't have a bullying problem. Says Tyrese and Bowman and the other faculty set a good tone and the cool kids and jocks got along and that nobody is bullied."

"That's even better to hear," I say.

"But what does that say about the motive?" he asks.

"That it's probably ol' garden variety psychopathology," I say.

"Which again would point to Mason and Dakota, right?"

I nod.

A car pulls up behind us and I turn to see that it's Reggie in her black sheriff's SUV.

"I came to talk to John, but I'm glad you're here, Merrill," she says. "This concerns you too."

"You want to sit?" I say.

She shakes her head. "Rather stand. Won't be long."

Merrill and I stand with her—partly out of respect and courtesy, partly so she's not blocking my view of my girls.

She looks at Merrill first. "I hear you're asking questions about the case over in Pottersville, investigating it as if you're more than a private detective."

"Don't know what more than a private detective means," he says, "but Tyrese asked me to look into it and because he's my favorite cousin and that's my school those little bitches shot up, I am."

"Which as a licensed PI is your right," she says. "But you know what my concern is . . . It's that you're bringing the info you uncover back to John so he can still work the case without appearing to work the case. And lo and behold I come to talk to John about it and here I find you two together in what looked like some deep-ass conversation."

"You can ask Tyrese," Merrill says. "He asked me to look into it. He really cares about the kids and the school and doesn't want to reopen without the killers being caught."

"I don't doubt that," she says. "Don't doubt any of it."

"I'm not working the case," I say.

"What the hell happened to your face?" she says.

"Derek Burrell's uncle," I say.

"Why haven't I heard anything about it?" she says.

"Because I sympathize with his point of view," I say. "I've done enough to that family. I'm not going to press charges against the distraught uncle of the kid I shot."

"But you'll damn sure try to figure out who put the two of you in the position to be shooting at each other in the first place, won't you?"

"I'm not working the case," I say. "I'm only leaving the house to bring the girls here and go to funerals."

"Do you have any idea of the pressure I'm under to fire you?" she says.

I shake my head. "I guess not. I wasn't aware of any."

"FDLE and everyone else, including the fuckin' FBI, is telling me what a shitty sheriff I am, and how I don't have control of my own people, and what the hell was one of my investigators doing at a school shooting in another county, and haven't you always done just what you want to, and—"

"I've always showed you the upmost respect and have done what you've told me to," I say. "You've actually thanked me for that before."

"Both can be true," she says. "I know I came into this job with very little experience and I know you're one hell of an investigator, but I'll be damned if I'm going to be made a fool of, if I'm going to be the laughing stock of the entire world—and that's who's looking at us right now. The entire fuckin' world. And if you'd get your drunk head out of your ass long enough you'd know that."

I start to say something but she cuts me off.

"Now, we still don't know where the investigation into your use of deadly force is going to go, but even if it goes your way, I'm not sure you should come back to my department. But between now and the ruling you think long and hard if you even want to and if you can follow my goddamn rules like everybody else. Because if you can't I can't work with you—no matter how much I like you personally or how good an investigator you may be."

53

We all do it, but only fools try to solve serious matters in the middle of the night. Clearly, we're all fools.

That night I had a dark night of the soul.

Unable to sleep, I pass the hours in silent contemplation, considering myself as objectively and honestly as I am capable of at this time.

It's the first night in a week I haven't had a drink.

I think about the shooting and my part in it and what I might have done differently to avoid shooting Derek.

After considering every scenario I can come up with, I conclude that, while tragic, what happened with Derek was an accident and that he was as likely to be hit by Kim or the SWAT team as me.

It doesn't make me feel any better about it, but regardless of what the FDLE investigation concludes or how public opinion sentences me, I'm clear on my role and responsibility.

What concerns me far more is my spiritual life and sobriety.

In my happiness and high life satisfaction-level to be with Anna and for us to be raising our girls together, I've been neglectful over my soul.

I've deceived myself that addiction was no longer an issue for me, that I had no need for meetings or a sponsor or a more active spiritual life.

It's the oldest trap out there and I stepped right into it.

I convinced myself of my own self-sufficiency and strength. I removed far too many forms of accountability from my life and have spent far too much time listening to my ego tell me how good and strong and capable I am.

I have rationalized.

I have justified.

I have been guilty of the most egregious forms of moral equivalency.

I have surrendered my sobriety and forfeited my serenity and have no plan in place to get either of them back.

I have overvalued and been overly dependent on the relative power of my own mind.

I have played to my strengths and ignored my weaknesses.

I haven't just done all these things. I'm still doing all these things.

Knowing is nothing. It's not enough to know what I'm doing wrong. It's not enough to take a searching and fearless moral inventory. Action is required. And it's not as if I don't know what to do. I do. But if I'm completely honest I have to admit to myself and my higher power that I'm not sure I'm ready to do anything just yet.

That makes me weak and lazy and unrepentant, but there it is.

54

When the shooting was happening I swore to myself that if I survived I was going to retire and never come back. I meant it too. I'm never stepping back into that building. If this is the world y'all are willing to put up with then y'all can have it. I want no part of it.

"The hell happened to your face?" LeAnn asks.

"You should see the other guy's fist," I say.

It's the next morning, the day before the memorial service at the high school, and Kim and LeAnn have come by to check on me.

LeAnn isn't dressed much differently than on any other day, but out of uniform, her hair down, in a sundress and carrying a big handbag, Kimmy bears little resemblance to Deputy Miller.

Though moving slowly, Kim has discarded her cane and the only evidence of her injuries is the bandage on her leg and the cast on her wrist.

Anna and Carla and the kids are in Panama City running

errands and grocery shopping, so the three of us sit at the kitchen table and have tea and biscuits and tupelo honey.

"We're worried about you, 'ol son," LeAnn says.

"That's sweet of you but—"

"We feel like we pulled you into this mess," Kim says.

"Actually that was Chip Jeffers," I say.

"It was, wasn't it?" LeAnn says, her bright red lips forming a huge smile. "Fuckin' Chip. Son of a bitch. Why isn't *he* over here checking on you? Never thinks about anybody but himself, does he?"

"Seriously," Kim says. "How are you?"

"How are *you*?" I ask. "You're the one who got shot." *And lost your boyfriend*, I think but don't say.

"I'm still in shock or in some form of postpartum depression."

LeAnn says, "Think you mean post-traumatic stress."

"It's nothin' like I imagined it would be," Kim says. "I'm just sort of out of it all the time. Feel distant from everything, including my own body. Keep wantin' to talk to Ace about it."

"I'm so sorry," I say.

"I miss the shit out of that big ol' lug," she says. "We were more like comfortable old friends than anything else. I could tell him anything. And that's what I miss most—how he could comfort me no matter what I was going through. Weren't exactly the last of the red hot lovers, but he was my best friend."

"Hey," LeAnn says. "I thought I—"

"You know what I mean."

"I've heard some really good things about him," I say. "Kids liked and respected him. Said he treated everyone the same."

She nods. "He did. Didn't matter how little athletic ability they had. I'm glad you heard good things."

LeAnn says, "There's some bad things being said too. Gossip. Small town, small mind shit."

"Really? Like what?"

"Saying he was a bully."

"I heard just the opposite," I say. "That he prevented bullying from happening at the school."

"Exactly," Kim says. "Thank you."

"The craziest ones are that he was sleeping with students and stealing money from the athletic programs," LeAnn says.

"Yeah," Kim says, "poor fella had some plumbing issues and—"

"Couldn't get it up very often," LeAnn explains.

"Yeah, I caught that," I say.

"And he lived in a rundown old trailer, drove a piece of shit old Camaro, and never had more than a few dollars to his name. I hate this town sometimes."

"It's better than the stuff they're saying about John," LeAnn says.

"True," Kim says.

"Or poor Janna."

"That's true too."

"Don't tell me what's being said about me," I say.

"You can guess it," LeAnn says. "You've probably heard it all."

"What about Janna?" I ask.

"Kind of stuff you'd expect. Took a different man home from the bar every night. Slept with Tyrese to get her job. Gang bang with students out in the art building."

"Why do people gossip?" Kim says. "Especially about the dead. Why do people believe it, spread it?"

LeAnn shakes her head, frowns, and looks wistful. "Just a little later and she would've been safe and sound out in the art building."

Kim looks at me. "Is everything as random as it seems? It all just seems so fuckin' full of chance, so like blind fuckin' luck."

I frown and nod.

"That wasn't rhetorical," she says.

"I'm probably not the person to be asking at the moment," I

say. "I'd have a hard time coming up with the meaning and grand design behind me shooting a kid."

"Exactly," she says. "Exactly."

"You haven't lost your faith, have you?" LeAnn asks me.

I shake my head. "My faith embraces chaos."

"Care to explain?"

"Now's probably not the best time, but . . . let's just say that for me, faith means trust and faithfulness to certain principals and truths. It's a practice, not belief or make-believe. And my trust in goodness and love and God is far more at the macro than the micro level."

"Let's change the subject," Kim says. "He said he didn't want to talk about it."

"I'm happy to talk about it another time," I say. "When I'm in a better place."

"Let's change the subject back to gossip and the real reason we came here," LeAnn says.

"I thought y'all came to check on me," I say with a smile.

"Yeah, yeah, we did," LeAnn says, "but listen to this. There's talk among the kids that there's going to be another attack—at the memorial service tomorrow."

55

Let me tell you, post-traumatic stress disorder is real. I have nightmares, anxiety, hyper-arousal, irritability, flashbacks, avoidance, and a hundred other things no one has even told me about yet. I will never ever be the same again.

When Anna walks in and sees my badge and guns on the kitchen counter her eyes open wide and her mouth drops open in excitement.

She is carrying grocery bags, which she quickly let slide from her hands on the nearest counter so she can rush over and hug me.

"Do those mean what I think they mean?" she says.

I nod. "Reggie dropped them off a little while ago. I've been completely cleared."

From the table behind me, LeAnn says, "I prefer the word *vindicated*."

Kim says, "We all knew you would be."

"Yeah," LeAnn says, "not like the criminal justice system ever gets it wrong."

"Exactly," Anna says. "I knew it was a righteous shoot, but . . . I was still worried. They concluded the investigation quicker than I thought they would."

"Reggie asked them to expedite it and she said Sam put in a word on my behalf."

"Did she apologize for how she spoke to you?" she asks. "Merrill told me what she said."

"Sort of," I say. "She was under a lot of . . . scrutiny. Just let it get to her. You know all the pressure she's under at home and work. She feels bad about it."

"Don't make excuses for her," she says. "There are none. When do you start back to work?"

"Monday."

"What is it, Mommy?" Taylor asks, trailing in with Johanna.

"Daddy?" Johanna says. "What's—"

"Everything okay?" Carla asks, coming in right behind them carrying John Paul.

"It's great news," Anna says. "And we've needed some."

Kim steps over and kneels in front of Johanna and Taylor. "Some important people said your dad did the right thing when he helped me last—"

"He always does the right thing," Johanna says. "Don't you, Daddy?"

"I always try to," I say. "But sometimes I mess up."

"Everybody messes up sometimes," Kim says.

"What did you do, Daddy?" Johanna asks.

"He saved my life," Kim says.

"Well, he helped," LeAnn says, "but it was really my work on the radio and watching the monitors that made the biggest difference."

"Oh, John," Anna whispers as she continues to hug and kiss me, "I'm so happy. For you. For us. We need to celebrate."

"That's sweet and I both appreciate it and second the sentiment, but . . . as long as the Burrell boy is in critical condition I can't . . ."

"No, of course. I completely understand that. I just meant I want to cook your favorite meal and maybe make some homemade ice cream or something."

"Ice cream," Taylor squeals.

"She loves ice cream," Johanna explains to Kim.

"Me too," Kim says.

"Nobody loves it more than me," LeAnn says.

"It's not a contest," Kim says, "but I do."

"Y'all haven't seen Taylor eat it," Johanna says.

"Well, they need to, don't they?" Anna says. "Why don't y'all stay and eat with us."

"We'd love to," LeAnn says.

"But we can't," Kim says. "We have to go prepare for the memorial service tomorrow."

Anna nods. "I hope I haven't been insensitive. I'm just so relieved that John—"

"Not at all," Kim says. "We are too. If it weren't for him I'd be in one of the caskets there tomorrow instead of having to go home to try to come up with something to say at the service."

"Well," LeAnn says, *me* and him."

Kim gives Johanna a big hug but Taylor has moved away, distracted by something else before she can hug her.

When Kim tries to get up, she struggles a bit until Anna takes her by her good arm and helps her.

"I'll sign your cast if you want me to," Johanna says.

"Would you?" Kim says. "I would love that. I was just about to ask if you would."

As Anna searches through our junk drawer for a Sharpie and Johanna tells Kim how her name is spelled and what it comes from, Carla steps over to me. I immediately reach for John Paul, though that is not why she walked over to me.

"I'm so happy for you, John," she says. "No one deserves it more."

"Thank you," I say, holding little John Paul to me, propping his tiny head on my shoulder.

"I know you're going through some things right now," she says. "I'm just glad something broke your way in the midst of everything."

I remember having a bottle and a good buzz going at Rudy's Diner late on the night when Nicole Caldwell had been murdered and how the much younger version of Carla had looked at me, how relieved she had been when Anna walked in. Anna and I weren't together then, but I remember the fire in her eyes when she told me not to dare use the death of that precious little girl as an excuse to get drunk.

"Thank you," I say again. "And thanks for being here with us and sharing this little fella with us."

"I keep thinking we're in the way," she says. "That we've outstayed our welcome."

"That's something you could never do," I say. "It's such a grace to have you both here."

"I can't believe it's taking them so long to get our apartment ready."

"I wish they would take a lot longer," I say. "We will be very sad to see you go."

As a couple of media trucks pull up to the end of our property, Anna says, "They must have gotten the word. I wonder if FDLE released a statement. I feel like I should write a statement and go read it to them."

LeAnn says, "I'm all for it as long as it has the words *suck it* in it."

56

I think the reason there's so many school shootings is that y'all don't allow God in schools anymore. We need God back in school. And prayer. We need prayer back. And spankings. We need God, prayer, and spankings.

I'm just about to start drinking when Merrill calls.

"Got time for a little ride?" he asks.

"Sure."

He pulls up and picks me up in his black BMW a few minutes later.

The night is bright, cool, and quiet beneath a nearly full moon. The streets are empty, dappled by faint nocturnal shadows.

"You remember D-Bop?" he asks.

"The drug dealer? Yeah? In prison, isn't he?"

"Out. 'Bout a year now. Back to dealing but he's expanded his product line. Moves some weapons now too."

"Picked up some new tricks inside," I say.

"Yeah, and contacts."

"Good to see our justice system working."

"Oh, it works," he says. "Just not the way John Q think it do."

I don't respond and we ride in silence for a moment.

I haven't heard Merrill slip into his playful, ironic use of ebonics in a while and it makes me smile. I'm sure it's because he's about to be mixing it up with D-Bop.

From his car's finely appointed sound system I can hear the barely audible, nearly imperceptible singing of Marvin Gaye's "What's Going On?"

"I'm pretty sure D-Bop the one sold the kids the guns used in the shooting," he says. "Want you to hear what he has to say about it."

I nod. "Where we meetin' him?"

"Old Rish cow pasture on 73."

I nod, grateful I've got my badge and guns back.

In the absence of our conversation I can hear Smokey Robinson's "Being With You." Being a trained detective I deduce that Merrill's system is tuned to a Classic Motown station.

"Got word today that the two pair of boots found—ones on the stage and the ones in the video production room—were clean," he says. "No traces of blood or gunpowder on either of them. What looked like blood on one of them was theatrical blood."

"You got the list of who was wearing black boots the day of the shooting?" I ask.

"In the folder on the backseat."

I reach around and grab it and begin flipping through it.

The list of who was wearing black boots the day of the shooting is far more important now that we know the boots found weren't worn by the killers.

I locate the list and scan it.

Mason Nickols.

Tristan Ward.

Zach Griffith.

DeShawn Holt.

Josh Blunt.

Casey Box.

Sierra Baker.

Chase Dailey.

Denise Royal.

Sage Dalton.

Randy Haines.

Ray Ray Hill.

Deandre Wilder.

Matt Houston.

"Only suspects from our list not on that one are Evan Fowler and Dakota Emanuel, right?" Merrill says.

"Yeah, but Dakota didn't have any shoes on," I say. "So he could've had boots on and gotten rid of them somehow. Probably need to see if Tyrese can search the school for them again."

"He'll need help," he says. "Maybe we can put together a crew for this weekend."

"Sounds good."

"Couple of rumors continue to persist," he says. "Teachers and students gettin' it on and that the bullyin' and abuse that could'a motivated this shit came more from staff than the other kids. I asked Tyrese. Says he's never heard even a whisper of either one, so . . ."

We ride the rest of the short way to the old Rish cow pasture in silence, Stevie Wonder's "Master Blaster" taking us in.

We find D-Bop's black Escalade idling in the middle of the pasture, the exhaust trailing up into the moonlight.

The fence of the old field is mostly gone and the pasture is a popular spot for drug deals because of the isolation and how easy it is to see anyone approaching.

As we roll up beside the SUV, the back window rolls down.

Merrill pulls out his .45 and places it on the seat between his legs. I reach down and unsnap my holster and let my hand hang there hovering over the butt of my 9mm.

Rolling down his window, Merrill comes to a stop next to the open back window of the Escalade.

After a few greetings and some bullshit, we get down to the reason we're here.

"I ain't know they'd be usin' my gats to blast no damn school," D-Bop says.

I wonder exactly what he thought they were planning to do with them, but don't ask him.

"We tryin' to make sure they don't do it again," Merrill says.

"I cool with that, long as I left out of it."

Merrill nods.

"I got your word?" D-Bop asks.

Merrill nods.

"Want his," he says, nodding toward me.

I nod.

"Well, so whatch y'all wanna know?"

"Who made the, ah, purchase?" Merrill says.

"Moved two ARs recently," he says. "All this renewed racism, tribalism, whatnot . . . good for business. One was to a white boy. Can't tell you much more than that."

"Can you describe him?" Merrill says.

"He's white."

"Anything else?"

"He a high school kid, sorta scrawny, stringy cracker-ass hair needin' a trim."

That describes most of the guys on our suspect list—maybe even all depending on his definition of *stringy hair in need of a trim.*

"Nothing else?" I say.

"Ain't got to the *oh shit* part yet," he says.

"Which is?" I ask.

"Had a partner."

"What can you tell us about him?" Merrill asks.

"That it wasn't. It was a her. She had the money. She seem to be callin' the shots. She didn't even get out of the car, but he had to run back and forth to ask her shit and to get the money from her."

"You describe her?" Merrill says.

"White girl. That about it. She stay in the car. Got big sunglasses and a hat on."

Someone from somewhere in the dark SUV says something I can't make out.

"Tall Boy say dude coulda been a light skin nigga, but, shit . . . I don't know. Maybe he was."

"What about the other AR you sold?" Merrill says.

"That the weirdest shit of all," D-Bop says. "These mother-fuckers man . . . sayin' shit like they heard I's in prison and if I got a taste for it they'd suck me off or let me fuck 'em for a discount. These some messed up motherfuckers. I ain't gonna lie."

"They get a discount?" Merrill asks.

"Man, fuck you," D-Bop says. "You know I don't fuck with no faggots. But yeah, they gots a discount 'cause I got a little punk in my posse that like white boy penis . . . so I knocked off a few bucks so he could hold one. Some sick shit. He did 'em both —*together*. And they brothers and shit."

"So you know who they are?" I say.

"That's the strangest part of the whole strange motherfucker," he says. "They them foster twins what were killed in the shooting."

57

Usually in school shootings the shooters shoot themselves. It's the only good thing they do. But they didn't do that in our shooting. They didn't do the one decent thing they could have.

The memorial takes place on the high school football field the next morning.

The stadium is surrounded by armed guards from various agencies and everyone who enters it is required to go through a metal detector and submit to a pat-down.

I and others had passed along the information about a possible second attack during the service and I'm glad to see the threat was taken seriously.

Instead of four coffins like Kim had imagined there might be, there are four enormous posters on stands with wreaths beneath them on a stage at midfield. A podium with Pottersville Pirates is in the center of the victims' photographs.

The stage faces the home bleachers, which are filled to capacity with alumni, family, and members of the community.

Current students and teachers sit on the field in folding chairs between the stands and the stage.

A single camera is centered on the field and is feeding all the networks and news outlets that want to carry the service. Media trucks and vans fill the side field near the gym, reporters and camera operators, who aren't permitted in the stadium, standing and sitting and reporting in front of them.

Tyrese leads the service, assisted by various community leaders and clergy. An individual eulogy is given for each victim, and they vary greatly in quality. Kim does the best job with Ace's, but ministers who do Janna, Hayden, and Hunter's struggle through them with generic sentiments and platitudes like they didn't know—and didn't take the time to get to know—the person they're eulogizing.

We decided our girls were too young to attend an event like this and that it was too dangerous for both of us to be here, so Anna is home with Johanna and Taylor. Carla was back and forth about whether to attend or not but at the last minute decided to —and to bring John Paul with her.

Merrill and I are standing near the bleachers along the waist-high fence that defines the field, observing the proceedings but mostly searching the crowd for threats and keeping an eye on our suspects.

Mason and Dakota are sitting together near the back of the student section, Tristan and Denise on the center right. Zach Griffith is perched on a riser on the left side videoing everything.

It'd be easy to take the guts out of a video camera and hide a gun inside it, I think. *Wonder if anyone checked it.*

As I look around and wonder if there's going to be another attack today, I can feel a surprisingly high level of anxiety that lets me know I haven't gotten over the earlier one.

I want to be at home drinking, and can feel myself looking forward to sipping my way toward oblivion late tonight.

Chase Dailey performed a song he wrote about the tragedy

earlier, then disappeared into the crowd, and I haven't been able to locate him since.

If Evan Fowler is in attendance I haven't been able to locate him.

Ever the helpful, exemplary students, DeShawn Holt and Sierra Baker, who earlier passed out programs and helped usher, are now going through the crowd with the hand fans the funeral home provided.

The bright sun is beating down on us, and seeing them pass out the fans reminds me just how hot I am and makes me acutely aware of the bead of sweat rolling down the length of my back.

"Anything?" Merrill asks me.

I shake my head. "You?"

"That Nickols boy keep lookin' back here glaring at us. I don't know about shootin' but there's gonna be some school violence at this bitch."

"He does have a very punchable smirky face, doesn't he?"

"I'm guessing based on what D-Bop said it's probably Tristan and Denise," Merrill says, "but I ain't gonna lie, I's really wanting it to be Mason and Dakota and I's sure hopin' their punk asses would resist arrest at least a little."

I nod.

"You figure anything out on why the twins would be buyin' an AR?" he asks, nodding toward the posters of Hayden and Hunter Dupree.

I shake my head. "Not so far."

"Could they've been involved and been double-crossed or something?"

"It's possible."

"*Shee-it,* virtually anything's possible," he says. "I'm asking for what you think happened."

As I'm about to say that I just don't know yet, Inez Abanes, who is giving the closing remarks at the podium, says something that causes the killers' picture to begin to come into focus.

"We have to live every day as if it's our last," she is saying. "Life can be capricious but we can't be capricious about life. We just never know. I keep asking myself, why didn't the shooters come into my room. Ms. Harper's asking herself the same question. They were right there at our doors. Why didn't they come in?"

I recall watching one of the shooters on the surveillance footage with Tyrese go from door to door in the northeast hallway, the way he looked inside and pulled on the door.

"We have to live our lives as if we never know when our door is going to be opened, because we never do."

I can feel certain connections start to be made but before they can be, I see Anna's Mustang turn off the main road and into the drive between the school and football field.

Knowing she wouldn't be here if it wasn't important—wasn't something she could've texted or called about, I begin to move toward the main stadium entrance.

By the time I'm nearing the ticket booth, she is coming into the arena, Taylor on her hip, Johanna on the opposite side holding her hand.

Even from several feet away I can see tears streaming down Anna's cheeks.

"What is it?" I say as I reach her. "What's wrong?"

At first she can't speak, just starts crying harder.

Then Merrill and Kim and Reggie are there behind me.

Reggie takes Taylor and Kim kneels and embraces Johanna, as Merrill positions himself between us and the media in the field across the drive.

Behind us I hear the last *amen* of the final benediction and the crowd standing to its feet, a big portion of it beginning to head in this direction.

"Take your time," I say to Anna. "Just breathe."

Apparently back on stage, Chase Dailey begins to play the song he wrote again, a longer version this time that incorporates the Potter High School alma mater.

"John," Reggie says, "we're gonna take the girls out before the crowd tries to exit through here. Take your time. We'll be over by the car when you finish."

"Thanks."

"I'm sorry," Anna says. "I know I'm making it worse. I didn't mean to cause a . . . I just had to be with you, had to be the one to . . . tell you."

"Tell me what?" I ask.

"Oh, John, I'm so sorry," she says, a fresh wave of tears flowing out of her red eyes and down her cheeks, "but Derek Burrell died a few minutes ago."

58

God, I just want to wake up and have everything be back to normal.
I've never had a nightmare this bad or this long before.

I killed a kid.

Regardless of the situation or circumstances, in spite of the outcome of FDLE's investigation, irrespective of anything else, the unalterable, devastating reality is I had killed a kid.

How do I live with that?

How can I even begin to process something like that?

Now I understand why Anna is so upset, why she felt compelled to rush to be with me and—

My knees buckle and I actually fall to the ground.

Merrill quickly steps over and pulls me up, as the throng of exiting mourners descends upon us.

"Let's move a little more over this way," Merrill says, and leads me and Anna farther away from the exit.

Anna hugs me and whispers how sorry she is and how much she loves me.

She doesn't try to downplay it or rationalize or justify my actions and their consequences. She knows enough to know how hollow all of that is in the face of the fact that I had ended the life of a child.

The slow moving herd has reached us and has bottlenecked at the exit.

I become aware of the crowd glancing over our way and several camera operators pointing their cameras in our direction.

I shake my head. "We can't do this here. Let's get the girls and get home."

Anna dries her eyes and quickly pulls herself together.

"Y'all ready?" Merrill says. "Follow me and I'll make a hole for us to—"

"Mr. Jordan, are you okay?" DeShawn Holt asks as he and Sierra walk up.

"Were you especially close to some of our victims?" Sierra asks.

Merrill spins around and looks at her. "*Our*?"

She nods. "Yes. *Our. Our* school. *Our* community. *Our*. What did you think I meant?"

"Whose class were you in during the shooting?" I ask.

"I was in Ms. Abanes's," Sierra says.

"I was next door in Ms. Harper's," DeShawn says. "Why?"

"And neither of your classroom doors were locked?" I ask.

They both shake their heads. "Ms. Abanes sort of panicked and was too scared to step out into the hallway to lock the door."

"Same for Ms. Harper," DeShawn says.

I think back to the video again.

"And the shooter came to the door but didn't come in?"

"Came to the door," DeShawn says, "turned the handle, even opened it a little, but then pulled it closed and moved away."

"Same for ours," Sierra says.

"Okay," I say. "Thanks."

"Are you okay?" DeShawn asks. "You don't look so—"

But I'm already moving Merrill and Anna away from them, farther down the fence and away from the crowd again.

"It wasn't random," I say. "The shooter could've gone into those classrooms but didn't. It wasn't a random rampage shooting. The victims were chosen for a reason. It was a cold, calculated, purposeful, and premeditated execution made to look like a school rampage shooting. It was done when it was done for a reason. The cameras that were taken out were specific and intentional. There's a reason why one of the outfits was spotless and one of the guns was barely used. There was only one shooter."

"Who?" Anna asks.

"Kim," I say. "Come on. She has Johanna."

"What?" Merrill says. "You sure?"

I nod as we begin to move toward the exit again. "When the first explosions went off the shooter wasn't even in the hallway yet. The security cameras confirm that. The bombs were on timers to take out the cameras. I think she put the first few up when she helped Tyrese and the others search for explosives that morning. It was probably her idea for them to do it. Instead of searching for bombs she was planting them. There was a level of sophistication and maturity that this attack had that other school shootings haven't. Her explosions worked perfectly. Even the ones she intended not to explode. That's never happened before. In all other school shootings, beginning with Columbine, most of the explosives didn't work. She planted several that she never intended to explode so it looked like kids were behind it, but the ones she meant to detonate did so with precision—and for the primary purpose of concealing her identity. After the first few explode, she goes up ostensibly to confront the shooter but actually quickly puts on the outfit and grabs the gun. With the cameras in that area out and the school on lockdown there's no one to see her. She wears a mask to hide her true identity and a hat and the duster collar up to hide her ponytail. And she deviated from the fingerless gloves to full gloves to ensure she didn't leave any prints. I thought the killers had done that to keep from getting caught so they could do it again, but it was actually just her way of hiding her identity—both by concealing her hands and not leaving any prints."

We have joined the slow-moving crowd near the exit, our progress halting to a near standstill. I continue to talk to them softly, the noise of the crowd and Chase's music ensuring no one can overhear me.

"She zip-ties the back doors and goes immediately to Ace's classroom and kills him—that was her first priority," I continue. "She then shoots randomly—at the library doors, the hallway walls, and makes a show of checking the classroom doors on that side of the hallway where the cameras were still on, but she didn't go into the classrooms that weren't locked. She was stalking Janna Todd and Jayden and Hunter Dupree. She did the shooting when she did because it was the only time Ace and Janna would be in the main building. The rest of the day Ace was in the gym and Janna was in the art building. She left the notes for Chip to find and had us all working to prevent a school shooting to help cover what she was really doing. She knew how Chip would react. She waited until a day when he was filling in for her to leave the notes. She was using all of us as witnesses to a school shooting. She wears black boots as part of her uniform. She sewed the school shooter uniform together and made a slit up the back and put velcro on it so she could get it on and off quickly."

"Why the two uniforms?" Merrill asks.

"To make it look like two shooters were involved, just like at Columbine, but also because she needed a second gun—a handgun she could use to shoot herself. She couldn't use the rifle for that. She shoots Janna and the twins, then takes off her costume and sticks it in the locker with the rifle. Then removes the handgun, fires it a few times, then shoots herself."

"Then Derek steps out in the hallway with his shotgun and . . ." Anna says.

"It's no wonder he was confused. No wonder the shooters just disappeared. No wonder he shoots at her. And she returns fire knowing he's just out there to help. She doesn't shoot him."

"No," Anna says, "she sent you around there to do that."

"Why?" Merrill says. "Why the fuck she do all this?"

"Jealousy. Rage. Retribution. Punishment. She was exacting her revenge on her unfaithful lover and his conquests. My guess is if he had just been having an affair with Janna she wouldn't have done all this. By the way, I'm not convinced he was having an affair with Janna—I just meant in her mind. But I think it was the twins that drove her over the edge. Think about all the rumors of teachers having sex with students and what D-Bop and others said about the troubled twins. Kim made a big deal about Ace being impotent because she was trying to hide the fact that her boyfriend was a pederast. At the baseball game that first night up on the video riser, Zach Griffith referred to Ace as Sandusky. If she turns him in, she suffers the ridicule and embarrassment and inevitable questions about her involvement or what she knew or why she couldn't satisfy her man. No, her pride couldn't allow that. And she wasn't going to be used and abused by men the way her crazy mom always had been. She's a cop. She's going to take the bad guy out and make sure his crimes are never more than rumors and suspicions. She had the twins buy the gun she killed them with. They thought it was to take out their abuser, which it did, but then she killed them to cover it all up. I don't know. That's all conjecture. I may be wrong about some of the whys but the evidence says she did it. She's the only one who could have. And right now we have to get our daughter away from her without letting her know we know."

"Then we need to slow our roll and not come in so hot on her," Merrill says. "Maybe even split up."

59

Sometimes I think we're all just fucked and there's nothing we can do about it. I mean goddamn it's not hard to come to that conclusion, is it? I know it doesn't have to be this way, but somehow we just keep not changing a thing, not a single fuckin' thing.

"Thank y'all for watching them," Anna says as we walk up.

We find Reggie and Kim and the girls under the partial shade of three random pine trees in the front corner of the overflow parking field for the football stadium.

Reggie is bouncing Taylor on her hip and singing to her while Kim is squatting down next to Johanna playing some sort of hand slapping game.

People are swarming all around us, making their way to their vehicles.

"Happy to help," Reggie says. "Is everything okay?"

"We just got word that Derek Burrell died," Anna says.

"Oh no," Reggie says.

"Oh John," Kim says. "I'm so sorry to hear— Why are you looking at me like that?"

She slides her hand into her huge purse.

"Like what?" I say. "I'm just upset."

Anna and I both step toward her to grab Johanna but Kim snatches her back.

Johanna lets out a little yelp and turns to look at Kim with a confused expression.

Shit! We should have discussed who was going to do what so one of us could've distracted her while the other got Johanna.

She is now holding Johanna's little hand so tight that the color has drained from it. Johanna is attempting to jerk it away from her and telling her to *Let go!*

"John, come take a little walk with me and Johanna," Kim says.

I step over to her.

She leans in and whispers to me, "I have a pipe bomb in my purse, so unless you want to introduce your daughter to Derek and apologize to him in person today, do exactly what I tell you to."

I nod, realizing that, like me and the other law enforcement officers at the event, she wouldn't have been subject to being searched and it would be expected that her gun would set off the metal detector anyway.

"Reassure your daughter and tell them to back off," she says.

I do.

"Okay, now walk me to my car."

We start walking.

"Don't keep snatching your hand," I say to Johanna. "Just relax it and walk with Kim to her car. Everything's going to be okay."

"Okay, Daddy," she says, and complies.

To Kim I say, "Will you release a little of the pressure on her hand? She's not going to try to get away."

She nods and seems to.

"Can we talk?" I ask.

"About?"

"What a bad, sick man Ace was," I say. "How you stopped him from abusing any other kids."

"Don't try to play me, John," she says. "Okay? All you bastards are bad—deep down. You gonna tell me you're not, you drunk fuck."

"Why didn't you warn me that Derek wasn't the shooter?" I say.

"How was I supposed to do that? Without letting you know I was . . . I didn't send you around there to kill him. I figured you'd see each other and realize what was going on."

I wonder if that's true or if she was hoping I'd eliminate a potential witness who could potentially raise questions about the disappearance of the mysterious shooters.

"Was Ace sleeping with the twins?"

"He was fuckin' fuckin' foster kids for fuck sake. But that's what predators do. They pick out the most vulnerable and they take them down and they hold them there and they do whatever the fuck they want to to them."

"Did you have them buy the rifle from D-Bop?" I ask.

"Told them we were gonna take the sick bastard out," she says.

"Why didn't you put them on your suspect list?"

She shrugs. "Started to, but . . . didn't want them looked at too closely."

"I understand why you did what you did," I say. "Everyone will. But if you hurt Johanna—"

"I'll be a child killer just like you, won't I?" she says. "You killed a fuckin' kid, John. A good, decent kid too. Not one of these little punks who walks around here like they'd blow up the world if they could. A gentle, kind kid. How you gonna live with that?"

I shake my head. "Not sure I'm going to be able to."

"Sorry," she says. "I really do feel bad for you both. Wish I could take that part back."

"You *can*—in a way," I say. "Let me take my little girl. I won't try to stop you. Just let me take her back to safety."

"There is no safety in this world," she says. "There's no such thing."

All around us there are people leaving the memorial service completely oblivious to what Kim is doing.

"Please," I say. "There can be for her. I will keep her safe. I promise. I'll keep her away from the Bowmans of the world."

"You were always so decent to me," she says. "Even back in school when all the other boys were such cocky little asses."

"I still can be," I say. "I can help you. I can be here for you if you'll let me."

"If I'd've had a boyfriend like you . . . Instead I get fuckers like that piece of . . . How many of my mother's boyfriends do you think had a go at me over the years? Just like Ace did those poor boys. I know they were evil, slutty motherfuckers but . . . they didn't start out that way. I didn't plan on killing them . . . but I could tell they knew it was me. I could see it in their lascivious little eyes and sick, twisted smiles. I lost it. That's the only time I did."

I think about how much worse that back hallway was than any other part of the school.

"They smiled like they had something over me," she says. "Like they not only owned my man but now they owned me."

"Please," I say. "Let us go. Turn yourself in. I swear to you that I will do everything I can to help you. LeAnn and I both will, you know that. We won't abandon you."

"*I* abandoned me," she says. "A long time ago."

"Kimmy, please."

She looks at me, some softness flickering in her eyes. "I'm sorry," she says.

She lets go of Johanna's hand and keeps walking.

"Goodbye, John," she says. "Good luck living with . . . Good luck."

I reach down and scoop Johanna up and hug her to me as I rush away in the opposite direction.

Glancing back I see Kim quickly get into her car, close the door, and reach in to her handbag.

When I turn back around, Anna, Reggie, and Merrill are standing there. Giving Johanna to Anna, I turn back and start running toward the car, yelling as I do, "Get back. Get away from that car. Get down. NOW."

People begin to scramble away from her car and it seems as if she pauses an extra moment to let them.

"Kimmy," I say as I reach the car. "Please don't do this."

She looks up at me through the driver's window. "Back away, John. I don't want you getting—"

"See?" I say. "You don't want me or any of these other people hurt. There is good in you. Please don't kill yourself."

"Good?" she asks, her voice wavering, her expression pained. "I've got good in me? I murdered that poor woman, Janna— because I was jealous of her. Because I thought she was sleeping with Ace, but I should've known better. He liked little boys, not grown women. And the truth is somewhere deep down inside I did know. But I killed her anyway. I just lost it. I was jealous of the time and attention he gave her and I . . . I don't deserve to live, John. But you do, so back away from the car right now. I'm deto- nating this bomb—and it's not a little one—in three . . . two . . ."

I can tell she means it.

I take a few quick steps, then dive and roll and feel the blast.

The loud bang of the explosion, windows being blown out, glass raining down on asphalt around me, smoke billowing out of the car, fire burning inside, burning what's left of my classmate's lifeless body.

60

When I came to admit that I was powerless over—well, everything —and that my life had become unmanageable, I took my first step toward having a better life. And it wasn't something I did just once, but over and over again.

It's a few days later.

I'm parked across the street from the old Episcopal Church in Pottersville.

On the seat next to me is a copy of the complaint I was served earlier today notifying me that Derek Burrell's family is suing me for the wrongful death of their son.

I've spent a lot of time thinking over the past few days. I've done little else. Thinking about our world and my future and a million trillion other things. I've thought about how I'm going to take D-Bop off the street again—even as I've wondered who the second set of kids were he sold the other rifle to. I've thought about all the victims, all the survivors, all the damage done. I've thought about my girls and how to best protect them. I've thought about how much pain people are in and what can be done about it. But mostly I've thought about the kid I killed.

I have just come from officiating Kim's funeral, where much of our graduating class got to hear one child killer eulogize another.

In addition to containing ample evidence against her, Kim's home revealed the sad, lonely life of a troubled woman who felt passed by and picked over, disrespected and wronged.

Following the interment, with Merrill keeping watch for his family, I visited Derek's graveside, kneeling down next to the fresh earth and funeral flowers to tell him how sorry I was for what I had done and to ask his forgiveness.

Anna and Merrill and Reggie and LeAnn and Dad and nearly everyone I know keep telling me the same thing—it was just a horrible accident, that Derek is Kim's victim not mine, that he shot first, and on and on, but nothing can mitigate the guilt and sorrow and remorse I feel.

When I had climbed up off my knees, which still had light, sandy North Florida soil on them, LeAnn was waiting for me.

"You did a good job with her funeral," she says. "No one could've done it better. You're good at what you do—both things you do."

I hug her.

"How could I have missed all the signs?" she says. "Looking back now I can see them so clearly—the way she was with men, her relationship with her crazy mother and her many boyfriends, the juvenile way she was with Ace, their lack of sex or anything serious and on and on and on—but I didn't see it, didn't put it together in the way I should have. I'm a licensed mental health counselor for fuck sake."

"The two people we often have the hardest time seeing clearly," I say. "Ourselves and those closest to us. You were a good friend to her. She was lucky to—"

"I failed her," she says. "And by doing so failed the school, the students . . . none of this would've happened if I had just done my damn job."

"The mental health of the school resource officer is not the responsibility of the guidance counselor."

"She was my closest friend. I was—"

She breaks down and begins to cry.

I hug her again.

"I miss her murderous ass so fuckin' much," she says. "I still can't believe she . . . that she . . . that any of this happened."

"Me either."

"What're we gonna do?" she asks.

I shake my head. "Haven't figured that out yet."

She frowns and nods and says, "I keep thinking about what you said about your faith embracing chaos, about it being trust and practice more than belief and . . . it's helping me."

When I reached my car, Frannie Schultz had been getting out of hers with a sad little bouquet of grocery store flowers.

"For Derek's . . ." she says, nodding at the flowers, then to his grave.

"Been thinkin' about all that happened," she says. "Can't imagine what . . . what you must be carrying around."

I don't say anything but my expression is a mixture of acknowledgment and sadness.

"I begged him not to do it," she says. "Pleaded. He had no business out in that hallway. Big dumb goof. But he's my hero."

"As he should be."

"You're my hero too," she says. "I know it's corny and . . . it's embarrassing, but . . . it's true. What you did for us, what people like you do all the time to help to keep us safe."

My weary, bloodshot eyes begin to sting again and I blink back tears.

"Just wanted you to know that," she says. "And that we don't blame you and you shouldn't blame yourself—not for some dumb, random, tragic accident."

Even now, sitting in my car outside the small, antiquated Episcopal church in Pottersville, her words provide some semblance of something like comfort.

Next to the copy of the complaint on the seat is a bottle of Absolut, its seal, for the moment, still intact.

I watch as slowly one by one the disparate, downtrodden men and women who number themselves among the countless friends of Bill W arrive and make their way around to the musty old Sunday School room in the back.

Most of the faces are familiar, but the few new ones mixed in have the same unsure but resolute look, the same hesitant but determined carriage.

I stare after them with respect and admiration and on more than one occasion grab my door handle to go and join them, but long after the last one enters the safe, sacred space, I'm still out here alone with my regrets, only the complaint and the Absolut to keep them company.

Eventually, I get out of the car, but instead of joining my anonymous friends, I enter the empty sanctuary to mourn the boy who would never become a man, the heroic teenager who just wanted to be helpful, who I had robbed of his first date with Frannie Schultz and everything he could've fit into the lifetime still due him.

START BLUE BLOOD NOW!

CHAPTER 1

"I'm not trying to be a martyr," Malia Goodman says. "I'd much rather live for the cause than die for it."

Author and activist Malia Goodman is a forty-something African-American woman with cinnamon skin so flawless it looks to have been airbrushed on by a skilled and careful artist who takes great pride in his work.

She is tall and athletic and attractive—exceptionally so, though her allure is as much the result of her bearing and her bruised soul as her big, bright, black eyes and the features of her heart-shaped face.

Merrill and I are in her hotel room at the Holiday Inn on MLK across from the mall in Panama City. Her handler, Rodney Livingston, a tall, bony, older black man, and her assistant, Tana Kay, a small, pale, plain-looking black woman in her late twenties, are also present.

The remodeled room is light and airy—a stark contrast to the dark, dramatic, Victorian whorehouse-looking decor with blood-red drapes it had once flaunted.

"I'm not particularly brave or heroic," she says.

She is both, and it speaks well of her that her self-deprecation seems genuine.

A social justice activist specializing in police-civilian relations and a *New York Times* bestselling author of books on the same subject, she is in a particularly poignant and unique position to speak about policing procedures and the criminal justice system.

Her new book, *Shots Fired*, is an in-depth look at police and policing techniques, including a look at the alarming number of shootings of unarmed citizens by law enforcement.

On an extended book tour that involves marches, protests, and rallies, she typically stays anywhere from two days to two weeks in each city she visits and attempts to expose injustice while there. Two police shootings—one out in Panama City Beach and one in Downtown Panama City—have brought her to town.

Though not officially associated with any other groups or movements, Malia's work often parallels and occasionally intersects them.

"Don't get me wrong, there are days when joining Graham and Malik is far more appealing than anything this world has to offer, but . . . I'm enough of a coward to want to die peacefully in my sleep of old age."

In separate and unrelated incidents, both Malia's husband, Graham, and her son, Malik, had been shot and killed.

Graham Goodman had been a detective with the LAPD who was killed in the line of duty by a drug dealer high on bath salts as he was attempted to question about the death of his girlfriend. Malik Jackson, an up-and-coming young rapper and aspiring actor, had been gunned down by police during a routine traffic stop. Malik, who was unarmed and happened to be black, was shot and killed by a white cop. Graham, who was a highly respected and decorated cop who happened to be white, was shot and killed by a black drug dealer.

At times Malia's writings and speeches sound like she's the

staunchest defender and apologist for law enforcement. At others she sounds like the angry mother of an unarmed son who was executed by those very same police. The truth is she is both, with both supporters and detractors on both sides—and recently someone from the second group has made both threats and attempts on her life.

That's why we're here. Well, that's why Merrill is here. He's interviewing to provide security for her while she's in the area for a series of speeches, protests, and book signings. I'm here because I'm on administrative leave and not in a good way, and Merrill has been taking every chance he can to get me out of the house and away from the alcohol and self-loathing I have stock-piled there.

"Anyway . . ." Malia says to Merrill. "You look like you'd be good for the job. Hell, you look like you could stop a scud missile, let alone a crazy with a gun, but . . . well . . . would you? Would you really put yourself in harm's way to protect me?"

Merrill nods, but doesn't say anything.

"That's it?" she says. "That's all I get? *A nod*?"

"I can verbalize it if you like," he says.

"I would like."

"I would," he says.

"Why?" she asks, trying to suppress an amused smile.

"Because I said I would," he says.

She nods as if she understands. "You'll risk your life to keep your word," she says.

He nods.

She waits for him to elaborate but he doesn't, and there is an awkward silence.

Like the colorful carpeted hallway, the room smells of commercial cleaning products and an air freshener questioning its identity. Does it want to be citrus or floral? It has so far been unable to decide.

"Your code includes death before dishonor?" she asks.

"That's not the way I would put it, but . . . something like that."

"And that's it?"

He shakes his head.

"Then what else?" she asks.

"In your case," he says, "there's more to it than just my word."

"Like what? Do you mind explaining it to me?"

"If I said I'd protect a white supremacist, I would," he says. "Even if it costs me my life to do it. But with you . . . Let's just say your views are far more in line with mine than a white supremacist's would be."

"All my views?" she asks.

"Most of them."

"On both sides of the issue—my support and defense of cops and my calls for reforms that would keep unarmed citizens from getting killed?"

He nods. "Some of my best friends are cops."

She gives him a radiant smile and something passes between them—something indefinable that includes both appreciation and attraction.

"*And*," Merrill adds, "though I am rarely unarmed, *I am* a black man."

"So you'll protect me more than you would the white supremacists?"

He shakes his head. "The same. I was just trying to reassure you, let you know what my answer to Marley's question is."

"Which question is that?"

"How long will they kill our prophets while we stand aside and look?"

She is visibly moved that he regards her as one of our social prophets.

"And your answer is?" she asks, her voice thick with emotion.

"No longer."

She nods. "You're hired. Rodney will handle all the details.

I've got a conference call I need to be on, but you're most certainly hired. And I'd like you to start as soon as possible."

Merrill nods.

When Malia stands, Tana and Rodney jump to their feet as well. Merrill and I also stand—just not as quickly or enthusiastically.

Malia shakes Merrill's hand and then mine, and then Rodney leads us out of her room. Before the door closes, she and Tana are already going over the talking points for the conference call.

As soon as Malia's hotel door is closed behind us, Rodney's demeanor changes. "Okay," he says, "now that we've got that out of the way we can have the real interview. And I'd really like to meet with Merrill alone."

Merrill starts to protest, but I cut him off.

"Sure," I say. "I have somewhere I need to be anyway."

"Cool," Rodney says. "It's nothing personal, just . . . you know."

"Don't go far," Merrill says. "I'll hit you up soon as I'm done."

CHAPTER 2

While Merrill meets with Rodney in his room upstairs, I meet with Merrick McKnight downstairs in the bar.

Like the rest of the hotel, the bar has been remodeled. It's lighter and brighter and more open.

I liked it better before.

Merrick and I were meant to get together later in the evening, but when I called him and told him my schedule had unexpectedly freed up sooner than I had thought it would, he said he was both close by and available to meet now.

"Cheers," I say, holding up my vodka and cranberry.

"Cheers," he says, clinking his bottle of Bud Light against my glass.

We both sip our drinks as an uncomfortable silence creeps in around us.

Merrick had asked to meet with me and had not said why, so I drink as I wait for him to introduce a topic of conversation, glancing occasionally at the basketball game on the muted TV monitor mounted above the bar.

It's my first drink of the day and it's all a first drink should be.

"I've never seen you drink before," Merrick says.

"Is that why things just got awkward?"

He shakes his head. "Well, maybe," he says. "But if it is, it's only part of the reason. The biggest is what I need to talk to you about."

I nod and wait and drink.

Near the open entrance of the bar, beyond which the mostly empty lobby can be seen, a balding black man with a too thick beard softly plays a grand piano.

"There're actually two things I wanted to talk to you about," he says.

"Is one any easier than the other?" I ask.

He nods. "A little."

"Well, why not start with it?"

He nods again, takes a long pull on his Bud and sits the bottle on the beige bar top in front of him.

"I'm worried about you," he says. "We all are."

I nod again slowly and say, "I can see why you would be and I appreciate it."

"That's not the first thing I wanted to talk to you about but it sort of sets it up," he says.

I take another drink.

A loud burst of laughter erupts from the lobby as three inebriated women in their late twenties pitch forward through the sliding glass doors, holding on to each other for support.

Please don't come into the bar. Please don't come into the bar. Please don't—

"*Oooh*, piano," one of them says. "Let's go into the bar. Let's 'o to . . . bar. Come on. Just one 'ore 'ittle drink."

"*Tiff*," one of her friends says with great emphasis, "*you promised*. Nightcap in the room then straight to bed."

"Er'ry par'y has a pooper an' at this par'y . . . and at 'is . . . You are it. *Hey, Mr. Pia'o Man.*"

Her voice grows even louder and the piano player stops mid-note on the chorus of "Walking in Memphis" and starts playing Billy Joel's "Piano Man."

The abrupt transition into the new tune is lost on Tiff.

"Hey, Mr. Piano Man," she says again. "My lame friends're makin' me go up 'o 'ed. See you 'nother time for some tic . . . tickle . . . ticklin' 'ose ivories."

The three young women stumble out of view and eventually out of earshot.

"How are you?" Merrick asks.

"I thought we just covered that. Probably about how I seem," I say.

He frowns. "Sorry to hear that."

He pauses a moment and looks around the bar. I follow his gaze.

Besides us, there are only five other people in the spacious bar—the bartender, the piano player, a middle-aged man in a business suit at the other end of the bar, and a couple at a table in the far back corner whispering intimately between kissing intensely.

"You've always been there for me," he says. "Always so under-standing and accepting and positive. I really appreciate the way you've always been with me and my kids."

The bartender looks down our way and asks if we're ready for another yet. Merrick shakes his head though his bottle is almost empty, so I assume he's only having one.

"Thing is . . ." he continues, "you do so much for so many . . . I wanna make sure somebody is doing something for you. I wish I could, but . . . I'm no counselor or sponsor or whatever, but . . . I know someone who is. A friend of mine happens to be a really great counselor. You two have a lot in common. I've often thought —even before . . . now . . .before what you're dealing with—that I should introduce you two because I know you'll hit it off. He works out of the country and is only here for a few weeks every three months. I've told him about you and . . . I think it'd really do you good to talk to him."

"Thank you," I say. "That means a lot. I really appreciate you thinking about me."

The pianist is now playing a rousing rendition of "Sweet Caroline," really banging the *bamp bamp bams*.

"Will you talk to him?" he asks.

I start to shrug, but stop.

"As a favor to me," he adds. "Will you? Please."

I nod.

"You will?"

I nod again. "I will."

"Ah man, you don't know how happy that makes me," he says. "How relieved it makes me feel."

His genuine delight at my willingness to talk to his friend on top of the kindness he is showing me stings my eyes and makes my throat constrict. I glance away, blinking and trying hard to swallow.

When I am able to look back at him, I say, "That was the easier of the two things you needed to talk to me about?"

He nods and smiles, but the smile quickly fades into a frown.

"No easy way to say it," he says. "So I guess I'll just . . . Reggie and I broke up."

"*Really?*"

I'm completely caught off guard. Based on the occasional offhanded comment made by Reggie, I guess I've known they've had issues—but what couple doesn't? I never suspected anything like this, had no idea they had already pronounced time of death.

"She hasn't said anything to you?" he asks.

I shake my head.

"That's so like her," he says. "Probably part of the reason we broke up—she buries most everything. Not really willing to talk about much of anything."

"I'm so sorry to hear that y'all are—"

"It's been comin' a while. Everything started so good between us—so damn good. Best ever, but then . . . I don't know . . . our differences started showing more, became more pronounced. We drifted apart. Started arguing more. And no matter what I tried she . . . she just wasn't willing to talk about it. It's so funny . . . you think it'll be the big things—somebody having an affair or going through some sort of crisis or you'll have some big issue related to sex or kids or money, but . . . and then it's just a million little things. You get so far apart you can't figure out how to get back together—or why you ever were in the first place."

"I really hate to hear that," I say. "How are you doing with it? You okay?"

"I'm okay. I really am. Like I said it's been a long time coming. I mean, I hate it, but . . . I'm okay. It wasn't all of a sudden like someone dying or something. It didn't catch either of us by surprise."

"Well, it certainly has me," I say.

"I wanted to talk to you because I knew I'd be seeing you less and I wanted you to know and to keep an eye on Reggie—to help her if she'll let you."

"Of course," I say. "I'll look out for her."

"I know you're going through your own shit right now."

"That's the best thing for it," I say. "Get out of my own cycle of self-pity by helping someone else. But I'll still see you."

"I'm actually moving over here," he says. "Casey already attends college and works over here and there's a good school for Kevin. I can't make a living as a journalist in Wewa. I've taken a job with the *News Herald*. I'm sure our paths will still cross occasionally but probably not nearly as often. That's why I wanted to go ahead and tell you in person—that and to introduce you to Dave."

"Dave?"

"My counselor friend I was telling you about."

"Oh. Gotcha."

"You up for meeting him tonight?" he asks.

"Maybe not tonight, but soon," I say.

"I just feel like if you don't meet him tonight you might not ever. Please. Just for a few minutes."

CHAPTER 3

"Now, look, my young brother," Rodney says when he and Merrill are in his room. "I'm glad you made a love connection or whatever that was with Malia. She needs to be comfortable with who's gonna be guarding her. But I gotta know you can do the job and that you're really worth the money. I'm the one bankrolling this operation. I'm the one calling the shots."

Merrill doesn't say anything.

"Oh, you a hard nigga, that it?" Rodney says. "Well, I guess that's good when you protecting the princess, but . . . you ain't gonna get the chance to do that, you don't convince me you the right man for the job."

Though Rodney's room is nearly identical to Malia's, something indefinable about it makes it seem like it's not as nice. It's not as bright and well lit. It doesn't smell as good. And it's not as fresh and clean. But Merrill decides the real difference is the absence of Malia herself.

"Thought I already had the job," Merrill says. "Ain't tryin' to be hard. Just listening to you and tryin' to get the lay of the land. Didn't realize Ms. Goodman wasn't in charge."

"Oh, she thinks she is," Rodney says. "And I'm happy for her to think that. She's very good at what she does. Makin' a real difference, but she's naive. The threats are real—from a lot of different directions. She wouldn't last a day out here on her own."

As Rodney talks, Merrill gets a good look at him for the first time. He's a tall, thin, older man in a cheap burgundy suit with long hands and bony fingers. His eyelids are loose and droopy and appear hooded. Peeking out from behind them, his small, watery eyes are wary and furtive.

"Maybe I'm a bad judge of character," Merrill says, "but she doesn't strike me as naive, and I'd say given what she's gone through, what she goes through every day, she's tough enough to handle most anything comes her way."

"I'm not sayin' she's not tough or strong, not resilient in a certain way," Rodney says, "just that she's . . . She's a . . . a visionary I guess you'd say. She's a big-picture type of person, not good with details. That's all. I'm not saying anything bad about her. Just letting you know—"

"Who calls the shots," Merrill offers.

Rodney leans back and studies him for a long moment before speaking. "You fuckin' with me, boy?"

Merrill's brow furrows as he looks up and squints, seeming to consider something.

"You have to think about it?" Rodney asks.

"About what?"

"Whether you're fuckin' with me or not."

Merrill shakes his head. "No, not that."

"Then what?"

"I's tryin' to remember that last time I's called *boy*. And what I did to the man who said it."

Rodney holds up his elongated hands, palms out, in a placating gesture. "Didn't mean it like that. Sorry. Got caught up in playin' the old man role a little too much. Tell you what . . . you let that one go and I'll let the fact that you were fuckin' with me go."

"The only reason I'm still here," Merrill says, "only reason I haven't knocked you on your old black ass, is how much I respect the lady and admire what she's doing and know I can protect her better than anybody else. But there are limits even given all that and we've about reached 'em. Hire me or don't, but get on with it."

"You should be the best for what you charge," Rodney says. "You come highly recommended by the right people, but goddamn you're pricey. I could hire three bodyguards for what I'd be payin' you."

"Get what you pay for," he says. "And you ain't just gettin' me. But I'm willing to give Ms. Goodman a discount for the cause."

"That's very generous of you and would be greatly appreciated. Thank you. But we've got to talk about who'd be helpin' you. The gentleman who came with you tonight isn't right for what we need."

"I say who's right to work for me and nobody's righter than John."

"Righter or whiter?" he asks. "And it ain't just that he's white. He's a cop."

"Two things Ms. Goodman obviously doesn't have an issue with."

"As I said she can be too naive for her own damn good sometimes," Rodney says. "The thing is . . . this isn't just about who can do the job but how they look doing it. I've got to consider the optics involved in everything we do."

Merrill turns without a word and leaves the room.

Rodney follows him.

Merrill steps down the hallway and knocks on Malia's door.

"Wait," Rodney says. "There's no need for . . . Don't disturb her. We can work this out."

Tana opens the door.

"Did you make sure it was us?" Merrill asks.

"No, I'm sorry, I just . . ."

"I need to speak to Malia a moment."

"She's—"

Malia appears behind her. "What is it?"

"Just came to say goodbye and to make sure you knew why I wasn't taking the job," he says.

"I thought you already had," she says.

"I did too, but evidently, Rot-ney here calls all the shots because he's bankrolling this little operation and he thinks I'm too expensive—even with my offer of a discount because I believe in what you're doing—and my friend is too white and too much a cop to be working for you. It was an honor to meet you. Keep up the good work. And maybe be a little more selective about who you surround yourself with."

With that, Merrill nods to her and turns to leave.

"Wait," she says. "Please."

AND THE SEA BECAME BLOOD

AND THE SEA BECAME BLOOD -- the 21st John Jordan Mystery Thriller and Author Michael Lister's response to living through Hurricane Michael, the Cat 5 hurricane that devastated John Jordan's beloved Gulf Coast.

The death of elderly loner Emmett Daughtry begins like any other murder investigation for John Jordan, but it ends in a thrilling cat and mouse chase during an existential storm of apocalyptic proportions.

Pre Order "And The Sea Became Blood" today and 25% of all profits will be donated directly to Hurricane Michael disaster assistance.

Go to www.MichaelLister.com to find out more.

CPSIA information can be obtained
at www.ICGtesting.com
Printed in the USA
LVHW011139120519
617538LV00003B/627/P